D.E.A.D. TILL I DIE

JAMES P. SUMNER

BOTH
barrels
PUBLISHING

D.E.A.D. TILL I DIE

FOURTH EDITION PUBLISHED IN 2022 BY BOTH BARRELS PUBLISHING LTD.

EDITING AND COVER DESIGN BY: BOTHBARRELSAUTHORSERVICES.COM

ISBNs:
978-1-914191-27-5 (HARDBACK)
978-1-914191-28-2 (PAPERBACK)

VISIT THE AUTHOR'S WEBSITE: JAMESPSUMNER.COM

JOIN THE MAILING LIST

Why not sign up for James P. Sumner's spam-free newsletter, and stay up-to-date with the latest news, promotions, and new releases?

In exchange for your support, you will receive a **FREE** copy of the prequel novella, *A Hero of War*, which tells the story of a young Adrian, newly recruited to the U.S. Army at the beginning of the Gulf War.

Previously available on Amazon, this title is now exclusive to the author's website. But you have the opportunity to read it for free!

Interested? Details can be found at the end of this book.

We finally got there...

DISCLAIMER

The following novel details what happened between the Adrian Hell novels, Deadly Intent and A Necessary Kill. It was first published in 2015 before being extended and re-released in 2016.

The version you are about to read is a complete re-envisioning of the story. This "director's cut" expands on the consequences of the original in greater detail and provides more insight into the three main stars of the series. While it can be enjoyed as both a standalone title and as the first official entry in the GlobaTech series, you will get more from the experience if you read it in context with the Adrian Hell novels mentioned above.

PREVIOUSLY...

Adrian Hell was arguably the world's greatest assassin. His reputation was legendary, and he was feared and respected in equal measure by criminal fraternities around the globe.

But in 2014, he retired. After a decade of killing bad people, he had found the peace he so desperately sought, and he hung up his guns. Using the vast fortune he had accumulated over the years, he moved to the quiet town of Devil's Spring, Texas, where he set up his own bar, met a woman, and finally began to enjoy life.

His best friend, Josh Winters, wasn't ready to retire. He had stood by Adrian's side most of his life—first in the military, as part of a black books CIA unit, then as his handler and confidant when he began working as a contract killer. He knew Adrian Hell better than anyone and was genuinely happy when he decided to settle down.

But Josh needed something more.

Having cultivated a relationship with GlobaTech Industries over the last few years, he began working for them. Specifically, for Ryan Schultz, the former U.S. Secretary of Defense and now acting CEO of the company. A previously rocky relationship had turned into a huge opportunity for Josh… one he was ready to seize.

On April 7, 2017, three men walked into Adrian Hell's small Texas bar to recruit him to a terrorist organization with plans of a massive attack. Adrian refused, incurring the wrath of the group. The body count started to rise. This led to GlobaTech's intervention, which, in turn, meant that both Adrian and Josh's paths would cross for the first time in over two years.

In no time at all, retirement was over, and they had slipped effortlessly back into their old ways…

PROLOGUE

On a military base that didn't exist, in a part of the world where no one would ever think to look for them, four people walked into a small, rectangular briefing room. Lights flickered into life and buzzed quietly overhead, triggered by a motion sensor above the door. Moments later, the nerve-shredding screech of metal legs scraping against the old, tiled floor filled the room as each of them took their designated seats around the oblong, wooden table in the center.

Mounted on the far wall was a sixty-inch screen that acted as a digital wallboard. In front of it stood a desk with a single chair nestled neatly underneath, looking out at the otherwise empty room.

Two sat next to each other at one end, facing the screen, with one sitting on either side of them. They each carried a tablet, which they propped up in front of them by folding the protective cover into a small triangle behind it.

A few moments passed, filled with minimal conversation that stopped immediately as a fifth person appeared. Jericho Stone was a shade over six-five, and his powerful frame filled the doorway as he strode confidently into the room. The muscles on his arms and torso bulged beneath his black T-shirt, developed over years of military service and combat missions.

He moved to the front of the room, stood with his back to the screen, and looked at the group of elite operatives he had commanded for the last seven years. He, too, had a tablet, which he held awkwardly in his left hand. He tapped the device, syncing it to the wallboard so that it displayed to everyone what he saw on his own screen. He tapped it again and brought up a satellite image showing an apartment building in the Upper West Side of Manhattan.

When he spoke, his voice was deep, weighted with authority, and his tone firm. "A little over two hours ago, a meeting between the director of the CIA and a high-value asset was interrupted by a man recently added to the Terrorist Watch List. There was an exchange of gunfire, and the assailant escaped with a laptop he stole from the asset. We've been tasked with retrieving that laptop at all costs."

"Do we know who this guy is?" asked Damien Baker, who was sitting at the far end of the table. He stood at six feet tall, or six-three if you included the bright red mohawk running along the center of his otherwise shaven head. His long, thick beard flowed down to his chest, and tattoos ran up the sides of his neck and down over his shoulders and pectorals, which were partially visible under his dark green vest.

Jericho looked at him and shook his head. "Intel's sketchy, but we believe he's an assassin known to the world's criminal fraternity as Adrian Hell. He's reportedly linked to an organization we believe to be planning some kind of attack on the United States. I've sent a profile to each of your tablets. Study it closely. There isn't much about this guy to go on, but what we *do* know is he has a reputation as a highly-coveted, extremely dangerous hitman."

Baker nodded. "And what's so special about this laptop?"

Jericho hesitated before answering. He felt uncomfortable feeding his unit a line passed down to him by his superiors, but in this particular situation, he had no choice. "I'm afraid that information's classified. No one here, including me, has a high enough security clearance to say otherwise. This matter is being viewed as a threat to national security. It doesn't matter to us what's on that laptop. We just need to make sure it doesn't find its way into the wrong hands."

"What do we know about this organization?" asked Charlotte LaSharde, the only woman in the room, sitting on Baker's left. She was incredibly toned and physically strong despite her slim build. A thin film of sweat coated her dark skin and glowed under the fluorescent lights. Her tank top clung to her body, further emphasizing both the fact she wasn't wearing a bra and that she had little reason to. She was as stunning as she was lethal, and in another life, she wouldn't have looked out of place on a catwalk. But her dark, alluring eyes betrayed no emotion. She was a true warrior.

Jericho snapped his gaze to meet hers. "Again, we haven't been granted access to as much intel as I would've liked, but we know it's a large terrorist network that's been actively recruiting for the last twelve months. We don't know who's running it or what they're planning, but we *do* know they've approached our target in the last few days."

She frowned. "So, how do we know they're planning an attack?"

"Analysts at Langley have seen an increase in chatter over the last few weeks. The same keywords are repeatedly being flagged in multiple communications, and right now that's the educated guess by the people who sign our paychecks."

"This is bullshit," she said, shaking her head. "We might as well just make it up as we go along..."

Jericho regarded her for a moment. Given the very nature of his unit's purpose, it was important to maintain an air of informality. They were funded by the CIA but operated independently, meaning there was zero accountability should they ever be captured while on a mission. For security, they dispensed with any structure or recognized chain of command. They all followed Jericho's lead—they didn't need a title or a badge to acknowledge that. In the military, that kind of comment would be viewed as insubordinate, but Jericho and his team knew each other well enough that respect went without saying. He understood her frustrations because he shared them.

He looked at each member of his unit before speaking. "Look, I don't like the fact there's so little to go on either, but the urgency with which this operation has been put together speaks volumes. As you know, our job is to carry out the missions deemed too sensitive, too dangerous, or too important to warrant sanctioning. Sometimes that means we have to operate on tight schedules and with minimal intel. Get over it. We know time is a factor, and we know our objective—intercept this Adrian Hell asshole and retrieve the laptop he stole. Questions?"

The man sitting to Baker's right raised his hand slightly. Rick Santiago was a computer genius and an expert with any kind of explosive device. Usually, he served as tactical support for the team.

Jericho gestured to him. "Yeah?"

"What do we do with him once we get the laptop back?" he asked.

Jericho stared blankly for a moment as he considered the question, clenching his jaw muscles as he chose his response carefully. "The mission parameters state the retrieval of the laptop is top priority. Bringing the target in for questioning isn't."

Santiago nodded, reading between the lines.

"So, how do we get him?" asked the man sitting across from him. Standing at a little over six-two, Chris Black was a career soldier and Jericho's second-in-command. He had chiseled features marked with dark stubble and brown eyes that always saw more than he acknowledged. He was a smart, capable individual whom Jericho himself had recommended to be recruited to the unit.

Jericho tapped the screen on his tablet, updating the board behind him for the room to see. He stepped to one side and gestured to the display. "We have intel that puts our target on a private plane by the end of the day, so we need to move fast with this." He looked over at Santiago. "Rick, I need you to find out exactly when and where that plane is due to take off and who's expecting it when it lands. Once we know that—" he turned to Black— "*you're* going to get on board and hide out in the cockpit. After take-off, you'll re-direct the flight..." He tapped the screen of his tablet again, displaying a satellite image of an abandoned airstrip. "...here. It's an old airfield, roughly fifteen klicks outside Cartagena, Colombia. We'll be waiting for you."

"What if the pilot resists?" asked Black.

"The pilot and co-pilot are expendable. Bottom line, ladies and gents, this mission came from way up high. Success goes without saying, and we're to leave no evidence we were ever involved. We clear?"

The group nodded and murmured their understanding.

Jericho eyed each member of the unit individually. "I want you all ready to roll in thirty minutes. Gear up."

The sound of scraping chairs echoed around the room once more as everyone got to their feet. Baker and Black were the first out. Santiago was next, and he peeled away into the operations center across the corridor, where he took his usual seat behind the main computer terminal and set to work finding the target's flight details.

LaSharde followed and quick-stepped until she caught up with the others. "This mission is bullshit," she said, her words sounding even more confrontational than intended on account of her thick, Bronx accent. "We've got no idea why we're doing anything. We never do."

"Relax," said Black, glancing over his shoulder at her. His voice was calm and his tone casual but assertive. "We're not here to ask questions. We're here to aim at whatever we're told to aim at and pull the trigger. It's frustrating at times, yeah, but it's nothing new. This is what we do, Charlie."

"Plus, Jericho wouldn't send us anywhere he wasn't happy with," added Baker. "He said himself, we don't have much to go on, but timing's crucial. Trust *him*, if nothing else."

LaSharde sighed heavily. "Whatever."

She pushed past the two men and stormed out of the building. The two men stepped out into the courtyard a few moments later, momentarily short of breath as the afternoon heat hit their faces. They both stared ahead as their hot-tempered colleague walked angrily toward the barracks.

Black turned to Baker and pointed to the armory. "You go and get ready. I'll see if I can cool her down a little."

Baker smiled and patted him lightly on his shoulder. "Good luck, amigo. I think you'll need it."

Jericho stepped out into the corridor as Baker was heading outside. He had heard LaSharde's concerns, but he wasn't going to defend his orders for a second time. He entered the operations center and stood behind Santiago, patting him on the shoulder with one of his large hands. "What have you got for me, Rick?"

"The target's due to fly from JFK just after nine tonight," he replied. "It's a private jet registered to GlobaTech Industries."

Jericho frowned. He had heard of GlobaTech—most people had nowadays. The company was a military contractor and responsible for nearly all the technology his unit used. He couldn't immediately see any reason why they would be helping a known terrorist, so he dismissed the concern a moment later. His orders were clear, and the *why* wasn't relevant—simply the *who*.

He checked his watch. "That gives us just over seven hours. I want a chopper here in twenty minutes to take Black to the nearest airstrip. Get him airborne and en route ASAP."

"Copy that."

Jericho walked purposefully out of the building, squinting slightly against the glare of the sun. Across the courtyard, he saw Black and LaSharde emerging from the barracks. He met them in the middle and quickly relayed the information from Santiago. LaSharde walked away to gear up for the mission, but Jericho tapped Black on the arm and gestured for him to hang back.

"Everything okay?"

Jericho nodded. "I just wanted to say, the target is deemed high-value until you land. We don't know his background, but we do know what he does for a living, so exercise caution. He's obviously had some kind of formal training because he was able to infiltrate a meeting between the CIA director and an agency asset. That place would've been swarming with agents."

"I've got this. Don't worry. Was there anything else?"

Jericho shook his head. "Just get ready. Your ride should be here in a little over fifteen minutes."

Black walked over to the armory to join the others. Jericho held the man in high regard. He had always known of his aspirations to one day run the unit, but he didn't view that as a threat. He was unquestioningly loyal and a formidable soldier.

He smiled to himself for a moment, amused as he thought how Black was likely under the impression his sexual relationship with LaSharde was a secret. He shook his head and made his way over to the rest of the team.

The three of them were standing in a line, wearing dark gray, unmarked Kevlar armor and holding their weapons loose. Jericho moved past them, toward a rack of weaponry attached to the back wall. He selected a FAMAS-G2, which was his preferred assault rifle. He took some spare magazines, loading one into the rifle and sliding the others inside the pockets sewn into the legs of his pants. He side-stepped right to the next rack and rested his weapon against it as he picked his own Kevlar vest from a hanger, quickly put it on, and strapped it in place. Picking up his rifle again, he walked back over to his team and stood in front of them.

Santiago appeared, having finished his work in the console room, and fell in line. "Boss, the chopper will be here in five minutes."

Jericho took a breath, stretching his shoulders back and standing to his full, impressive height. "Thanks, Rick. All right, everyone, listen up. This operation is now live." He looked at Black. "Chris, your chopper's going to fly you to

Augusto Cesar Sandino International Airport, where you'll board a cargo plane that'll take you Stateside. You need to be in place on the target's private jet by 20:30 hours local time." He looked at Baker, LaSharde, and Santiago in turn. "The rest of you are with me. We're heading to the airfield in Colombia. We'll sit tight and wait for Chris to arrive with the target. Questions?"

No one spoke. Outside, the sound of a chopper gradually filled the air. Jericho stepped out into the courtyard and looked up as it approached and hovered overhead, slowly descending and landing out of sight behind them.

He looked at Black. "Move out, soldier."

Black nodded. "Copy that." He looked at the rest of the team in turn, his gaze lingering a split-second longer when his eyes met LaSharde's. "Stay safe," he said to them before turning and disappearing around the corner to the waiting helicopter.

Jericho walked over to the Humvee, stopping near the passenger door. "Rick," he called over, "you're driving. We'll cross the border into Costa Rica and rendezvous with a chopper to take us the rest of the way."

The team piled into the vehicle, and Santiago started it up, slid the stick into gear, and eased out of the garage. The barrier lifted automatically, and he drove out of the gates and turned right, speeding along the dirt track that led them to the main road.

It was after midnight as the plane made its final approach. There was a light breeze blowing across the deserted airstrip, cool and refreshing in the otherwise humid climate. Standing in the doorway of the long-abandoned control tower, shrouded in shadow, Jericho and his squad looked on as the private jet touched down, the screeching of the tires amplified in the ghostly silence. It taxied to a stop just ahead of them, and the door opened out, triggering a small flight of steps to automatically lower to the ground. Two men appeared in the doorway and exchanged a brief word before descending.

Jericho Stone looked on, watching as the first man, their target, stepped down onto the blacktop. Chris Black was a few paces behind him, aiming his gun with a professional steadiness at his prisoner. After a moment, the target got down on his knees, crossed his ankles behind him, and put his hands on his head.

Weapons ready, the squad made their way over to the runway. Jericho had taken point, with LaSharde and Santiago behind him, and Baker completing the diamond formation at the back. Stopping a few yards from the target, they formed a neat line in front of him.

The large moon dominated the clear night sky, shining down unobstructed and illuminating the scene with its pale, silvery-white glow. Jericho stepped forward and moved to the center, staring down at the target.

He regarded the man for a moment. He had a shaved head and two-day-old stubble on his chin. He was a decent size—a strong build but lean, not overly muscular. He noted the man's eyes; they were ice-blue and glimmered with subdued violence as they stared back at him. He didn't look panicked but exuded an almost arrogant calmness despite his current predicament.

"Adrian Hell?" asked Jericho, adjusting the grip on his FAMAS for effect.

The man shrugged. "Used to be."

"Welcome to Colombia. On your feet."

Adrian stood, looking around with an absent curiosity.

Jericho pointed his gun casually at him. "Now where's the laptop?"

Adrian settled his gaze on the mountain of a man standing before him and frowned. "What laptop?"

"The one you stole approximately fourteen hours ago. It's government property, and you're going to hand it over immediately."

"So, you work for the government?"

Jericho didn't answer. He simply stared back at him, intrigued by the man's approach to the situation. His face, however, gave nothing away.

"You guys have me confused with someone else, clearly," Adrian continued. "The laptop *I* stole belonged to a known terrorist. I'm actually trying to help the government that you may or may not work for. But it's okay. You weren't to know. I'll just get my things and be on my way. I don't suppose one of you can fly this plane, can you?"

Everyone leveled their rifles at him. Black had moved around to join the rest of the unit, standing at the end of the line to Jericho's left, his weapon trained on Adrian.

Jericho felt his own uneasiness growing as the seconds ticked by. Something wasn't right. No one would act so confidently when faced with five armed soldiers who had just kidnapped them, no matter who they were. "I won't ask you again. Give me the laptop."

Adrian rolled his eyes and let out a frustrated sigh. "Like I said, I stole the laptop from a terrorist, not a government employee. I did so on behalf of a private military contractor as part of an ongoing operation. And you people obviously wouldn't be interested in that, would you?"

Jericho's eyes narrowed. "What operation?"

"I've been targeted by a terrorist group who want to

recruit me. As you say, I'm Adrian Hell, whether I'm retired or not. I refused, and they came after me. Some friends of mine happened to be investigating these assholes anyway, so I agreed to help them out. I managed to get in the same room as one of them and steal his laptop, which I've since handed over to my PMC friends. But that has nothing to do with the government, so I'm at a loss as to why you'd be sent after me..."

Jericho fell silent as his mind processed the new information. Behind him, he could almost feel the looks of concern from his team. Their uncertainty was palpable in the quiet moments that followed. But he didn't care. He just wanted to do what was right, and the way things were going, the mission was beginning to make less sense.

"Who sent you after me?" asked Adrian with increasing persistence.

Again, Jericho stayed quiet.

"Come on, get on your comms and ask the question. You know you want to."

Jericho tensed his jaw muscles as he considered his options. He could tell when people were lying to him, and he believed Adrian when he said he wasn't in possession of the laptop anymore. The problem was he also believed the other things he was saying, which was making him doubt the mission his unit had been tasked with. He knew he had his orders, and following them unreservedly was ingrained into his DNA, but he had always trusted his gut, and the information Adrian was giving him contradicted the parameters of his operation.

Jericho let out a taut breath. He had made his decision. For the time being, at least, he wanted to keep the man alive until he could put his mind at ease.

"Watch him," he said, looking quickly at his unit but

speaking to no one in particular. He stepped away from the group and spoke into his comms unit. "Sir, we have the target. There's no package—I repeat, no package. Please advise... over."

On the other end of the line, speaking from inside the CIA Headquarters in Langley, Virginia, a familiar voice replied, "Jericho, this is Jones. What exactly did the target say to you?"

He briefly summarized the conversation. A few moments of uneasy silence followed before another voice came on the line. Jericho recognized it immediately, even though he had only spoken to the man a handful of times.

"Soldier, you're to terminate your target immediately and destroy the plane," said General Matthews, the director of the CIA. "Leave no evidence behind. Understood?"

Jericho frowned. "I understand, sir. But... can you please clarify the threat here? If there's a chance what he says is true, shouldn't we make contact with the PMC and follow up from there?"

Matthews sighed heavily down the line. "Just do as you've been ordered. Terminate that man *immediately* and leave the area."

Jericho caught a hiss of static in his ear and didn't hear the last part.

"Say again, sir..."

Matthews repeated the order.

Jericho took a deep breath. "Understood, sir."

For a few moments, he stared blankly ahead of him, a whirlwind of doubt in his mind. He knew his job, but he also knew to trust his own instincts. Despite the fact Adrian Hell was an assassin, he believed he stole the laptop from a terrorist. He could see it in his eyes. They never lied, and so far, neither had he.

He was conflicted, and in that moment, he found himself doing something he had never done before: questioning his orders. He had heard the desperation in Matthews's voice when he gave the kill order. It wasn't urgency. It was panic. Coupled with what Adrian had already told him, he knew there was more to this than he was being told, and he didn't want to involve his unit in something that could potentially come back to them.

He composed himself and walked back over to the group, moving back in front of his target and raising his rifle at him once more. "My orders are to kill you," he said matter-of-factly. "But... I want to know who you're working for."

Adrian raised an eyebrow. "Why?"

"Because there's an ongoing mission I think could benefit from that information."

"What's the mission?"

Jericho shook his head. "Are you serious?"

"Worth a try." He shrugged. "I know you have your orders, but I'm not the enemy here. You have my word."

"And what is the word of a two-bit hitman worth, exactly?"

"Two-bit?" he scoffed, seeming genuinely offended. "Try *world's greatest*, you ignorant prick. And I'm many things, but I'm not a liar. I'm trying to help. I don't trust you enough to give you everything I know, but I *can* tell you I've seen solid intel that suggests a pending terrorist attack that nobody else currently knows is coming."

The revelation stunned Jericho. He glanced over his shoulder at the rest of his squad, fighting to suppress the growing uneasiness currently welling in the pit of his stomach. They all exchanged nervous glances and shuffled awkwardly on the spot. He ignored their obvious concerns, turning back to his prisoner and locking eyes with him.

"I'm trying to help," Adrian continued. "And I'm offering my help to you now. I'm not the enemy, and given what I know, I suspect your orders are bogus, unjustified, and given by someone who doesn't want the world to know they're implicated in a terrorist attack."

Does he mean Matthews? Jericho wondered.

"And you can prove this?" he asked.

"Yes."

Jericho sensed movement to his left. Before he could turn his head, a split-second of bright light burned around him. Then he felt himself falling as the dimly-lit airfield quickly faded into a vast, all-consuming darkness.

D.E.A.D. TILL I DIE

GLOBATECH: BOOK 1

1

April 19, 2017

Chris Black stood in front of his squad, regarding each one of them silently as they muttered among themselves. They were sitting in a neat line; their chairs had a small fold-away table attached to the right arm, like in an exam. Overhead, the buzz of the fluorescent lighting was barely audible over the chatter in the large, yet mostly empty meeting room.

Since the chaos of their mission in Colombia eight days ago, they had received only two communications from their CIA contact, the first of which officially put him in charge and told him to sit tight and await further instruction.

It had been a difficult week. Two days ago, the world had changed. In a short and sudden turn of events, every nuclear power on the planet had seemingly turned its missiles on one another and fired. Unprecedented global devastation rocked every corner of the globe.

The second communication Black had received contained information about Project: Cerberus, the top-secret satellite program designed to prevent the very catastrophe that had recently occurred. It also contained intel from CIA analysts that suggested GlobaTech Industries—who helped build the satellite—were responsible for the attack.

Finally, it contained orders.

Black had struggled with the time spent in limbo. He didn't regret for one second obeying the order that came through to terminate Jericho, but once the dust had settled, tensions had started to run high. He had acted quickly to maintain order and earn the team's faith in his ability to follow in Jericho's footsteps as the leader of the unit. Now he stood in front of *his* unit with a mission brief from the people who signed their paychecks.

"Okay, settle down," he said to the room. He waited as they fell silent and turned their attention to him. "Look, I know it's been a long wait, but under the circumstances, it was necessary. I've heard from Langley today, and they have a mission for us."

He picked up his tablet from the table to his right and pressed the screen, syncing it wirelessly with the large digital wallboard behind him. He stepped to one side, so his squad could see the display.

A large profile picture filled the left of the screen, with writing appearing down the right. He cleared this throat. "This is Daniel Vincent. He's an engineer for a private contractor. We have intel that suggests Mr. Vincent has stolen classified information. We don't know what his intentions are, but due to the sensitive nature of the material, this is being treated as a matter of national security."

"What's the information?" asked Damien Baker, who was sitting on Black's right.

"Classified," he replied sharply. "I wasn't told because we

don't need to know. The only thing that matters is retrieving it before he has the chance to do anything stupid with it. He's been under surveillance for the last forty-eight hours. He's smart. Staying off the grid—using public transportation, paying cash, and his cell phone is turned off. Langley suspects he's trying to make contact with someone. Maybe a buyer for the information. He has a wife and daughter, and we've been monitoring them in case he tries to get in touch, but there's been nothing so far."

"Where is he now?" asked LaSharde.

"At the moment, we don't know," conceded Black. "The last confirmed sighting of him was in a coffee shop in Berlin. He was heading toward Central Station, and that's when surveillance lost him. He could be on a train to anywhere. Langley has analysts scanning every camera, cell phone, and satellite at their disposal to find him. As soon as they do, we'll move to intercept."

"Are we sure this intel is good?" asked Santiago.

Black glared at him, and even the others turned and looked surprised at the question. Santiago was typically a quiet man by nature and rarely spoke unless he had to.

"What do you mean?" asked Black.

"I mean, our information was way off in Colombia. Our target didn't have the laptop, like we were told. In fact, I'm not sure our target even *was* a target. I know Jericho didn't think so..."

Black held his gaze, clenching his jaw muscles with frustration. He took a moment to compose himself before responding—a slow, deep breath to help remind him of his new position. "The intel has been verified. Once we know the location of the target, we'll move to intercept. That's all for now." He nodded curtly to the room. "Dismissed."

The chairs scraped loudly on the floor as everyone

stood. Baker left first, followed by LaSharde. As Santiago neared the door, Black stepped toward him.

"Rick, you got a sec?" he asked as calmly as possible.

Santiago turned and hung back, waiting until the others had left before closing the door.

"What's up?" he asked informally.

"Do we have a problem?"

Santiago shrugged. "I don't know... do we?"

"You've been unhappy since we got back from Colombia."

"I know. The real question is: why haven't you?"

"And what's that supposed to mean?"

Santiago struggled to control his frustration. "What the hell do you think? You shot Jericho in the head, homie! How are you okay with that?"

Black took another step toward him, trying to exert some of his newfound authority. "It's not about whether I'm okay with it. I was following orders. Something Jericho had developed an issue with. He was talking with our target like he was a goddamn colleague! He knew Langley was listening, so what happened is on him, not me. He disobeyed a direct order."

Santiago shook his head. "That's because it was a stupid-ass order," he countered. "That was Jericho, homie! He was our boss for over seven years, and you blew him away like he was nothing!"

Black moved so that he was standing almost nose-to-nose with the slightly smaller Santiago. "I followed an order given by the director of the CIA—that was all. We're soldiers, and this is a war. Get in line, or get the hell out—it's your call. But make it fast, *homie*, because I won't tolerate my authority being questioned in my unit."

"Your unit, huh? Just like that?" Santiago shook his head

and took a step back, holding his hands out to the side. "Whatever, man. Like you say, we all soldiers, right? Just tell me which direction to shoot... *boss*."

Black held his gaze for a few tense, silent moments and then nodded. "We're done here."

Without a word, Santiago turned on his heels and walked out of the room, leaving Black standing there, breathing heavy with adrenaline and anger.

Once the door was closed, Black waited a few moments to give Santiago a chance to walk away and then picked up his tablet and launched it across the room. It hit the far wall with such force, it smashed into pieces and scattered across the floor. He leaned forward on the desk, staring at nothing in particular.

"Sonofabitch," he muttered under his breath.

He knew he had to deliver on the next mission. All eyes would be on him, especially after Colombia and the events of the past couple of days. He knew that if he couldn't hold things together and get the job done, Langley would find someone else who could.

Did he regret having to kill Jericho? A little, maybe. But orders are orders, and he had waited his whole life for a chance to head up a unit like this one. He wasn't about to let one man's insubordination get in the way of that.

He left the room and headed outside into the courtyard. Santiago was making his way over to where Baker was preparing the weapons and equipment, getting ready for the next mission. He watched as the men began talking, but he was too far away to hear what they were saying. Judging by their body language, he guessed it was about him.

He shook his head in a moment of anger and walked across to the barracks, where LaSharde was just disappearing inside. Hearing the crunch of his footsteps on the gravel, she turned and held the door for him.

"Thanks," he said as he reached her.

The air was just as humid inside, and it momentarily took their breath away. They made their way along the dimly-lit corridor side by side until they reached the door to her apartment, which was the farthest one from the entrance, on the right-hand side, opposite the stairs.

LaSharde stepped in front of him, putting her body between him and the door. "Are you all right?"

"No, I'm not," he replied with a heavy sigh. "There's so much going on right now. I dunno... I feel like I'm out of my—"

She placed her index finger on his lips. "Hey, it's okay. Come here." She stood on her tiptoes and pressed her lips against his, stroking the back of his head with her hand. They parted a few seconds later, both smiling. "That better?"

He nodded. "Yeah, thanks."

She grabbed his hand. "C'mon, we have some time. I want you to show me *exactly* who's in charge."

She led him inside her apartment and kicked the door closed behind her.

2

Jericho Stone gasped as he snapped awake, opening his left eye as he bolted upright in his bed. He felt as if someone had ripped him from a nightmare.

"What the hell?" he shouted, his voice filled with an uncharacteristic panic. He looked around the room, using his training to quickly absorb every detail and determine if there was any immediate threat.

He was lying in a bed, in what appeared to be a very specialized hospital ward. An assortment of technology beeped and flashed away on either side of him. He looked down and saw a variety of wires both on him and *in* him, which connected him to the machines.

There were no windows. The room was bright and clean and looked like something straight out of a sci-fi movie. Every surface he could see was white. He wrinkled his nose at the faint smell of disinfectant.

On the right, a large door stood open, offering a limited view of the corridor beyond. There was a man standing casually at the foot of his bed, partially blocking his view of a large, flat-screen TV mounted on the wall opposite. He was dressed in a shirt and jeans and stared at him with an expression of bemusement and disbelief.

On Jericho's immediate right was a nurse, wearing a white overcoat. An ID badge clipped to the pocket over her left breast stated her name was Julie Fisher. She was looking at him with professional concern, her hand on his forearm as a gesture of comfort.

"Where... where am I?" asked Jericho, still taking in quick, deep breaths.

Julie squeezed his arm gently. "You're—"

"I'll take this one," interrupted the man, holding up his hand as he spoke. He took a step toward the bed. "Jericho, you're in a medical research facility in California. You've been in a coma for just over a week. You woke up for the first time yesterday, and you've been drifting in and out ever since."

Jericho frowned. "California? But you're... you sound British."

The man nodded and smiled. "That's because I *am* British—but please don't hold it against me. I'm Josh Winters. I work for GlobaTech Industries."

Jericho frowned again as the name registered in his brain with a familiarity he couldn't immediately explain. He knew GlobaTech was one of the largest private contractors in the world. They specialized in contracted security, were industry leaders in the research and development of technology and weaponry, and worked in conjunction with agencies such as the CDC, focusing on healthcare advances. But the name was familiar to him for another reason that he couldn't quite put his finger on.

Jericho set his jaw with determination and, with what

felt like a colossal effort, re-positioned himself in his bed so that he was resting upright against his pillows. When he spoke, he sounded more alert and a little concerned. "What am I doing here?"

Josh was quick to pick up on the change in tone. "You're safe, Jericho, I promise. I'm not naïve enough to think you'll trust me straight away, but I need you to believe we mean you no harm. You're recovering after undergoing an emergency medical procedure that ultimately saved your life."

Jericho stared blankly ahead of him, trying to wrap his head around what was happening. He fought desperately against the dark fog clouding his mind in an effort to recall the events that led to him being there.

"Do you remember what happened to you?" asked Josh.

"Mr. Winters, please..." said the nurse, interrupting before Jericho had a chance to respond. "I must insist you let this man rest. He's been through an incredible trauma. He needs *time*."

Josh looked at her. "I understand that. I do. But time isn't a luxury we have right now. He's a big boy. I'm sure he'll manage."

Jericho let out a heavy sigh and closed his eye for a moment, focusing his mind and trying to remain calm. When he re-opened it, he fixed Josh with a hard stare. "I remember being in Colombia. I was on a... on an airstrip. Something went wrong... I don't..."

Josh held his hands up and gestured for Jericho to take it easy, seeing the man was still disoriented. "It's all right. Relax, mate. I'm sorry to push you. It's just that we have a limited time frame to work with, and you have a lot of catching up to do. Rest up—I'll be back soon to see how you're doing."

He turned and left the room, closing the door gently behind him. The nurse then set about monitoring the various machines and documenting the information on a chart attached to a clipboard.

Jericho regarded her quietly as she worked. He thought she was attractive in a subtle way. She wore her brown hair up, held by a clip, and her hazel eyes darted back and forth, scanning the information with practiced efficiency.

"How did I get here?" he asked her after a moment.

She looked at him quickly before turning back to the machines, as if she wasn't sure what to say. "It's... it's really not my place to say. I'm sorry, but it's my job to make sure you recover. Mr. Winters can tell you the rest."

Jericho leaned over, placing his hand gently on her forearm. "Please," he implored. "I need to know what happened to me. To the mission..."

She held her breath for a moment. Jericho looked into her eyes. He noted her slight frown and pursed lips, recognizing the signs of an internal debate, which he presumed was over how much information to divulge.

Finally, she relented, letting out a heavy sigh before speaking. "Look, all I know is you came in here a week ago with a gunshot wound to your cranium."

Jericho raised an eyebrow and relaxed back into his pillows. Letting go of her arm, he gazed ahead of him, staring at the TV but not really seeing what was on it. "Huh..."

She continued. "Truth be told, it's a miracle you're still alive. The wound itself was bad enough, but you also lost a *lot* of blood. You were flown here and operated on immediately upon arrival."

Jericho blinked slowly with his one good eye and took a

deep breath. "So... how am I not dead? I mean, it sounds like my injuries were pretty bad."

"The bullet penetrated your forehead, just above your brow line. It narrowly missed your brain, essentially grazing the bone. The damage to the area was extensive but ultimately not lethal. We were able to insert a metal strip, which will hold the bone together securely until it's had time to fully heal."

"I have a metal plate inside my head?"

She nodded. "You do, yes. But it's not as bad as it sounds, I promise." She smiled weakly. "Listen, you need to rest. There'll be plenty of time later for you to worry about what's happened, but you need to get your strength back before you do anything."

Jericho nodded slowly and closed his eye once more, trying to make sense of everything.

Who shot me in the head? Our target was unarmed...

He struggled to remember but couldn't. There was a black hole in his mind where his memories should be. He took some deep breaths and soon felt himself drifting back to sleep.

When he awoke a few hours later, Jericho found it a far less traumatic experience, having avoided any further nightmares. After quickly realizing the wires and IV lines had been removed, he pushed himself upright in bed again, which proved easier than last time as more of his natural strength had returned. He moved his right arm, turning his hand and clenching his fist, feeling like his old self.

As he looked around the room again, he realized he was struggling to gauge the distance of things. It took him a few moments to realize he could still only open his left eye, for which he had yet to be offered an explanation. Tentatively, he moved his hand to his face and slowly pressed his fingers against his skin. He moved them gently across, feeling the bandage around his head and over his eye.

"What the..." he muttered.

Just then, the door to his room opened, startling him. He dropped his arm and looked over as Josh entered the room. "You've been out for over three hours," he said as he approached the bed. "How are you feeling?" His British accent sounded excessively cheerful, which, under the circumstances, Jericho found mildly irritating.

He took a deep breath before replying. "Better, thanks." He moved his hand back to his face momentarily. "What happened to me?"

Josh smiled apologetically. "That's a... big question. One step at a time, eh? Let's get you dressed and into the conference room. I think it's about time you were fully de-briefed."

On cue, Nurse Fisher appeared behind him in the doorway, holding some clothes in her arms. She stepped inside, moved past Josh, and stood next to the bed. "I've brought you something to change into," she said, raising her arms slightly and gesturing to the new outfit. "They're not exactly the height of fashion or anything, but..."

Jericho flashed a polite smile. "That's fine. Thanks." He looked back at Josh. "I want answers. No bullshit."

Josh nodded. "Fair comment. I haven't fed you any so far, and I have no intention of starting now."

Jericho took a moment before swinging his legs out from under the covers and resting his feet on the cold tiles. Placing his hands on the edge of the bed, he gradually put more pressure on his legs until he felt comfortable enough to stand. Slowly, he did, inhaling as he stood to his full, impressive height.

Jericho was an intimidating sight. On his legs, he wore hospital scrubs, which were at least two sizes too small. His bare torso was incredible, with large, well-defined muscles on every inch of it. His entire body was almost triangular, with his broad shoulders narrowing to a natural six-pack on his waist. Occasional scarring decorated his otherwise impeccable chest and abdomen.

His huge arms were adorned with extravagant tattoos. The head of a very detailed Chinese dragon covered his right shoulder, and the body wrapped itself around his arm and ran all the way down, with the tail finishing in a circle around his wrist. His other arm sported an equally detailed —and slightly more impressive—Renaissance piece, complete with images of clouds and cherubs. Michelangelo himself could have painted it.

Jericho glanced at Josh, whom he estimated was close to six-one or six-two. The Brit was looking him up and down and had a weird smile on his face. "Holy crap... you *are* a big fella, aren't you?" he observed.

Without replying, Jericho turned to the nurse, who held out the clothes to him. He noticed her gaze never left his own and that she was seemingly less impressed with his physique than Josh was. He took the outfit from her, dropping the items on the bed behind him.

"It's Julie, right?"

She nodded.

He pointed to the bandage covering his head. "Can I take this off, Julie?"

She exchanged a glance with Josh, which Jericho was quick to notice and interpreted as concern, though he said nothing. "Your wounds are still healing," she said finally. "We'll assess how well you're doing later, but for now I need you to keep it on."

Jericho nodded and turned toward the bed, picking up the T-shirt from the small pile of clothes. He pulled it on over his head, slowly feeding each arm through the short sleeves before tugging it down over his body, finding it a tight fit.

He picked up the beige cargo pants and paused, looking over his shoulder at both of them in turn. "Do you mind?" he asked, gesturing to the pants.

Josh smiled. "I'll be outside when you're ready."

He stepped outside into the corridor, reaching behind him and holding the door open for Julie, who let her gaze hold Jericho's a second longer than was necessary before following.

Left alone in the room he had apparently spent the last week or so occupying, Jericho sat on the edge of the bed, quickly getting dressed. After he finished lacing his boots, he paused for a moment before standing, his hands gently feeling the bandage around his head and over his right eye again with inevitable curiosity. He ran his fingers across his forehead as if expecting to feel metal beneath them. He moved a hand to his right eye but stopped himself from touching it. He had no idea what damage had been caused and suspected he wasn't going to like any answer he was given, should he ask.

Finally, he stood and stretched, moving his arms out to the sides and easing them back. He opened the door and stepped out into the corridor. There was no sign of the nurse, but Josh was waiting for him, leaning against the wall opposite with one leg tucked up behind him.

"All set?" he asked as Jericho appeared.

He nodded once. "I want to know everything. Like I said before—no bullshit. If you lie to me or hide anything from me, I'll know. And bandage or no bandage, I *will* beat the crap outta you, understand?"

Josh seemed to suppress a smile as he nodded. "You're

just like him..." he muttered cryptically as he pushed off the wall and set off walking along the clean, gray corridor, toward the elevator at the far end.

"Just like who?" asked Jericho, confused.

Josh spun to face him, continuing to walk backward, smiling. "Come on, big guy. We don't have all day."

3

The conference room on the fourth floor looked out over the vast expanse of GlobaTech's headquarters, located at the base of a small mountain range on the outskirts of Santa Clarita, close to one of the two national forests that bordered the city. The whole area looked like a small town. There were buildings, stores, living quarters, helipads, a network of roads... even an airstrip. The entire micro-community was teeming with activity.

Jericho stood by the window, squinting in the glare of the bright California sun as he watched groups of Globa-Tech operatives busying themselves around the compound, avoiding the huge trucks that navigated the enclosed community, transporting weapons and technology between different buildings.

He was impressed with the facility and found himself wondering why it looked so busy. He expected a fair amount of hustle and bustle as standard, but he thought all the activity outside seemed excessive.

Behind him, Josh was sitting at the end of a conference

table, leaning back in his chair with his hands behind his head and his feet resting up on the desk.

"It really is something, isn't it?" he said.

Jericho looked over at him and shrugged. "Looks like any other military base to me. Except on this one, I guess you can do whatever you want, right?"

Josh was quick to notice the flippant hostility but chose to ignore it. He figured Jericho would be feeling on edge and a little defensive under the circumstances. He simply smiled. "You'd think, wouldn't you? But while we might not answer to any colonels or the president here, we *do* have a board of directors and a whole host of corporate investors, which, believe it or not, is actually much scarier."

Jericho went to respond, but the door behind him opened, distracting him. Another man walked in, dressed similarly to Josh—smart and casual, with his shirt tucked into his jeans, brown shoes, and an open sports jacket. He was portly compared to his British colleague and looked older than he actually was. Jericho recognized him immediately but didn't fully understand why he was there.

The man extended his hand and spoke with a distinctive Texan drawl. "Jericho Stone. It's damn good to see you back among the living, son. I'm—"

"Secretary Schultz," interrupted Jericho, shaking his hand. "I didn't expect to see you here..."

Schultz smiled. "Call me Ryan. I've not been the secretary of defense for a while now." He gestured to one of the chairs around the table. "I'm lending a hand around here for the time being. God knows they need all the help they can get at the moment. Take a seat, son."

Jericho hesitated momentarily before sitting at the opposite end of the table to Josh, with his back to the window, facing the door. Old habits of planning his exit long before he needed it.

He looked around quickly. To his left, a large TV screen was mounted on the wall, facing the table, with a camera just above it for video conferencing. Apart from that and the table itself, the room was devoid of any features or decoration.

Jericho glanced over his shoulder and out the window as he heard a chopper flying low overhead. He saw it begin its descent but couldn't see from his seat where it actually landed. He looked back around and caught Josh observing him with curiosity. He frowned. It wasn't the first time he had seen him staring like that, and he was beginning to feel like a sideshow attraction.

Schultz sat beside Josh and leaned forward, resting his arms on the table and clasping his hands together, looking at Jericho. "Son, I'm just gonna get straight to it because we're short on time and long on problems."

Jericho nodded. "I appreciate that, sir." He gestured with his hand at Josh. "As I've already said to your friend here, I want the truth. I don't like it when people lie to me or try to hide things from me. I'm not a kid or a wet-behind-the-ears rookie fresh out of the academy. I've served this country a long time, and I'm a very capable soldier. If I think you're not being straight with me, that'll make me angry, which would be a problem for all concerned."

"Would we not like you when you're angry?" asked Josh with a deadpan expression. "Do you turn green? Because honestly..." He paused to gesture with his hand at Jericho's body. "...that wouldn't surprise me."

Jericho glared at him, his eyes narrowing as he subconsciously tensed his considerable arm muscles.

Josh recognized the look of irritation and quickly held

his hands up in apology. "I'm sorry," he chuckled. "I'm just kidding. Lighten up, okay? We're on the same side, and we want to help you."

Jericho stared at him for a moment longer and then took a deep breath, relaxing.

"Do you remember anything about what happened to you back in Colombia?" asked Schultz.

Jericho furrowed his brow as he fought to recall how the mission went down. Vague silhouettes of memories floated around inside his mind, but everything remained stubbornly unclear. He cursed to himself, frustrated, and shook his head regrettably. "Nothing concrete. Just flashes, mostly."

"Well, tell us what you *do* remember, and we'll try to fill in the blanks," said Josh.

Jericho tilted his head slightly, regarding each of the men in turn before his gaze settled on the British man. Josh Winters looked youthful, with his neatly styled, short blond hair and clean-shaven features, but his tired eyes betrayed his age.

Jericho smiled humorlessly. "Sounds to me like you already know what happened. So, you can stop with this... *help me help myself* routine and get to the point. What's going on around here? Why do you want to help me?"

"We want to help because my spider sense is telling me you're one of the good guys, and you just want to do the right thing. I honestly think we can help each other, so I thought it would be best for all concerned if we could protect someone with your credentials."

"*Spider sense?*" he said with mild disbelief. "What are you, like, five?"

Josh smiled. "It's just one of my things. I like pop culture references—no situation is complete without one."

"You're a very strange man."

"It's been said…"

Jericho shifted uncomfortably in his seat, sitting up straighter and massaging the base of his neck, which had started to ache. He didn't feel comfortable going into too much detail about his last operation, but he trusted Globa-Tech enough to feel he wasn't in any immediate danger. Plus, the former secretary of defense was there, which made him feel more at ease about co-operating, at least until he figured out what was going on.

"All right," he said reluctantly. "I was on a mission to take down a known terrorist who had stolen a laptop from a CIA asset. My unit and I were ordered to capture him, retrieve the computer, and then dispose of his body."

"That was your exact mission brief?" asked Josh. "That the man you were sent after was a terrorist?"

Jericho frowned as more previously repressed details came flooding to the forefront of his mind. "He said he wasn't. He said he was working for… for you."

He glazed over momentarily as he began remembering segments of his conversation with the man in Colombia, but Josh's voice distracted him. "In a manner of speaking, yes, he was. Do you remember his name?"

Jericho let out a short breath. "Adrian Hell."

"That's right. Did your briefing give you any more information on him?"

"Just that he was on the Terrorist Watch List, and he was a hitman. There was very little information at all about the mission."

Josh smiled. "Well, he *was* a hitman. He retired. But I can tell you, he's definitely not a terrorist."

Jericho frowned. "You're talking like you know him."

"He's my best friend," he said without hesitation. "I used

to work alongside him, handling his contracts and his finances while he did all the hard work."

"What, and you went from running an assassin to working in the private sector?"

The disdain in his voice wasn't hard to miss.

Josh nodded. "That's right. Now all that's a long story for another day, but I can promise you one thing: he's not your enemy, and neither are we. Now, in the interest of time, let me summarize everything that's happened while you were in a coma." He paused to take a deep breath. "An organization tried to recruit Adrian to work for them. When he refused, they sent... literally *waves* of people to kill him. And he sent them all back dead, which pissed off a lot of people."

Jericho massaged his temples as he felt the onset of a full-blown headache taking hold. He was frustrated and struggling to make sense of what he was being told. "What does any of that have to do with my mission?"

Schultz cleared his throat. "The man you were sent to capture *did* steal a laptop, but it wasn't from a CIA asset, as your briefing said. It was, in fact, taken from a goddamn terrorist sonofabitch."

Josh smiled and turned to Schultz. "Nicely put, Ryan. Poetic, as always."

"That's what he said to me," said Jericho.

Josh nodded. "And he was right. The laptop contained classified information about a government satellite program codenamed Project: Cerberus. You heard of it?"

Jericho shrugged. "I've *heard* of it, yeah, but I don't really know anything about it, other than what was released to the public—a government-funded satellite designed to monitor all communications within the United States and track any potential terrorist threat before it happens."

Schultz nodded at Josh and then looked at Jericho.

"That's right. Straight off the disclaimer. Now you received a new order from your superiors, specifically telling you to ignore any new leads on the whereabouts of the laptop and kill Adrian, didn't you?"

Jericho nodded.

"Yet, you didn't. Why?"

"It didn't feel right," he explained. "My gut was telling me to believe what the target was saying, even though it made no sense. Then the kill order came through, and it set alarm bells ringing. I remember thinking it sounded like a desperate move, which didn't sit right. I tried to find out more information from your friend, but I don't remember what he said."

Josh pointed his finger at Jericho. "And *that's* what got you all kinds of shot. The CIA doesn't like people who question things. They never have, and they never will."

"And how the hell would *you* know that?" he challenged.

He sat forward in his seat. "Jericho, this is me being completely honest with you—full disclosure, all the cards on the table, et cetera. I know you ran the D.E.A.D. unit, which, y'know... absolutely wasn't, in any way, shape, or form, a deniable, clandestine unit secretly funded by the CIA."

Jericho clenched his fists, using the action to suppress both his anger and his concern. "I don't know—"

"What I'm talking about? Yes, you do. And I know you do because I used to be a member of the same unit, albeit before your time. In fact, I was there when it was created, way back when. So was Adrian. He used to run it, just like you did."

"That's not possible. The briefing would've—"

"Mentioned that? No, it wouldn't. We both know you guys don't exist, in the same way we didn't back in the day—

tary support, healthcare, food, temporary housing—you name it—to all the affected nations."

"That's just... I can't believe it. How did this happen? I thought Cerberus was designed to *detect* potential threats, not cause them."

"It was," replied Schultz. "But the problem was our own satellite was being used against us from the very beginning. You see, in reality, there was no Armageddon Initiative."

Jericho frowned and shook his head. "I don't understand. You just said—"

Josh smiled sympathetically, cutting him off. "I know how you feel, but bear with us, okay? The CIA recruited a terrorist called Hamaad El-Zurak to act as the front man for all of this. He handled all the preparation for the attack, and his propaganda diverted attention away from the people really responsible for it all."

"You can't mean...?"

Schultz nodded. "The goddamn CIA."

"That's just not possible. No way. I'm not buying it. This is... insane!"

Schultz sighed. "That doesn't make it any less true. Bottom line? The CIA director is at the center of a terrorist plot. Now you might not want to hear this, but your D.E.A.D. unit was—and probably still is—being used to cover his tracks, so the world doesn't find out about his involvement in what happened."

Jericho felt his heart rate increasing as a surge of adrenaline rushed through his body. His mind was trying to deal with things it couldn't and didn't want to understand. He felt vulnerable, betrayed. His instinct was to run. To put distance between him and the information he couldn't fathom as well as the people relaying it.

"I'm sorry, but it's true," added Josh. "I know this is difficult to hear, but we have evidence that *proves* the CIA manufactured intelligence reports to make it look as if both GlobaTech Industries *and* Adrian Hell were responsible for the attacks. We also know with unequivocal certainty that it was Director Matthews *himself* who pushed the button that launched the missiles."

Jericho sat quietly, numb with shock. His aching head had reached the point where it simply refused to comprehend any more words.

Josh continued. "These bogus reports were then distributed to other agencies, such as the FBI and the NSA, so they would pursue *us* in their investigations. You can't trust anyone anymore, Jericho."

"But none of this makes any sense! Why would the CIA want to cause a war?"

Schultz shook his head. "They didn't cause a *war*, son. There was no *fight*, no... drawn-out conflict. They wiped out practically every corrupt and broken nation east of Italy. This was someone pushing a great big reset button, removing any potential threats or enemies in the process."

Jericho stood and walked slowly back over to the window. He clasped his hands behind his back and stood at ease, looking out at the compound before him, allowing his mind to wander, to make sense of everything.

No wonder it's so busy down there, he mused.

He looked over his shoulder at Schultz, turning his body toward the table when his vision blurred because of his covered right eye. "What would be the point of such an attack?"

"You tell me," Schultz said. "Who would benefit from it?"

Jericho shook his head. "I can't see how *anyone* could

44

benefit from something like this. Quit stalling and tell me already."

"You're still thinking like a company man," said Josh. "You can't see the bigger picture because you've not accepted the fact that you can't trust the people who used to sign your paychecks. We're not stalling. We just know from experience this is a lot easier to comprehend if you come to the conclusion on your own."

Jericho moved to the end of the table, opposite Schultz. He stood with his back to the TV screen, facing the room. He leaned forward and rested his palms on the table. "Okay, fair enough. But I can't honestly think how anyone could benefit from such a catastrophe."

"When in doubt, follow the money," prompted Schultz. "Matthews was behind the terrorist façade. He orchestrated it all. He physically launched the missiles. Who signs *his* paychecks?"

Jericho frowned as he realized there was only one answer to that question, and it seemed too far-fetched to be true. Nevertheless, he replied, "The president?"

"We have a winner!" said Josh facetiously.

"Are you saying President Cunningham masterminded this?"

"We are," said Schultz. "All that money he made this country from his radical reforms on drugs and prostitution... he used it to fund his own bat-shit crazy plan to reshape the world to his own design."

Jericho shook his head as he paced slowly around the room for a moment before finally re-taking his seat. "And you can prove this, I assume?"

"We have the evidence to prove every single word, yeah."

"Show me."

"We... we can't," said Josh hesitantly. "Not right now, anyway. Adrian has it all on a flash drive."

Jericho frowned, finding it impossible to hide his instinctual dislike for the former assassin despite what Josh had said about him. "I didn't think he would still be alive. Why does *he* have it?"

"Because, despite the CIA dedicating a large proportion of their resources to hunting him down and killing him, he's the only person who can act on that information right now. Like you, he's a loose end who knows too much, and they can't afford to risk letting him live in case he exposes them. But luckily for us, he's the toughest bastard alive, and so far, he's been able to stay ahead of the game and take out anyone who's found him."

"Right. So, will he?"

"Will he, what?"

"Expose them?"

Josh thought about it for a moment and then shook his head. "Probably not. Right now, I imagine he's figuring out a way to kill every last one of them."

"But do you trust him?"

Josh nodded. "With my life. And you should too—he kept you alive and safe in Colombia until medical assistance arrived on the scene. He told me about it afterward, which was how I was able to track you down and get you transferred here, to give you the help you needed."

Jericho fell silent for a moment. "Who else knows about all this?"

"Outside of this room? Just Adrian Hell and an FBI agent we trust, although we're trying our best to keep him out of it —mostly for his own good. But probably everyone who works here has heard rumors."

"So, why not just go public and expose them yourself? Why put Adrian in that position?"

Schultz leaned back in his chair and stretched. "We already thought of that, son. Hell, it was the *first* thing we considered doing. But the CIA has already made *us* out to be the bad guys in all this and then the president came out and publicly backed us as the face of this country's global support effort, which essentially tied our hands. For us to turn around now and start pointing the finger at *anyone* just makes us look petty and ungrateful."

Josh nodded in agreement. "He's right, Jericho. Even though we have proof, the CIA would simply say we manufactured it. It would be a long, drawn-out battle in both the world media *and* the courtroom. Even with proof, it'd still boil down to our word against theirs because of who they are. Sure, we'd probably win... eventually... but the fact it would take so long would damage GlobaTech's credibility. Right now, Adrian has nothing to lose, so he's the perfect person to take the fight to them. We're doing what we can to help him. Quietly."

"Is that all you're worried about?" asked Jericho scornfully. "Your *image*? You leave things in the hands of a goddamn psychopath because you're scared to lose face?"

Schultz shook his head. "Not at all. But take a look outside. Take a look at the news. We're the only ones able to provide the level of support needed to all the affected nations on this planet. We can do it quickly and effectively because we don't need anyone's approval to release funding, travel overseas, send manpower and supplies... none of the bureaucratic bullshit your government would have to deal with, whether they were corrupted or not. If the public stops believing in us, they'll stop accepting our help. We're smart enough to know that our ability to help people far outweighs our need to prove somebody wrong. At least for the moment."

Jericho relaxed in his seat. He was feeling slightly more reassured that GlobaTech was on the level, though it was little comfort given everything he had just learned.

"But you can't just let them get away with this," he said after a moment. "Are you even *trying* to stop them?"

"Yes, we are," said Josh. "Of *course,* we are. For the most part, I'm leaving that to Adrian. Like I say, he's got a plan of sorts, and he's staying off the grid until he can figure things out."

"I can't believe you're leaving the fate of the free world in the hands of a professional killer."

Josh looked away for a moment, choosing his reply carefully. "I appreciate you're still a little unsure of things, Jericho. I do. I also understand your feelings toward someone who was once a target for you. But you need to ease up on the judgment and hostility toward Adrian."

Jericho shrugged. "I'm grateful for his help after Colombia—don't get me wrong—but he's still a paid assassin. Forgive me if I'm a little skeptical about all this being left to someone like him."

"*Someone like him?*" Josh slammed his palm on the desk, which startled Schultz. "Let's not forget who *you* are, Jericho. You ran the same black ops unit for the CIA that he once did. Just because the government paid you instead of criminals, it doesn't make you all that different from him. The only thing separating you two right now is the fact that Adrian understands what needs to be done, and he's risking his life to do it. So, why don't you climb down off your ivory tower and pick a fucking side!"

Schultz placed a hand on Josh's arm. "Take it easy, will you?"

Josh shot him a glance before looking back at Jericho. "And I'll tell you something else, Mr. Stone—there's no one more qualified and no one I trust more to do this than him. That man's like a brother to me, and I'll do whatever it takes to help him, with or without you."

Jericho wasn't used to being spoken to like that. He didn't respond. He just got to his feet again and paced back and forth, trying to wrap his head around it all. He was a military man, born and raised on bases all over the world and bred for combat. He considered himself a patriot, loyal to his country. But everything he'd just been told had turned his entire world upside-down.

He stopped and stared out the window again, thinking about what Josh had just said to him. He didn't care for the man's tone, but he conceded that maybe he had a point. He was so angry, shocked, and confused, he just wanted someone to blame. He didn't like it, but he knew Josh was right. He needed to stop thinking like a CIA operative. He still didn't fully understand the reasons, but one thing was becoming painfully clear to him: his days with the agency were done. They had left him for dead because he questioned an order. Seven years of his life erased with a single gunshot.

He turned and looked directly at Josh. He wasn't about to apologize; he believed saying sorry was a sign of weakness and doubt. He simply nodded once at him. "Okay. So, what about me?" he asked. "Where do I stand in all this?"

"Right now, as far as we know, the CIA believes you're dead," replied Schultz. "And I, for one, would like to keep it that way—at least for the time being. If they knew there was another loose end that tied Matthews to everything that's happened, they'd come after you with everything they've got. You wouldn't last a day."

Jericho frowned. "Hey, if Adrian can manage it, I'm damn sure I could!"

Josh took a breath to calm himself and then shook his head. "He manages for two reasons. One, he has absolutely no moral compass. You'll never meet a nicer guy, but the man won't hesitate to kill anyone if he believes it's the right thing to do. Where you kill only because you're ordered to, he kills because he chooses to, which means he's more likely to do what's necessary when it counts. And two, he doesn't have the D.E.A.D. unit hunting him, whereas you almost certainly would the moment you step outside. I'm sure you don't need telling how dangerous that unit is. Even Adrian would struggle to survive against them on his own. You're not even close to a hundred percent, Jericho. This isn't your fight. Not yet."

Jericho nodded thoughtfully and then sat back down in his seat once again, looking at both men in turn. "So, what can I do to help? I need to do *something*..."

"I know you do, and I have just the thing. We're putting together a team. A small unit—tactical, discreet, off the books. Not an investment we intend to declare at the next shareholders meeting, if you understand me. We want to use this unit to help Adrian bring these bastards down, and I'd really like you to be a part of it."

Jericho thought about the prospect of working to help the assassin. Then he thought about what was at stake. If GlobaTech could focus on the greater good and put their own battles on the back burner, why couldn't he?

After a moment of hesitation, he nodded. "When do we start?"

4

Josh cast a tense look at Schultz before speaking to Jericho. "Well, there's... one more thing you should know," he said.

Jericho narrowed his eye skeptically. "What?"

He gestured to the bandage covering Jericho's head. When he spoke, his tone was softer, more sympathetic. "I'm sure you're wondering why you only have the use of your left eye at the moment."

Jericho moved his hand slowly toward his right eye and gently ran his fingertips over the material that covered it. "It had crossed my mind, yeah," he replied with a hint of impatience.

Josh got to his feet and began pacing aimlessly back and forth, pausing briefly at the window before turning to address Jericho.

"Here are the facts," he began. "The bullet you took in Colombia did significant damage to your head."

Jericho nodded. "I know. Nurse Fisher told me about the metal plate you put in there to keep my skull together."

"That's right. The bullet grazed across your forehead,

about a quarter-inch into the skin. It essentially scratched your skull all the way across."

Jericho shrugged. "But it'll heal, right? How does this affect my eye?"

"You were very unfortunate in that the bullet hit you at a slight angle, meaning the farther across your forehead it went, the deeper it burrowed. It damaged your optic nerve as it exited your skull, rendering your right eye permanently useless."

The news hit Jericho like a freight train. He felt the breath taken from him momentarily. He absently moved his hand to his bandage again, hovering cautiously over it. "So, what are you saying? I'm blind in one eye?"

Josh massaged the bridge of his nose between his right thumb and index finger as he let out a long, heavy sigh. "Yes... and no..."

Jericho was pretty good at reading people's body language. Josh's eye movements were rapid and restless, which he knew was a sign that he was thinking very hard and very quickly about something. He also hadn't stopped fidgeting with his hands, whether it was brief massages, scratching his head, or putting them in his pockets only to take them out again a moment later. All were telltale signs of awkwardness and uncertainty. Neither were great indicators that the person talking is someone he should trust.

He glared angrily, switching his gaze between Josh and Schultz. "What have you done to me?"

Josh turned to face him, holding his hands up as he flashed an uncomfortable smile. "Now I need you to stay calm and let me finish what I'm about to tell you before you react, okay? This is important."

Jericho slowly got to his feet, flexing his shoulders and standing to his full height. He had learned from a young age that he had an intimidating physique. With the confidence and experience to take care of himself in almost any situation, he was accustomed to people doing what he told them. "Start... talking."

Josh took an involuntary step back. "All right, take it easy, *Bruce Banner*—we're on your side, remember? When you came in, it wasn't certain you'd even live through the surgery. Once it became evident you *would*, we started looking at the rest of your injuries. We knew we'd have to remove your damaged eye and saw an opportunity to—"

Jericho's good eye went wide with rage. He clenched his jaw and his fists, a physical effort to restrain himself from grabbing Josh by his throat. "What... did you... do to me?"

Josh held his hands up. "We saved your life and hopefully your sight. We've made some amazing advances in stem cell research, and—"

"You *experimented* on me while my life hung in the balance?" Jericho yelled.

Any trust he had invested in them since waking up was gone in an instant. All he could think about was the most basic of human instincts: self-preservation. He reached behind him and flung his chair across the room with one hand. It crashed into the wall just to the left of the TV, causing Schultz to jump in his seat.

"What gives you the right? You're supposed to be helping people, not treating them like lab rats!"

Suddenly, the door to the conference room burst open, and four men entered. They were all dressed similarly to Jericho, in GlobaTech-issue uniforms, except each of them had a sidearm holstered to their right thigh, a hand hovering over it. The men weren't as big as him, but they were big and capable all the same.

"Sir," said one of them, addressing Schultz. "Is everything okay in here?"

Josh took a step toward the group, holding one hand out at them and the other at Jericho. "Boys, we're fine. Just... stand down, okay? Jericho, listen to me—we're not your enemy. Maybe I was out of line before, but I stand by what I said. You need to stop thinking like a company man. You're on the outside now, like the rest of us. I know the CIA turning on you will have left you with a bitter taste in your mouth, but not everyone is out to get you. We did what we had to do to save your life. You have to calm down and trust us. If you leave now, and the CIA finds out you're still alive before we want them to, you'll be dead within the hour."

Jericho was standing in a loose fighting stance, his arms up in a low boxing guard, his muscles flexed. He felt like a caged animal. His instinct was to run. Not through fear but because he knew he had to distance himself from everything and everyone until he could figure out his next move.

He took a challenging step toward the group of men.

"Jericho, stop!" pleaded Josh. "There was no easy way of telling you about your injuries, and I'm sorry if you feel we violated your rights, but you need to let us explain!"

"Don't tell me what I need to do!" he shouted back, losing all control of his emotions. He felt an adrenaline rush surge through him, like a wave of fire touching every part of his body. He made no attempt to control it. He needed time, and this was the only way.

Without another word, two of the men moved toward him. Jericho responded by moving toward them and throwing a straight, heavy right hand at the man to his left. He gave it very little backswing, knowing the majority of the power lay within the first inch or two of movement. It was basic physics—the farther you travel, the more momentum you lose. The punch exploded forward, catching the man just below the cheekbone. The strength and fury contained within the blow sent him crashing to the floor, where he landed in an unconscious heap.

The man to his right attempted to grab him. Sensing the movement, Jericho turned and gripped the outstretched arm, pulling him sharply toward his own body. He then threw a short, quick elbow, jabbing the man just below his Adam's apple. The guy dropped to his knees, eyes wide with panic as he clutched at his throat, choking. Jericho turned his body sharply, slamming his knee into the guy's temple, sending him crashing into the wall.

Jericho turned toward the door as the remaining two men charged him. He leaned forward, dropped his right shoulder, and met the man on his left head-on. They collided like two primal animals, knocking the wind out of the GlobaTech operative. Jericho scooped him up with ease and launched him into the nearest wall. His body was five feet off the floor when it smashed into the TV screen. He landed heavily, the remains of the TV dropping on him a second later.

The remaining operative threw a kick, aiming for the ribs, but Jericho saw it coming in the corner of his good eye and turned to meet it. He caught the leg by hooking his arm around it just above the ankle. He held the man steady for a moment and then swept his other leg out from under him. Keeping hold of the guy's ankle as he fell flat on his back, he hooked both hands around it and twisted violently. He snapped it expertly, leaving the foot facing inward at a ninety-degree angle. The man screamed in pain, clutching at his deformed extremity.

Josh and Schultz stood motionless, both impressed and shocked in equal measure at the display of power and capability they had just seen.

Jericho paused for a split-second to look at them before bolting from the room. He turned left and headed along the brightly lit corridor, lined on either side by rooms just like the one he had left. He was on the fourth floor and knew it would be difficult to get out of the building and the compound without attracting further attention.

Reaching the small vestibule at the end, where the elevators were, Jericho glanced over his shoulder as he pressed the button, but no one was following him. He figured they would simply be calling ahead to have more men waiting for him downstairs.

The doors slid open, and he stepped inside, pressing the button for the second floor. He knew they would be expecting him to head straight for the first floor, so he would get off early and take the stairs in an effort to throw them off their game.

After a few moments, the elevator dinged, and the doors opened again. Jericho stepped out onto a crowded office floor, bustling with noise and activity. He glanced around and estimated there were close to two hundred people in front of him, all busying themselves at their desks or navigating walkways made from the spaces between banks of computers and filing cabinets.

No one paid him any attention as he strode urgently through the office toward the fire exit he had seen halfway along on the far side. At first, he thought it strange, but then he realized he was dressed like a GlobaTech operative, so it made sense that he would blend in.

He made it to the exit without incident and pushed the door open, casually stepping inside the cold, concrete column that he assumed ran the full height of the east wall. He descended the metal steps quickly, his footsteps echoing in the otherwise silent stairwell.

He opened the door at the bottom, and a blast of warm air hit him. He looked around the compound spread out around him, squinting while his eye adjusted to the glare of the sun. Units of soldiers were still marching in formation, and vehicles were still traversing the small, impressive community.

He couldn't see any way to get out of there. Even though he was dressed like everyone else, he was hardly inconspicuous. Aside from his hulking frame, the bandage around his head and over his eye made him stand out even more. He knew he didn't have much time before people located him. He broke into a jog and headed across the compound, hoping to hide in plain sight among the other operatives while he figured out how to escape.

Within seconds, a man dressed identically to him, though much smaller, approached from inside the next building along. He produced a weapon and pointed it at Jericho's chest. "D-don't move!" he yelled. "You need to come with me, r-right now!"

Jericho completely dismissed the man as a threat. His hand was shaking, which meant the gun was anything but steady. He was only standing twenty feet away, if that, yet Jericho was certain any bullet fired would still miss its mark.

He ignored the gun and stepped in close to the man, keeping the gap between them to a minimum, restricting whatever movement and options he might have had. He looked him in the eye and smiled with little humor. "No, I don't. I'm having a really shitty day, and I have bigger things to worry about than you. So, *move*."

The man held his ground, which was likely down to him being frozen to the spot with fear more than anything. Jericho saw the flicker of doubt in his eyes and reacted in a flash. He grabbed the guy's outstretched wrist and pulled him sharply toward him as he raised his right arm. The incoming face was met by Jericho's outgoing elbow, which connected sweetly with the man's jaw. His head whipped back from the impact, and his body fell limp almost instantly. Jericho let go of the wrist, catching the man's handgun as the body hit the floor.

There was a flurry of movement away to the right, which Jericho caught in his peripheral vision. A group of ten men, all wearing the same uniform, appeared and lined up in front of him, their weapons drawn and aimed with every intention of being used. It was a diverse group in terms of physical size, but each of them displayed far more confidence than the last guy.

"Jericho Stone," said one of the men. "Put the weapon down and come with us. We *will* use force if necessary."

Jericho spun to face them, holding the recently-acquired gun with both hands, ready for action. He eyed each man individually, finally resting his gaze on the one who spoke. He still seemed hesitant, as if lacking confidence in his own words. He kept looking over his shoulder for reassurance from his colleagues.

Jericho shook his head in disbelief. Ten guns aimed at one man, yet *they're* the ones who were nervous. That said, he'd had years of experience dealing with situations far worse than this, which gave him a considerable advantage. He knew it was all about confidence. If you stand tall, control your breathing, and don't blink, you can look incredibly intimidating to a lot of people. It didn't hurt when you had a physique that looked as if it were carved out of a mountain either.

Before anyone else could speak, Josh appeared, pushing his way through the group and standing in front of them. He was out of breath and looked more than a little disheveled.

"Don't do this, please," he said to Jericho. "You've got us all wrong. We're the good guys. We can help each other here..."

Jericho shook his head. "Illegal human experimentation isn't what good people do! I'm leaving, and I swear to God, I'll shoot the first asshole who tries to stop me."

He stared at Josh, who held his gaze longer than most people normally did. The group of men shuffled restlessly, gesturing with their weapons and preparing for the slightest movement.

The sound of an engine gunning away to Jericho's left distracted everyone. He turned and saw a Jeep speeding toward them from across the compound. It braked hard, skidding to a stop with a loud screech of tires, separating him from Josh and the group of operatives. The passenger door opened from within, and he quickly looked inside at the driver.

It was his nurse, Julie Fisher.

"Get in!" she shouted.

Jericho didn't need telling twice. He didn't trust anyone, but he figured not trusting them on the way out was preferable to not trusting them while still trapped inside. He quickly climbed in, and they sped off toward the security hub, only a few hundred yards away. She joined the network of roads at speed, navigated her way past a large truck, and took a right, sliding wildly and kicking up dust behind them. She hit the gas and sped toward the gate.

Two men appeared from inside the security hut but had no time to react. Jericho braced himself, and Julie gripped the wheel until her knuckles turned white as she blasted through the barrier with a loud crash. She immediately slammed on the brake, turned left, and then put her foot to the floor once again, accelerating west, away from the compound.

5

Rick Santiago sat facing the bank of computers in the communications room, across the hall from where Black had confronted him earlier. He was alone in the D.E.A.D. unit's operations center. Black and LaSharde were off-base together, and Baker was still in the armory, checking their equipment.

Santiago had a rough childhood, growing up in a small, underprivileged neighborhood in Santa Fe, New Mexico. Military service in his early twenties saved him from what would likely have been an early death—a result of a misspent youth, running with gangs and committing increasingly serious crimes. He carried the scars and the tattoos on his body as a constant reminder of what might have been.

He was slightly below average height, but his courage and his natural aggression more than compensated. He had proven himself a capable soldier early on in his career, but it wasn't until he discovered a previously unknown affinity for computers and technology that he really hit his stride. Nowadays, he typically ran support when the unit was on a mission, providing intel while they were on the ground. Only occasionally would he join them out in the field, though he was always a welcome and notable addition when he did.

He also had an instinctively suspicious mind, and something over the last week or so had been bothering him. Seizing a rare opportunity while alone, he used the unit's systems to hack into the CIA mainframe and pull the audio recordings from the Colombia mission. He scanned through the files, clicking an encrypted transmission with a time stamp that didn't fit in with their official mission log. He lowered the volume and leaned forward on the desk, listening intently.

"Chris Black, this is the Director of the CIA. Do not acknowledge this communication. Just listen. We're monitoring your mission in real time at Langley, and we believe your commanding officer, Jericho Stone, is jeopardizing the integrity of an ongoing investigation. The laptop you've been sent to retrieve belongs to an undercover asset named Yalafi Hussein, whom Adrian Hell believes is a terrorist. Find out what he knows and silence him. I am officially executing Alpha Protocol. You know what that means, soldier. Do your duty."

Santiago frowned and replayed the message.

Black didn't even hesitate in carrying out that order, he thought. *How could he go against Jericho like that?*

There was a noise behind him, and he quickly closed down the file and spun around on his chair.

"What are you doing?" asked Black, who had appeared in the doorway.

Santiago shrugged casually. "Nothing important. Just doing some research while I had the spare time." He turned back around and pressed a few more keys, quickly deleting any trace that he had accessed the file while trying to remain as nonchalant as possible. "There—I've finished up now. Do you want me running comms once we know the location of the stolen intel, or am I on the ground with the rest of you?"

Black stared at him, his eyes narrowing with suspicion. "I want you monitoring the satellite feeds," he replied after a moment. "I doubt we'll be the only ones looking for this Vincent guy, and I want to know if we have company down there."

Santiago nodded and stepped to the side as Black moved forward, inspecting the console. "Makes sense. I'll make sure I give the local authorities a heads-up too, so there's no resistance should anything not go according to plan."

Black slowly looked away from the bank of computers, meeting Santiago's gaze. "Good. We need to get this information as quietly as possible."

"And we definitely don't know what it is that Vincent's taken?"

Black took a short, impatient breath. "No, we don't. And I don't see why it would matter..."

"I'm just thinking out loud," he said, shrugging innocently. "If we knew what it was, we might have a better idea about who, if anyone, would be coming after the target besides us. It'll make things easier."

"Don't you worry about that. Just concentrate on keeping us safe while we're out there."

Santiago sighed. "You're the boss."

Black took a small step toward him. "Yeah, I am. Something you'd do well to remember."

They were standing just a few feet apart, with neither man backing down. They held each other's gaze for a few tense, silent seconds and then Santiago rolled his eyes and let slip a small smile before walking out of the room.

Black watched him leave and then quickly moved over to the console, desperately searching for evidence of what Santiago had been doing before he arrived. He checked the logs to see what files and systems had recently been accessed, but there was nothing that looked suspicious.

He slammed his fist down on the desk with frustration. He leaned forward, resting his hands flat on the surface, staring at nothing in particular and breathing heavily. After a moment, he reached into his pocket and pulled out his cell phone, dialing a number from memory. The call was answered on the third ring.

"Jones."

"Julius, it's Black. I think we might have a problem."

"What is it?"

Black took a deep breath before speaking. "I've got a bad feeling about Rick Santiago—the way he's been acting since Colombia. Are you able to arrange a search against his profile to see what systems and information he's accessed in the last six hours?"

"You can do that yourself," replied Jones, somewhat dismissively.

"I know, and I have, but there's nothing there."

"So, what's the problem, Chris?"

"I think he might have deleted his usage history in some way. The only person I know skilled enough to work around that is him. Can you get one of your analysts to do it?"

"What's this really about?" Jones asked, lowering his voice. "You've been on edge all week. Did we choose the wrong man for this job?"

Black closed his eyes for a second, cursing himself for prompting that line of questioning from Langley. "No, of course not. It's just he's been vocally opposing both myself and the orders you're sending me. But discipline isn't the issue. I think he's up to something. It's not like him to question things."

Jones sighed. "Okay, leave it with me. I'll be in touch."

Black clicked off the line and pocketed the phone as he walked hastily out of the room, toward the entrance.

6

Jericho leaned back in his seat, casting a glance sideways at Julie. He saw a thin film of sweat on her brow. Her eyes were narrowed, focusing intently on the road ahead. They passed a sign that said the freeway was two miles out.

"Why are you doing this?" he asked her after a few minutes of silence. "Why help me?"

Julie's hands began to shake as they gripped the wheel. The concentration on her face waned slightly, and tears welled up in her eyes. When she spoke, her voice cracked with emotion. "I... I don't know. What they did to you wasn't right. I... I tried telling them to wait until you woke up, but—"

Jericho gently placed a hand on her shoulder. "It's okay. Just relax. I'm grateful, whatever your reasons." He glanced over his shoulder, looking through the back window to check if they were being followed, but couldn't see anything suspicious. "Just try to stay calm and focus on the road. Forget about everything else for now, okay?"

Julie took a deep breath and nodded. After a half-mile in

light traffic, Jericho pointed to a gas station just ahead of them. "Pull in here."

She drove in and killed the engine in front of an unoccupied pump. She turned in her seat and stared at him. "Now what?"

"Now we drop off the grid while I figure out my next move," he replied.

He opened the door and stepped out of the vehicle. The strangely pleasant smell of gasoline hit his nostrils. He looked up and down the road but still couldn't see anyone he thought might be a tail, which he thought was strange. In his experience, if someone escapes from somewhere and starts running, the first thing you do is run after them. After everything they had told him, it didn't make sense that they would just let him leave.

Julie got out, stretched, and then walked around the front of the car to stand with him. She pointed toward the store. "I'm just going to use the restroom. I think I need to freshen up a little bit."

He quickly stepped in front of her and grabbed her arm firmly, holding her still. He shook his head. "They'll have security cameras everywhere in there. We need to limit our visibility as best we can and keep a low profile until I know what I'm dealing with here."

He glanced around and saw a white sedan parked in front of the pump just ahead of them. It was rusty around the edges and hadn't been cleaned in an age. It wasn't flashy, and it had local plates. No one would look twice at it. It was perfect.

He couldn't see anyone inside the vehicle. He took a couple of steps toward it, glancing casually through the window of the store, and saw a small line of people by the checkout. He figured the owner was one of them, so he looked over at Julie and said, "Come on, quickly."

He made his way over to the car, pausing for a moment to discreetly slide the gun he had into a trashcan, not wanting to risk being caught with it, and slid in behind the wheel.

Julie climbed in beside him a moment later. "What the hell are you *doing*?" she asked with disbelief.

"I'm borrowing this car," he replied, as if it were the most natural thing in the world. "We need to stay off GlobaTech's radar for a while, which means ditching their vehicle. They'll have it LoJacked, which means they can see wherever we are." He looked across at her and smiled reassuringly. "Trust me, okay? I know what I'm doing."

She held her breath and nodded.

He started the engine and eased away from the gas station, turning left and heading back the way they had come.

Julie frowned. "I thought you wanted to get away from GlobaTech? Why are we heading straight for them?"

Jericho glanced at her. "They saw us go left. Human instinct is to keep running from danger. It won't occur to them that we'd stop and turn around, so we'll head the other way, free and clear."

"And then what?"

"Once we're out of the city, I'll think of something."

It wasn't long before they shot past the main compound. They continued on for another twenty minutes without speaking. The sun was blazing, and Jericho had the window wound down, resting his arm on the frame. The car didn't have air conditioning, and while the speed created a mild breeze, the heat made it far from refreshing.

"Should you be driving with only one eye?" asked Julie,

breaking the silence. "It'll affect your ability to judge distances."

"It's fine," he replied with a shrug. "I've driven under worse conditions in my time."

Progress slowed as the traffic got heavier, but Jericho wasn't concerned. He figured they had bought themselves at least twenty-four hours. He checked his rearview every few minutes out of habit but still saw nothing that raised the alarm.

They sped past a sign informing them Los Angeles was thirty miles away, which he estimated would take about forty-five minutes if the traffic stayed as it was.

Julie had noticed the sign too. "We're going to L.A.?"

Jericho nodded but didn't take his eye off the road. "It's a big place—easy to hide and stay hidden. I need time to think."

She didn't say anything. She just leaned back in her seat and let out a slow, heavy sigh. Jericho flashed a glance across at her, watching for a moment as she stared blankly out the window. He was grateful to her for sticking her neck out for him the way she had, although he still couldn't understand why. It was a gutsy move for a nurse with a small frame and innocent eyes. But he wasn't complaining. Without her, he would still be fighting a small army of GlobaTech operatives.

Fifteen minutes passed before either of them spoke again.

"So, what's your story, anyway?" asked Julie.

"How do you mean?" replied Jericho.

"Is it true you worked for the CIA before this?"

Jericho paused before answering, choosing his words carefully. Even after everything that had happened, he still wasn't sure if he could fully trust her and thought it best to keep his cards close to his chest.

"In a manner of speaking, yes," he said, vaguely. "I ran a specialized unit that focused on preventing large-scale threats to both national and international security."

"Wow!" she said with a small, shocked laugh. "That sounds... really important. Is that what D.E.A.D. was, then?"

Jericho threw her a sideways glance and flicked an eyebrow questioningly.

She smiled weakly. "I overheard Mr. Winters talking while you were in your coma. What does it stand for?"

"It means 'Doesn't Exist on Any Database'. It means I'm a ghost." He shook his head to himself, letting slip a small smile, thinking how silly it felt to say that after everything that had happened. "Or at least I used to be."

"So, do you remember what happened to you?"

He shrugged. "I'm getting there. I know that a member of my old unit turned on me—shot me in the goddamn head."

"That's unbelievable. I mean, why would he even do something like that?"

Jericho shook his head. "That's one of the things I need to figure out. Winters and Schultz offered me an explanation, but I don't believe them. I *can't*... I need to find out for myself what happened."

"Mr. Winters is a good man," said Julie. "And Mr. Schultz is... well, his heart's in the right place." She laughed a little, but Jericho didn't react. "It's just, with everything that's going on right now, they're pretty much in charge of supporting the world, y'know? That's GlobaTech's mission. Just... go easy on them, okay? They're not your enemy, regardless of how they've treated you."

Jericho stopped at a red light and looked over at her, holding her gaze. He had always believed he could learn everything he needed to know about a person by looking into their eyes. She seemed nervous and tired, but she had an innocence that shone through more than anything. A genuine, kind nature that made him believe she was being honest with him.

"How did GlobaTech get involved in the first place?" he asked. "Surely, after an attack of this magnitude, the U.N. would arrange relief and foreign aid?"

"I don't know the specifics, but I know we lost one of our directors, Robert Clark, during the terrorist attack. Mr. Schultz was originally with us as a consultant, but given his history, the board of directors didn't blink when they gave him the role of Acting CEO, and he believes GlobaTech is the best option to support everyone affected. We have the money and the technology, so it makes sense."

He set off again, turning right and settling at an inconspicuous cruise.

"It's still an awful lot of responsibility for a company whose primary function is to act as an army-for-hire," he said.

"You really don't trust them, do you?"

"Can you blame me? I wake up from a coma to find they've done some kind of experiment on me..." He paused for a moment, his mind focusing on his bandage and what might lie beneath it. "Then they feed me some crazy story about the CIA being responsible for everything that's happened to the world in the last forty-eight hours."

Julie shifted in her seat. "Have you... have you seen the news?"

He shook his head. "I've not really had time to stop and watch TV."

"It's just... tragic. Some of the images... entire cities

reduced to dust... millions of bodies..." Her voiced started to crack with sadness, and she sniffed back tears. "People are saying this will change the world forever."

"They're probably right," he replied casually. "And I'm sure whoever's responsible will be brought to justice."

"President Cunningham was on TV yesterday saying they've already captured the man behind it all."

"And you believe him?"

Julie shrugged. "I know what people are saying at Globa-Tech, about a conspiracy. It seems a little far-fetched to me."

"And me. But your bosses seemed pretty convinced."

Traffic slowed to a crawl as they closed in on the City of Angels. Jericho sounded his horn as a van cut him off and gestured with frustration as he narrowly avoided slamming into the back of it.

"Asshole," he muttered under his breath.

Julie continued. "But what if they're right, Jericho? I know it sounds crazy, but what if the CIA really *did* cause all this? And what if the president is pulling the strings?"

"Well, they're big ifs," he replied. "But *if* the CIA is responsible, and I'm somehow involved... being used as someone's instrument... I'll find out for sure who's behind it all and make them pay."

That last statement finished the conversation, and they entered the Los Angeles city limits in silence. They passed Dodger Stadium on their left, heading into the Chinatown district. It didn't take them long to find a no-name hotel on the main street, overlooking a row of restaurants opposite.

They pulled into the small parking lot at the back and stopped in a space near the rear entrance.

"Do you have any money?" asked Jericho, looking over at Julie.

She shook her head regretfully. "I left work in kind of a hurry. My bag's still there, and my credit card's inside it."

"All right, it's not a major issue. We need to use cash anyway, so they can't trace the transaction."

He started the engine again and eased back out of the parking lot, turning right.

"Where are we going?" Julie asked.

"To make a withdrawal," replied Jericho tersely.

7

The sun had almost completely disappeared behind the skyline, and the sound of the city's nightlife awakening floated in through the open window, growing louder as the remaining slivers of daylight faded. They had grabbed some lunch using cash they found in the glove box and spent the afternoon and early evening staying mobile, staying no more than an hour in any one place before moving on. It might have been overly cautious, but Jericho didn't want to take any chances.

He guided the sedan along the busy street, absently scanning the sidewalks as they went by, which were crowding up with people out for the evening. He wondered how many of the attractive, scantily-clad women he saw were aspiring actresses—somebody's daughter, putting herself on the line for that one big break.

He caught the eye of a tall, stunning blonde, who was teetering precariously on her six-inch heels. He rolled the sedan along slowly as the queue of traffic filtered through the intersection ahead of them. Momentarily distracted, he flashed the young blonde a polite, innocent smile. She reciprocated for a split-second before her gaze rested on his bandaged head. Her eyes widened, and she looked away, quickly gossiping to the brunette she was walking with. Despite the multitude of problems facing Jericho, he still found himself disheartened by the girl's superficial reaction.

Again, he moved his hand slowly up to his head, feeling the rough material beneath his fingers.

"So, how exactly are you going to get cash?" asked Julie. "You've been stalling all day..."

Jericho snapped back into the moment and looked over at her. She was smiling a little, which he took as a mixture of sympathy and embarrassment. He decided to ignore the fact she had probably seen what just happened.

"The thing with places like L.A.," he said, "is that, if you know where to look, you can lay your hands on pretty much anything... including money. You just have to wait for the right time."

He turned left when he reached the lights ahead of them, which led them to a small but popular district filled with exclusive nightclubs and restaurants. Between two particular establishments, which both had modest crowds congregating out front, was an alleyway, dimly lit and partially obscured by a thin mist from the air vents of the buildings on either side.

"Wait here," he said, getting out of the car. He looked up and down the street briefly and then crossed over, casually blending himself in with the throng of people on the sidewalk. After a few moments, he discreetly stepped away and headed down the alley, which opened out into a small square a couple of hundred feet in. It was surrounded by tall buildings, with just a narrow passage leading out the other side.

"You lost, son?" said a voice to his right.

He turned and saw a black man leaning against the wall, dressed in a large overcoat and loose-fitting jeans, with expensive-looking sneakers poking out the bottom. He wore a baseball cap high, with the peak almost vertical. He was clean-shaven, maybe late twenties.

Jericho glanced over his shoulder, back to the street. No one was paying any attention. He turned to face the man. "Not lost," he replied, shaking his head. "Just looking."

The man stepped closer, stopping only a couple of feet in front of Jericho. "That right? And what you lookin' for, big man?"

He was quick to pick up on the confidence in the man's voice. He knew the type. Low-level dealers, earning enough coin to live the life their limited imagination allowed them to dream of, deluded by their own arrogance. The man showed no hesitation or concern, as if he didn't feel threatened at all despite Jericho's intimidating presence and physique. He almost certainly had back-up hiding somewhere nearby, most likely listening or watching.

He smiled to himself, amused at the man's unjustified swagger. Then he gestured to his bandage, which he knew was far from inconspicuous. "I need something for the pain."

"You're a big guy," said the man, shrugging. "I reckon you can manage."

"I don't know... I'm in a *lot* of pain."

"Oh, you about to be, homie..."

The man's gaze flicked momentarily to his right. Jericho spotted the look and glanced over his shoulder. Two more guys appeared from the opposite alleyway, dressed in similar outfits. They made their way over slowly, as if making a point that they were in no hurry, that he wasn't important and could wait for them.

Jericho looked back at the first man as his friends moved either side of him, forming a close triangle around him. "Is this really necessary? I'm not here to—"

"You damn right this is necessary, fool! I'm a business-man, and this is how I do business. You don't like it, get to steppin', you feel me?"

Jericho held his hands up apologetically. "Fair enough."

"So, are you a cop, big man?"

Jericho arched an eyebrow. "Do I look like a cop?"

"Yeah, you kinda do," he replied with a humorless smile.

"Huh... really? Well, that's a pain in the ass. I'm *not*, by the way, and you shouldn't judge a book by its cover. Tell me, do you treat all your potential customers with such prejudice and contempt?"

"Whatever, man. In my line of work, you're guilty until proven innocent, y'know what I'm sayin'? Now my boys here are gonna search you. I hope, for your sake, we find nothin' but cash. Otherwise, you gonna have a problem, you feel me?"

Jericho smiled regrettably. "Look, I appreciate you need to be careful in your line of work. I do. But I swear to God, if any of you lay a hand on me, I'm gonna break it."

The man took a step back, his face a split-second picture of shock before lighting up with a large, white and gold smile. "Ah, shit—you just gone and got yourself *killed*, bro." He turned to his friends. "Mess this fool up!"

Jericho turned to look at them as they moved toward him. Their bulky frames and weathered faces gave the impression they were professional muscle, but he knew they posed no serious threat. Their barrel chests proved they worked out, but their slumped shoulders suggested a laziness or inability to fight hard and effectively on a moment's notice. Also, their feet were too flat on the ground. They were too heavy, which meant they were too slow. All of which told Jericho everything he needed to know.

He took one giant step forward and met the guy on his left head-on. Before he could move, Jericho thrust his left leg forward without breaking stride and kicked him hard in the groin. The man buckled over instinctively. As his head lowered, Jericho took another step and lifted his right knee, smashing it into the man's face. He felt the cartilage in the nose break under the impact and watched as the guy crumbled to the ground like a dead weight.

Jericho turned to face the other man, who hesitated briefly before throwing a looping punch at his face. Jericho caught it in his large right hand, stopping it dead. The impact stung his palm, but his face betrayed nothing. He stared into the man's shocked, wide eyes and saw a wave of fear sweep across them. He threw the man's hand down and launched one of his own—a quick, stiff jab that connected flush on the bend of the jaw. The man flailed backward and landed hard next to his friend, stunned but not unconscious.

Jericho spun around to face the first guy again, breathing heavily from the surge of adrenaline. It felt good to get involved again—to feel capable. His world had been turned upside-down, and being able to take down a bunch of lowlifes made him feel... himself again.

The man produced an old Colt Python, with a four-inch barrel that fired .357 rounds, aiming it directly at him. He was standing maybe ten feet away. Jericho noticed the faintest of quivers in his hand. He stared into the man's wide eyes, seeing the fear etched onto his face.

He was right to be afraid.

"Give me whatever cash you have, and maybe you get to

walk home unaided tonight," said Jericho, feeling that was a perfectly reasonable proposal.

"Sc-screw you!" replied the man. "I'm gonna shoot you!"

Jericho smiled. "No, you're not."

The man frowned. "And what makes you so sure, fool? I got a gun pointing right at you."

Jericho nodded. "Yes, you do... but you've got the safety on."

The man shifted his gaze to the weapon. In that split-second, Jericho charged forward, covering the minimal distance between them in the blink of an eye. He grabbed the guy's wrist, twisting it away from his body, so the reflex caused him to loosen his grip and drop the weapon. As it clattered to the ground, Jericho launched a thunderous right elbow—the point of which, along with the bulk of his large forearm, connected with the man's left temple. He let out a low grunt as the consciousness was smashed out of him, and he landed with a dull thud.

Jericho took a step back and scanned the area, making sure no one else was coming. Satisfied he was alone, he checked the man's pockets and found a handful of small bags, each containing varying measurements of crystal meth.

He shook his head and muttered, "Unbelievable."

Even though the president had legalized cocaine, people still sought to make money from selling cheap—and presumably poor quality—narcotics to gullible idiots looking for a quick score.

He put the drugs back in the guy's pocket and continued his search, quickly finding a roll of cash and a cell phone. He counted close to a thousand bucks, which was useful. He stuffed the money and the phone in his pockets and reached over to retrieve the gun, which had landed a couple of feet away from them. He stood, admiring it for a moment. It looked small in his giant hand.

He glanced at the man, who was still out cold. "It doesn't even have a safety, asshole."

He flicked open the barrel and emptied the bullets onto the ground before tossing the gun away. He checked the other two guys but found nothing besides a couple of hundred dollars between them. He added it to his new wad, looked around one last time, and then made his way back to the street.

He re-entered the crowd of eager partygoers, mingled casually for a moment or two, and then strolled back across the road and climbed in behind the wheel of the sedan. He reached into his pocket and pulled out the cash, dropping it on Julie's lap.

She stared at it, surprised. "Where the hell did you get all that? There must be close to a thousand dollars there!"

"A little over twelve hundred, actually," corrected Jericho, shrugging. "Like I said, a place like this... you just have to know where to look."

He gunned the engine, spun the car around, and drove back to the hotel they had found earlier in the day, parking in the same space as before.

They walked in through the main entrance and across the small foyer. Jericho looked at Julie. "Book us in for one night. It'll be better if you do it as you're less memorable."

"Gee, thanks..." she responded, sounding slightly disgruntled.

He rolled his eyes. "I just mean we're trying to keep a low profile, and if anyone's questioned, they're more likely to remember a guy who's six-five with half his head wrapped in a bandage."

"I know what you mean. Relax," she said, smiling. "Will one night be long enough?"

Jericho nodded. "By the morning, I'll know exactly what we need to do. Don't worry."

Julie approached the young woman sitting behind the desk while he hung back, casually checking out the place. The décor was simple, yet effective. There was minimal furnishing in the entrance, with a stand in the left corner by the door that had several different pamphlets detailing local attractions. The floor was plain, clean tiling, and the front desk was a simple counter, about waist height, with two people sitting behind it. The elevators and stairs were off to the right.

After a few minutes, Julie returned, holding a swipe card. "They only had a double left," she said, looking sheepish and a little awkward. "Sorry."

Jericho shook his head. "That's fine—I'll take the chair. I've slept on worse." He turned and strode over to the elevator, pressing the button to call it. "Which floor?"

Julie checked the key and replied, "Third."

The doors opened, and they stepped inside. Jericho hit the button for the third floor, and within a minute, they were walking toward their room along a featureless hallway, with peeling paint on the walls and a threadbare carpet underfoot.

Julie worked the door and opened it, stepping inside and holding it open behind her for Jericho. He paused, quickly checked up and down the corridor, making sure there was nothing suspicious, and then followed her inside, locking the door behind him.

The room, like the reception area, was basic but functional. A double bed against the right wall. A window facing them, offering a view of the street below and the restaurants opposite. A bathroom off to the left, with a shower cubicle in the corner. It was luxury compared to some places Jericho had spent the night.

He walked over to the window, glancing down to the street before closing the drapes. He turned and saw Julie sitting awkwardly on the edge of the bed, staring at the floor. He couldn't imagine what she must be going through right now. The things she'd done... the things she'd sacrificed to help him. She didn't even know him.

"Thank you," he said. "For everything. I'm really grateful."

She smiled weakly. "It's okay. I was just trying to do the right thing." Her voice lowered. "I hope I have..."

Jericho regarded her for a moment. She was still wearing her white uniform and nametag. Her flat shoes fitted shapelessly to her feet. She wore her shoulder-length, light brown hair down, tucked behind her ears on both sides. She looked deflated and afraid.

"First thing in the morning, we'll get a change of clothes," he said. "Then I'll disappear, and you can return to your normal life. Now sit tight. I'll be back soon."

She sat upright, looking at him with concern. "Where are you going?"

"I need to make a call. I took a cell phone along with the money. I can trash it once I'm done. I won't be long."

"Are you sure it's safe?"

"Honestly? I'm not sure of anything anymore. But I need to make this call. I know what I'm doing. Don't worry."

Julie nodded reluctantly. "Don't be long, okay?"

Jericho flashed a smile. "Just stay here, don't use the phone, and don't open the door for anyone besides me. Understand?"

Julie nodded again.

"You'll be fine," he reassured her.

"Promise?"

"Promise."

He took the keycard from her and left the room. He paused outside long enough to hear her lock the door behind him before walking back along the corridor and taking the elevator down to the lobby. He headed outside and stood on the sidewalk for a moment. He took a deep breath, tasting the stale air of Los Angeles.

He was wracked with uncertainty. He didn't know if he should believe what GlobaTech had told him. He didn't know if running from them was the right play, and he had no idea if the phone call he was about to make would help or make things worse.

He navigated the sea of pedestrians with a grace not befitting a man his size, walking for two blocks before stopping in the doorway of a store that had closed for the day. He took out the stolen cell phone and dialed a number from memory.

"Birchwood Savings and Loans. How may I direct your call?" asked a professional, direct female voice after a couple of rings.

"I'm calling to check my balance," recited Jericho. "My account number is three, three, two, three, alpha, nine."

"One moment please, while I retrieve your account information."

There was silence on the line for a few moments and then a click as the call was transferred. Jericho heard the faintest of sounds on the line but remained quiet.

"This account has been closed," said a male voice, deep and weary. "Who is this?"

Jericho hesitated, unable to shake the doubts implanted in his mind by Josh Winters. "It's me," he said eventually.

He was greeted with a moment's silence. Then a familiar voice said, "Jesus H. Christ! Jericho? What the hell happened to you? You've been dark for over a week."

The voice belonged to Julius Jones, a thirty-plus year veteran CIA analyst and the coordinator of the D.E.A.D. unit. Jericho's minimal obligations to the agency involved providing a weekly update to Jones on the progress of any missions. The last time they spoke was nine days ago, on an airstrip in Colombia.

Jericho decided to play it safe.

"I... don't remember much," he explained. "What happened back in Colombia? Did we retrieve the laptop?"

More silence followed. He assumed Jones would be putting a tracer on the call, so he figured he had maybe forty seconds before they tracked him down.

"You need to come in for a full de-brief," Jones said after a few moments. "Where are you?"

He took a breath to calm himself. He wanted to feed them a lie, to cover himself while he pressed for information to back up what Josh and Schultz had told him. The biggest sign that someone is lying is an elevated heart rate, which, with the right training, you can learn to detect in the person's voice.

"I'm not sure that's such a good idea," he replied. 'I woke up in a GlobaTech Industries medical facility. They let me leave, but I think they're following me. I've no idea why, but I think it's best I keep a low profile. Just tell me what happened, Julius."

"Wait a second... *woke up*? What happened to you?"

"They told me I'd been in a coma for over a week."

"Shit," muttered Jones. "Okay, listen to me very carefully. What have you said to them?"

Jericho clenched his jaw muscles and glared angrily at

the ground. He detected a hint of panic in Jones's voice, which wasn't a good sign.

"What do you mean?" he asked. "What could I have said to them? I don't remember anything after our target arrived in Colombia."

"Okay," said Jones, sounding relieved. "Did they say anything to you?"

"They said a lot of things, yeah, but nothing that made any sense to me."

"Jericho, you have to come in right away. If you do, maybe we can fix this."

"Fix what, Julius?"

Jones sighed heavily but said nothing.

"You still haven't located the laptop, have you?" Jericho persisted.

"No."

Jericho took a deep breath. He had managed to find out where the CIA were up to, and what they knew and didn't know, which was useful. He was aware the clock was ticking, but he needed more answers. He needed the truth.

"Why did you betray me, Julius?" he asked.

He heard a gasp, which was quickly subdued. "So, you *do* remember?"

"Yeah, I do. Answer the damn question."

"Because you compromised the goddamn mission!" hissed Jones, his tone changing in an instant. "You know how this works. Why didn't you do what you were ordered to?"

"Because it wasn't the right call," snapped Jericho, forgetting himself. "The mission was the laptop, and we were never going to find it with Adrian Hell dead. End of story. I was in charge of the unit, and I made the decision to—"

"*That* wasn't your decision to make," Jones interrupted. "I'd always been comfortable giving you the freedom to run that unit as you saw fit, and you never let me down. But when the CIA director gives you an order, it's non-negotiable! Christ, I thought you were smarter than that!"

Jericho went quiet, thinking about what GlobaTech had told him. He stepped out of the doorway, pacing slowly back and forth across the width of the sidewalk, ignoring the frustrations of people trying to get by.

"And why did the director feel he had to step in?" he asked finally. "Why was he so keen to terminate the target when there was no real reason to?"

His question was met with even more silence.

"Okay, do you know what was on the laptop that was so important?" he continued, curious to see if Jones would inadvertently confirm what GlobaTech had already told him.

Jones sighed heavily. "Look... how it went down was out of my hands. I don't know what information the laptop contained. Director Matthews gave the order, and he was under no obligation to justify himself. Jericho, if you come in now, voluntarily, I can help fix this. You have to trust me, all right?"

"Trust you? Answer my goddamn question, Julius. You can't honestly sit there and expect me to believe you had no idea why Director Matthews wanted Adrian Hell dead?"

"I don't know, all right?" He sighed again. "It's been a crazy few days, Jericho, and now isn't the time to be asking those types of questions. I can't talk over an unsecure line, but if you come in..."

"I'm not coming in, Julius. If you don't know anything about the laptop or why Matthews wanted the assassin taken out, that's fine. But I was shot and left for dead by someone I trusted, who was carrying out an order from *your* office. An order that could only have been given by the director. I want to know why."

"I know you're pissed, all right, but you know how this works. You know the world we live in."

"I *did*... but from what I've seen, the world's changed a little since I woke up." The line went quiet. Jericho shook his head in disbelief. In his experience, silence usually preceded guilt. "Julius, I swear to God, if I find out you had anything to do with anything that's happened, there won't be anywhere you can hide from me."

"We go way back, you and I," said Jones, sounding defensive. "I brought you in, helped train you..."

"Like you did with Adrian?"

"What? How did you—"

"I know a lot of things, Julius. Which makes me very dangerous."

"Look, Jericho, don't make this any worse for yourself. Come in. We'll talk..."

"We're done talking. I'm gone. Do you understand me? I'm out."

"You're *out*?" Jones laughed, exaggerating it to make a point. "People like you and me, we don't get *out*, Jericho. If you go down this path, there's no going back. Do you understand? If you do this, I can't help you."

Jericho felt a burst of anger inside, and he clenched his jaw tight to suppress it. He took some deep breaths as he stood in the middle of the sidewalk, forcing people to walk around him. "I don't need your help, you sonofabitch! You've spent the last week believing I'm dead. Let's leave it at that."

"You know I can't do that, Jericho. If you're alive, the agency will want you brought in. They'll want to—"

"If anyone comes after me, I'll send them back in a

bucket. Are we clear? And as for you... you're right. We've known each other a long time, and I can't just forget the respect I had for you, which means you get a pass this time. But you better hope and pray I don't see you again."

Jericho clicked the phone off, dropped it on the ground, and stamped down hard on it. He walked quickly back toward the hotel, cursing himself as he realized that was much longer than forty seconds.

8

Chris Black was sitting alone in the meeting room, leaning back in his chair with his feet resting up on the table in front of him. The rest of the squad were sleeping, but he couldn't settle his mind enough to do the same. Having spent the evening with LaSharde, he wanted to avoid waking her with his restlessness, so he had left her in bed, resting peacefully.

Over twenty-four hours had passed since his conversation with Jones, and he attributed his growing uneasiness to the fact he had yet to hear anything.

Suddenly, his phone rang, disturbing him from his anxious musing. It was on the table next to him, and the vibrating was amplified in the silence. He looked at the display, recognizing the number immediately.

"About damn time," he muttered. He put his feet down and leaned forward, resting on his elbows and stroking his chin as he answered. "Black."

"There's been some developments," said Julius Jones, dispensing with any pleasantries. "This is the first chance I've had to call."

Black sat up straight, disciplined and alert. "What is it?"

Jones sighed before speaking. "First of all, your mission. We've tracked Daniel Vincent to a hotel in Prague. You need to leave ASAP. We've got the jump on this, but our advantage won't last long."

"Copy that. I'll round up the team immediately. We'll be airborne in thirty minutes."

"Be aware that your target is employed by GlobaTech Industries. That means, in all likelihood, they will be actively searching for him as well. Be on your guard and avoid any unnecessary conflict. Am I clear?"

"Crystal."

"This mission must remain covert at all costs. Now, before you go, there are a couple of other things you need to know."

Black detected the change in Jones's tone. He assumed whatever was coming next wasn't good. "Go on..."

"I've spoken with Director Matthews regarding your concerns over Mr. Santiago," Jones began. "Your suspicions were accurate. He hacked into our secure mainframe and listened to an encrypted audio file—a recording of the director giving you the order to execute Jericho Stone."

"I knew he was up to something!" hissed Black. "That's why he's been asking so many questions..."

"The director no longer wishes Mr. Santiago to be a part of your unit. Do you understand what I'm saying to you, Chris?"

Black took a deep breath, clenching his jaw and glaring into space. "I do."

"You'll allow him to arrange your transport and then you will terminate his contract before you leave. Am I understood?"

"Copy that."

"Good. And finally, Chris, you personally have a very large problem."

He frowned. "What do you mean?"

"It's Jericho. He's still alive."

The words hung in the silence. Black stared blankly ahead of him, trying his best to comprehend them.

"That's not possible," he said finally. "Sir, I shot him in the head!"

Jones scoffed. "Whatever you did, it didn't work. I've spoken to the man personally. He's very much alive and is more than a little pissed off with the CIA."

"Where is he?" asked Black, getting to his feet. "I'll—"

"You'll do what you're told," said Jones, cutting him off. "Jericho's with GlobaTech, so you can't get to him. But I suspect he'll come to you very soon, so be ready."

Black was angry in a way he didn't know he was capable of. He knew that anger was directed more at his own failure to take out Jericho than anything else, and his mind was already racing to think of a way to redeem himself.

"If he's working for GlobaTech now, he'll definitely be in Prague," he said after a moment.

"That's my thinking too," agreed Jones. "Which is all the more reason to watch your back while you're over there and keep this whole thing quiet."

Black hung up without another word, pocketed the phone, and began pacing back and forth in the room, like a caged lion. As he neared the table again, he let out a guttural scream and slammed his right fist down on the surface.

"Shit!"

Fifteen minutes later, Chris Black stood facing the three members of his unit, summoned on a moment's notice to prepare for action. He had taken a little time to compose himself before waking them, wrapping his head around what he must do and what was to come.

"I've received information from Langley," he announced. "Daniel Vincent works for GlobaTech Industries and is currently hiding out in Prague."

"GlobaTech?" queried Baker. "Those guys are golden at the moment..."

"I know," agreed Black, "which is why this mission needs to happen quietly. We suspect they'll be sending a team to retrieve him, so we need to get there first and bring him back. We absolutely do not engage any hostiles unless we have to."

The team exchanged glances before nodding their understanding.

"There's something else," continued Black. He paused for a moment, taking a breath, preparing himself for what he was about to say. He quickly thought of all the different ways he could say it, but in the end decided to just come out with it, like ripping off a Band-aid. "Jericho Stone is still alive, and he's working for GlobaTech."

The sound of a collective intake of breath filled the room.

"How?" asked LaSharde, her eyes wide with shock and disbelief.

Black shook his head. "I honestly don't know, but he's already made contact with Langley and threatened to go after Jones. My guess is he'll want revenge, and he won't understand that everyone was just following orders. We all need to watch our backs until he's taken care of."

"What makes you think he'll want revenge?" asked Santiago quietly, speaking for the first time.

Black looked at him like he was an idiot. "Wouldn't you? I know I would..."

"No offense, boss, but you're not Jericho. The man I knew was a soldier and a patriot. Revenge wasn't really his thing."

Black took a step forward and glared at Santiago, who was sitting with an impassive look on his face that only served to anger him further. "I'd watch your mouth if I were you. Just remember who you're talking to."

Santiago smiled. "Yeah, well, you're not me either. And I wasn't following orders—you were. I think you're afraid. And if *I* were *you*, I'd be afraid too."

The two men held each other's gazes for a few tense, silent moments. Eventually, Baker cleared his throat and intervened. "All right. Let's take a breath, fellas. Chris, what's the plan for getting Vincent?"

Black looked over at him, pointing at Santiago. "Assuming it's no trouble for *him* to arrange, we need to be airborne in thirty minutes."

Santiago shrugged. "Piece of cake, homie."

Black took a breath and stepped away, turning his back on the unit for a moment. Then he spun around again, refocused on the task at hand. "Baker, LaSharde—head to the armory and gear up. Santiago, console room. Get us in the air ASAP."

He strode out of the room, heading out of the building and across the dusty, moonlit courtyard toward the barracks. There was something he needed to get before they left.

Five minutes later, he joined LaSharde and Baker in the armory. They were already kitted out—tactical vests, assault rifles, handguns... the works. They were standing side by side, facing Santiago, who had just started speaking as Black approached.

"The chopper's three minutes out," Santiago explained. "It'll fly you to our usual airfield, where a Lockheed C5 will take you directly to Prague. When you land, there'll be a transport vehicle waiting to take you straight to the target's location. You'll have the full support of local law enforcement while you're there too, and I'm watching via satellite, so—"

"Actually," interrupted Black, "I've just got off the line to Langley. There's been a slight change to the mission brief." He shuffled slightly to his right, putting his body mere inches from Santiago's. His left hand slowly moved behind him, and when he spoke, he addressed LaSharde and Baker. "Director Matthews himself has advised that due to the sensitive nature of the mission, Langley will be monitoring the mission via a comms link to their local station..." He paused and turned to Santiago. "Which means we no longer need your services."

In a flash, he produced a KA-BAR combat knife and whipped his body clockwise, thrusting the seven-inch blade into Santiago's gut, just to the left of his navel. His eyes went wide. The shock counteracted the pain, which would inevitably follow shortly.

The others gasped, and Baker instinctively took a step forward, but LaSharde stopped him. Black ignored them both, placing his right hand on the back of Santiago's head and leaning in close.

"If *you* were *me*," he hissed angrily, "you wouldn't have asked the same questions that got that steroid-induced freak disavowed and shot! I'm just following orders here, Rick... it's nothing personal."

He withdrew the knife and let go of his head, smiling

into Santiago's bulging eyes as he watched him drop to the armory floor, clutching at his stomach wound. Blood pumped out, soaking his hands and the dusty concrete around him, staining it a dark crimson.

Black wiped his blade on his leg and slid it back into its sheath before turning to face the others.

"That," he said, pointing to Santiago, "is what happens when you disobey a direct order from the director of the CIA. I trust the three of us are on the same page here?"

He knew LaSharde was with him, for obvious reasons. He assumed Baker was as well, but there was no harm in proving a point. After a moment, they both nodded.

The chopper sounded overhead, interrupting the scene. Black looked up and smiled, quickly moving to grab his gear as it made its descent. Moments later, the three of them were airborne and bound for Prague.

9

April 20, 2017

The next morning, Jericho left Julie sleeping and headed out to buy them both a change of clothes and some breakfast. He was still dressed like a GlobaTech operative, and she still had her nurse's uniform on, so they were both in need of a wardrobe change.

He found a department store that opened early, so he picked the first thing he could find that fit his large frame— a pair of light blue jeans, a plain white T-shirt, and a tan, zip-up hooded sweater. He kept the boots he was wearing.

He guessed Julie's size and picked out a similar outfit for her, quickly finding a feminine sweater and skinny-fit jeans. He also sprung for a pair of sneakers, which he figured she would prefer. He never professed to know much about women, but he knew that, where possible, comfortable shoes were always a good thing.

He changed into his new clothes in the store and paid for everything in cash. He put his old clothes in the first trash can he found and made his way back to the hotel, stopping in a Starbucks on the way to pick up two coffees and a couple of bagels.

He opened the door to the room just as Julie was stepping out of the bathroom, dripping wet and wearing a short towel wrapped around her slender frame.

She gasped as their eyes met, placing her hand to her chest, startled. "Oh my God!" she said, breathing heavily. "You scared the crap outta me!"

Jericho stood, momentarily frozen with embarrassment, staring at her. He couldn't help but cast a quick, approving eye over her before regaining his senses and respectfully turning his back.

"I'm sorry. I didn't realize..." He took a couple of steps back without looking around and held out the bag containing her new clothes. "Here—I hope they fit."

Julie took the bag and looked inside. "Thanks." She gestured to the bathroom with her thumb. "I'll just go and... y'know."

"Yeah... of course. Sorry."

He turned only when he heard the bathroom door close.

"Jesus..." he muttered to himself, unable to suppress a small smile.

He placed the coffee and bagels on the table near the door and sat on the edge of the bed, waiting patiently. After a few minutes, the door opened again, and Julie appeared, dry and dressed in her new outfit.

"What do you think?" she asked with a shrug, cocking her hip out to the side in a light-hearted pose.

Jericho looked at her approvingly. The sweater was a little big, but she seemed comfortable enough in it. The skinny jeans were a perfect fit. It was the first time he had seen her in anything other than the nurse's uniform. She had a great figure, her legs deceptively long and toned.

"You look great," he replied, which he noticed made her cheeks flush a little. He nodded at the table. "Breakfast is over there. Hope you like coffee."

"Who doesn't?" she said, eagerly taking a sip. She closed her eyes, savoring the taste before looking back at him. "How did you sleep?"

Jericho shrugged. "I've slept enough over the last week. You?"

"I got a few hours but nothing significant."

She handed him his coffee, which he took gladly. He had a mouthful and moved over to the window, looking down at the street below. The sun was rising, and the new day was already in full flow. He turned back to look at her.

"What did GlobaTech do to me?" he asked her, gesturing to his bandage.

Julie took a deep breath and a sip of her coffee before replying. "If I tell you, are you going to freak out and run, like you did before?"

Jericho smiled, feeling a little embarrassed. "No, I promise. I just need to know."

She took a seat on the bed, where he had sat a moment ago, holding her coffee in both hands. "Okay... your right eye was damaged beyond repair by the bullet. You know that already, right?"

He nodded. "Josh mentioned it, yeah."

"Well, they had to remove it completely during surgery."

Jericho's left eye went wide, and he gestured angrily to his bandage. "What? Are you telling me I have no eyeball under this thing?"

Julie went silent, avoiding his gaze.

"What? Tell me."

She took a deep breath before continuing. "GlobaTech has been doing a lot of research on stem cells as part of an ongoing healthcare program designed to aid the recovery of damaged limbs. It started out as a project to help injured soldiers, but early success prompted further investment, the plan being for a more commercial application."

Jericho frowned. "Josh started to say something about stem cells. Isn't that to do with, like, cloning or something?"

Julie nodded. "About a month ago, GlobaTech manufactured a right hand in their labs and were able to successfully attach it to a field operative who lost their own during a skirmish. Since then, they've been able to grow... pretty much anything."

She trailed off, and Jericho quickly put the pieces together. "I have an artificial eyeball in my head? What the hell!"

"Hey, you promised you wouldn't freak out!"

"Yeah, but that was before I found out you'd put a fake... real... whatever, eyeball in my skull! Jesus!"

"The surgery was successful," she explained. "It just needs time to... settle, for want of a better word, before you start using it."

"So, what's going to happen if I take the bandage off now?" he asked. "Is it going to fall out or something?"

"I doubt it," she replied, smiling. "Personally, my only concern is the stitching across your forehead. If that's not properly healed, you run the risk of re-opening the wound, which would result in rapid and significant blood loss."

Jericho stroked his chin, feeling the stubble scratch against his fingertips.

"This is ridiculous," he said, mostly to himself. He took some deep breaths, subduing the surge of adrenaline coursing through him, brought on by both his anger and his confusion. "Right, well, we need to try. If I'm going to lay low for a while, I need to be invisible." He tapped the tourniquet covering the left side of his face and head. "This thing's got to go."

She thought for a moment and then nodded. "Okay. Come into the bathroom, and we'll take a look."

Jericho followed her in, put the toilet seat down, and sat on the edge. Julie stood in front of him, pulling the cord for the light above the sink. She leaned forward, close to him, her face inches from his. He could smell her scent, and while he figured it was just the body wash from her shower, he still thought it was nice. He looked into her brown eyes as she examined his bandage, her fingertips carefully touching his forehead.

"I think we'll be okay removing it," she said after a few moments. "Hold still."

Slowly, she began unraveling it from around his head, revealing more and more of his face. Instinctively, Jericho closed his eyes. He still didn't fully understand how he could have an eyeball in his head that was made in a lab. He felt apprehensive about opening it once the bandage was off, simply because he didn't know what to expect.

It took Julie a couple of minutes to remove all the layers of dressing. Jericho gradually opened both eyes and was pleasantly surprised when he found he could see normally with both of them. He blinked tentatively a few times and looked around the small bathroom. It was like it always had been—two eyes, perfect vision.

Julie took a step back, looking at him. She raised her eyebrows.

"What?" he asked, seeing the expression on her face, suddenly feeling self-conscious.

She smiled. "See for yourself," she said, nodding to the mirror mounted on the wall over the sink.

Jericho stood and took a deep breath, turning to face the mirror, ducking slightly so that he could see his face. The first thing he noticed was the laceration across his forehead, roughly six inches long. It was a thin, dark line, with small, neat stitching running the full length of it. He knew that beneath the surface was a metal plate essentially holding his skull together. That in itself was a lot for anyone to wrap their head around.

Then he looked at his right eye. It wasn't brown, like it used to be. It was a light blue. He covered his left eye with his hand, just to be sure. He could see perfectly, although it felt slightly sensitive in the light.

"Are you okay?" asked Julie.

"It's weird," he said, shaking his head. "But yeah, I can see fine. They could've made it the same color as my other one though..." He pressed and prodded around his eye socket with absent curiosity.

"Well, I don't know the intricacies of growing eyeballs, but I'm sure there's a good reason why it's different. At least it's a nice color..." She smiled at him, which he returned. "Just go easy until it properly adjusts. Maybe wear sunglasses when you're outside for the time being, okay? We'll pick some up on our way out of town."

She turned and headed out of the bathroom. Jericho frowned and followed her, pausing in the doorway and leaning on the frame. "*Our* way out of town?"

She turned to face him, standing in front of the bed and folding her arms across her chest. She shrugged. "Well, I figure you'll need someone close by should that stitching re-open. Besides, I don't think there's anything left for me at

GlobaTech now. Even if I go back, they'll probably fire me for helping you escape. Or arrest me... whatever."

Jericho smiled but didn't get a chance to reply. The door to their room suddenly flew open, causing a loud bang as it slammed against the wall. Reacting in a split-second, Jericho pushed Julie backward. She bounced off the bed and landed on the opposite side, on the floor in front of the window.

"Stay down!" he yelled, turning to confront whoever kicked the door in.

Three men, dressed head to toe in black, rushed into the room, single file. Jericho's military instincts took over. He quickly assessed the threat. They were all armed with silenced handguns, their movements sharp, practiced, confident...

He didn't need to know anything else.

He stepped toward the man in front, grabbed him by the throat, and jabbed him twice, hard, in his side. Both blows found the liver, as intended. The man grunted from the impact and dropped his weapon. Jericho pushed it away with his foot as he slammed an elbow into the man's temple, knocking him out cold.

The part of the room near the door was narrow and opened out behind Jericho. He wanted to keep his body between the intruders and Julie, but he was limiting the space he had to fight in as a result.

Keeping hold of the first guy, Jericho put both hands on his chest and thrust him into the other two, momentarily knocking them off-guard. Knowing he wouldn't have time to retrieve the gun from behind him, he dropped his right shoulder and charged them, forcing the two men out of the room. Losing his footing as he collided with them, he went sprawling to the floor. As he stood back up in the corridor outside, he found himself in the middle of the men. Each of them aimed their weapons at his chest.

"Jericho, we *will* shoot you if you don't cooperate," said the one on his left.

He didn't respond. He looked back and forth between them. Each had their gun roughly three feet from him. One step in either direction and it would be within reach. He knew he had to act quickly.

He opted for the man on his left, figuring he was the more senior because he was the one who spoke. Jericho stepped toward him quickly, grabbing the outstretched arm. Turning so that he was standing in front of the guy with his back to him, he faced the remaining man in black. Using both hands, he controlled the gun and fired twice, hitting the other man in the chest. He flailed backward, landing awkwardly on the floor.

Jericho quickly snapped the wrist he was holding, reached behind him, and hooked his arm under the guy's armpit. Hoisting him up and over, he slammed him down on the floor in front of him. Jericho crouched beside him, quickly retrieving the gun, and fired twice, hitting the man with both rounds at close range in the chest.

He stood and rushed back into the hotel room, putting a bullet in the first man's head without looking as he passed him. He dropped the gun on the bed and moved toward Julie, who was standing by the window, rigid with shock.

He placed both hands on her shoulders, leaning down to look at her. "Julie, we have to get out of here right now. Do you understand?"

Jericho's voice distracted her from her distant staring. She looked him in the eye and nodded.

He bent down and picked up the first gun, which had landed nearby, and handed it to her. "Take this," he said, clicking the safety on. "Just put it under your sweater till we reach the car."

He picked the gun up off the bed as he walked past, heading out the door without hesitation. He aimed it in front of him, keeping it pointing in the direction he was looking at all times, gripping it in his right hand and cupping it with his left for steadiness.

"Come on," he called behind him. "Stay close."

Julie appeared next to him, holding the gun in both hands by the barrel, like a baseball bat. Jericho noticed it but said nothing. If that's how she felt comfortable holding it, so be it. It wasn't going to go off, and in the interest of time, it ultimately didn't matter. They just needed to get out of there. Fast.

They made it to the elevator at the end of the hall and stepped inside. Less than a minute later, they walked out into the deserted lobby. They went left, eager to avoid any security cameras as they ran past the mini bar and out the service entrance, to the parking lot at the back.

They stepped outside, hit by a light breeze that masked the deceptive heat of the early sun. Just ahead of them was the stolen sedan that had brought them there, surrounded by six men, all wearing the same black outfits as the three Jericho had taken out in the room.

"Oh my God!" screamed Julie as the men saw them. They took aim, fanning out to form a semi-circle with three on either side of the car.

Jericho clenched his jaw muscles with a mixture of anger and frustration, flicking his aim to each of the men in turn. His breathing remained steady and deliberate as his brain worked hard to figure a way out of what appeared to be, on the surface, an impossible situation.

Suddenly, a bright light appeared in front of him,

followed by a wave of intense pain that hit the center of his head, behind his eyes. He grimaced and staggered back, disoriented. He dropped his gun and sank to his knees, clutching the left side of his face. He felt a hand on his shoulder, startling him.

"Jericho, are you all right?" asked Julie. "What's happening?"

"Ah! I don't know..." he replied through gritted teeth. "My eye feels like... it's... burning!"

With his hand clamped over the right side of his face, he turned to Julie, frowning as he looked at her. She seemed different somehow. Calmer, more disciplined. Maybe even a little frustrated. The confusion over her sudden change in demeanor and body language momentarily distracted from the pain in his head.

"Shit," she muttered.

Before he could say anything, one of the men by the car shouted over. "Both of you, on your knees; hands where I can see them. We've been ordered to bring you in."

Julie looked down at Jericho, tilting her head slightly. Jericho recognized the look immediately—an unspoken plea for forgiveness.

Jericho shook his head. He didn't understand. What would she be feeling sorry for?

"Just stay here," she said to him. "Your eye's reacting to the influx of sunlight. Keep it covered."

Without another word, she got to her feet and tossed the gun she was holding into the air. She caught it again by the butt, flicked the safety off, chambered a round, took aim, and started firing. She ducked low, moving forward, scooping Jericho's handgun up as she went. She continued her shocking onslaught, taking out three of the six men with the first few rounds.

The remaining three dove for cover, but she seemed to anticipate their movements. She aimed both guns to the right and fired, catching one of the men as he moved away to the side; both shots hit him in the face. He dropped to the ground and slid to a lifeless halt.

The final two men emptied their clips but inexplicably hit nothing. Julie ran forward, throwing both guns away to the sides as she approached them. At full speed, she charged at the man farthest to her left, using her right foot to step on his thigh. She ran up his body, pushing off first with her foot and then with her knee on his shoulder to elevate her into the air. She moved her arm, positioning the point of her elbow above his head before slamming it down on the center of his skull. He crumpled to the ground and she landed on top of him, straddling his chest.

In a flash, she turned her body to the right, just in time to catch a kick aimed at her head. She caught it in her arms, displaying a natural strength one wouldn't expect from looking at her. With very little movement on her part, she held the man's ankle high in her left hand and thrust her right forearm through his knee from the side, snapping his leg. He fell to the side, screaming with obvious and under-standable agony. She looked back down at the man between her legs and threw a quick right hand at his face, ensuring he was out.

She stood and dusted herself down, looking quickly around to make sure all the men were taken care of before turning back to look at Jericho.

He was stunned. The pain in his skull was temporarily forgotten as he watched Julie—a slight, timid, innocent nurse—single-handedly take out six armed men with more ease than practically anyone he knew.

She walked toward him, but he sprang to his feet and

stepped back, bringing his left arm up into a loose fighting stance, his right hand still covering his eye.

"Stay away from me!" he shouted. "Who the hell are you?"

"Relax, Jericho. I'm on your side," she said. She placed a finger on her ear and glanced to the side. "Sir, it's me. Someone's found us—probably the CIA. I had to break cover. Jericho's dressings are off, and his eye's struggling with the sunlight."

Jericho took a step toward her, forgetting any concerns he had or any pain he felt, succumbing to the fresh feeling of anger. "Who are you talking to?"

She walked over, taking an earpiece from her pocket and holding it out to him.

Jericho frowned. He didn't know whether he should be angry, confused, or grateful. "Seriously, what's going on?"

"Put this in," she said. "You want answers? They're on the other end of the comms."

Reluctantly, Jericho took it and placed it in his left ear as lightning bolts of pain shot through the right side of his head. He grimaced as he activated the earpiece.

"Who... who is this?" he asked, grunting through a fresh wave of agony.

There was a brief crackle of static and then a familiar British voice sounded out. "Jericho, it's me—Josh. Are you all right? What's happening?"

"Josh? What's happening is I feel like a thousand burning knives are stabbing my brain! What have you people done to me?"

Josh sighed. "Bollocks. Okay, try to relax. We thought there might be a reaction to the light at first, but it's only temporary. Keep it covered, and we'll check you over when you come in."

"Screw you, all right? I'm not coming back!"

Josh sighed. "Jericho, listen to me. Those men Julie just disposed of for you and the ones in your hotel room? They were part of a CIA unit sent to kill you. Not bring you in... *kill* you. Do you understand me? Do you get what's going on here? Thanks to your phone call yesterday, they now know you're alive, which means you have a very large bullseye on your back. You'll be dead within twenty-four hours on your own. We can help you."

Jericho paused, feeling a second's reprieve from the pain inside his head.

"Why would you help me?" he asked, conceding that Josh made a valid point.

"Because we're on the same side," he implored.

Jericho looked over at Julie, who stood resting against the hood of their sedan, her arms folded casually across her chest. She smiled as if understanding his reluctance. "Jericho, you need to come with us. You shouldn't have made that call to your old boss yesterday, but I had to let you see for yourself that you can't trust them anymore."

He glared at her. "How do you know who I called? And why would I go anywhere with you after you lied to me? I mean, it *was* all a lie, right? The helpless nurse, the frightened girl who can't hold a gun... even you 'rescuing' me yesterday... it was all for show, wasn't it?"

Julie stared at the ground for a moment before answering. "I'm sorry, but we had to. It was the only way..."

"You *had* to? You didn't *have* to do anything!"

"Don't be angry at her," interrupted Josh on the comms. "It was my idea. The only way you'd believe us is if you figured out for yourself what was going on here, like Julie said."

"I'm not going anywhere with her," he replied. He stared

at Julie. "Give me one reason why I shouldn't kill you right now."

She shrugged. "How about... because you couldn't if you tried?"

She stood up straight, turning her body slightly away from him, visibly tensing her muscles.

"All right, easy, tiger," said Josh. "Julie, stand down. Jericho, you have no real choice. We need to take a look at you to ensure there's no permanent damage to your eye. If there is, it will be excruciating and potentially fatal. Plus, you have no allies in a war where the opposing side is far bigger than you can imagine."

Jericho shook his head. "Enough!" He looked at Julie. 'If you try to follow me, I *will* put you down—I don't give a shit *who* you really are. Understood?"

She held her hands up passively and nodded without a word.

"I thought you were different," continued Jericho, "but you're not. You're just like everyone else. There's always a hidden agenda. I just want someone to be straight with me!"

"We *are* being straight with you," she insisted. "I know this is hard, Jericho, but we're not your enemy. The real enemy is the CIA, and these guys..." She gestured to the bodies scattered around them. "They were just the beginning. They're not going to stop now they know you're alive. Do you understand that? You're a loose end, and they'll do whatever it takes to finish what they started in Colombia."

Jericho thought about what she was saying. He knew she made a good point, in spite of everything else running through his mind. And after speaking with Julius Jones the night before, he was convinced something was amiss. Even if he didn't want to believe everything GlobaTech had told him, he was beginning to realize that didn't mean they were wrong. Jones was very keen to get him back to Langley and quick to jump on the defensive when he questioned the CIA's position.

Besides, no matter the reason, there was no escaping the fact they had just killed nine people between them in a Los Angeles hotel. The CIA would probably cover it up, but that wouldn't stop the cops from heading here to investigate shots being fired. They were likely already en route.

Jericho took a deep breath and stared at Julie, watching her. His anger slowly subsided, and he knew there was only one logical way forward. He sighed. "So, you're not a nurse, I'm guessing?"

She smiled. "I'm a lot of things, but no, I'm not a nurse."

He lowered his left hand and let out a reluctant sigh. "Fine, I'll play along... for now. But this doesn't mean I trust you."

"Atta boy, Jericho," said Josh. "Just give us a chance to prove ourselves to you, okay? That's all I ask."

"Whatever," he said. He walked over to the sedan and opened the driver's side door, but Julie appeared beside him.

"I don't think so, handsome," she said, laughing. "I'm driving."

Jericho hesitated, but realizing he should probably keep his right eye covered with one hand, he stepped aside, allowing her to climb in behind the wheel. He shook his head and walked around the car, sighing as he slid into the passenger seat and slammed his door closed.

Julie started the engine and pulled out of the parking lot, turning right and heading back toward Santa Clarita.

Jericho rested his head back in the seat.

"Better the devil you know..." he muttered.

10

The drive back to GlobaTech's headquarters took less than an hour and passed mostly in silence. The pain in Jericho's head had subsided, which he was relieved about, although he still kept a hand over his eye as much as possible.

The traffic was steady, and the mid-morning sun was behind them. Julie had remained quiet, calmly focusing on the road. He noted the change in her body language, as if someone had flipped a switch and turned her into a completely different person. She was more relaxed, comfortable... confident. He couldn't deny being impressed with her fighting abilities—despite his anger at being deceived by her and by the people who had spent the last thirty-six hours asking for his trust.

She turned into the compound, slowing to a stop in front of the security barrier guarding the entrance. On the other side of the roadway, a team of three workmen were replacing the barrier they broke the day before, during their staged escape. Two guards came out of the hut in the middle and approached the car. Jericho recognized them both from the large group who had tried to stop him before Julie's intervention.

They moved to the driver's window, which Julie buzzed down, resting her arm on the frame as she leaned out. "Hey, fellas. We're here to see Mr. Winters."

They exchanged an uncertain glance, ducking slightly and staring at Jericho. Julie spotted their concern. "It's okay, guys. He's with me."

Both guards relaxed and walked back into their hut. A few moments later, the barrier lifted. She eased through, heading left, toward a large building in the far corner. It was a tall glass structure that wouldn't have looked out of place against the skyline of any major city.

She navigated the network of roads as Jericho gazed out the window, looking at the industrious citadel that surrounded him. Despite having seen it from inside the conference room a little over twenty-four hours ago, he hadn't really appreciated just how big the place was.

Small, six-person transport vehicles with the GlobaTech logo emblazoned across the sides whizzed by in every direction, carrying people wearing a mixture of suits, fatigues, and overcoats to wherever they needed to be.

The roads formed a large square around the center and branched out to the corners of the compound. In the middle were a helipad, a large SAM site, and units of troops all kitted out in high-tech uniforms running drills.

"How can you afford all this without any government funding?" asked Jericho, both curious and impressed.

Julie laughed. "Don't ask me. I just work here."

He glanced across at her. "Yeah, about that... who are you? Really."

She smiled. "I've worked here for the last six years," she said. "I did a lot of security work in South Africa for the first eighteen months. Then I was brought in to work for Robert Clark."

"He's the guy who died in the terrorist attack, right?" asked Jericho, recalling his brief conversation with her yesterday.

She nodded. "He was a good man and deserved better than that. We had a... bit of an issue a few years back with internal security. Someone who worked in our Finance and Logistics section—something Jackson; I can't remember his first name—tried to sell land GlobaTech owned to a domestic terrorist group. Robert headed up the investigation following Jackson's death and uncovered corruption at the highest levels. I was part of the unit that took out the trash. Once that was behind us, the company restructured its hierarchy, sought investment from reputable, private sources, and was able to quickly turn itself into what you see today."

Julie pulled over beside some steps that led up to the main entrance of the building. As they got out of the car, the doors slid open, and Josh Winters appeared. Jericho looked over and then raised an eyebrow at Julie.

"Be nice," she said. "He's here to help."

"Whatever..." he muttered in response before setting off up the steps.

Josh greeted him with an extended hand. Jericho stopped, looking first at the hand, then into Josh's eyes. "Let me be clear," he began, "I don't like being lied to." He quickly swapped hands, placing his left over his right eye and shaking Josh's hand firmly with his right. He tightened his grip to hold him there. "I told you before I wanted you to be straight with me, and you weren't. If it happens again, I'll break your neck. Understand?"

Josh smiled, continuing to shake hands and appearing

unfazed by the threat. "Jericho, you are one *scary* bastard, d'you know that?" He laughed a little nervously. "I'm sorry things went down the way they did. I didn't feel as if I had any other choice, and if you think I've wronged you, then I'm sorry. Now come on, let's get you looked at. No more games."

He walked back into the building, and Jericho followed him through the automatic doors. Inside was a large, open lobby. It looked incredible—the floor was dark marble, and there was a large, circular enclosure in the middle containing trees and plants. Along the right wall was a front desk with two attractive women sitting behind it, working feverishly away at their computers. Behind them, embedded in the wall, was an enormous TV screen with a graphic of the company's logo spinning around. All the way around, the walls were adorned with framed images showing the work that had been done and the things GlobaTech had accomplished over the years. On the left, standing side by side, were three glass elevators.

Jericho let out a low whistle as he looked up, unable to mask how impressed he was. Two massive chandeliers hung from the roof, six floors above them. Each level was square, built around the central column of space.

"This is our primary Research and Development building," said Josh, looking over his shoulder. "This is where our technology is born and tested. We have a medical facility on the top floor similar to the one you stayed in."

The women behind the desk stopped working and looked up as Jericho walked past, smiling, which he did his best to ignore. They headed for one of the elevators, and Josh pressed the button, looking up to see it descending toward them. A few moments later, it landed with a ding, and the doors opened. Jericho stepped inside first, followed by Julie and finally Josh, who pressed the button for the sixth floor.

"We'll get you checked out, and once we know you're okay, we'll discuss how we want you to help us. Now you're not gonna get angry and do a runner again, are you?"

Julie smiled, but Jericho frowned. "*Do a runner*?" he asked, not fully understanding the reference. "I won't try to leave again, if that's what you mean."

"Excellent, because now the CIA knows you're alive, we're not just running low on time—we're out of it."

The doors opened again, and Josh stepped out, heading left down a bright corridor. It was naturally lit by the outside wall, which was made entirely of tinted glass. Jericho and Julie followed, and they all walked through a large set of double doors at the far end.

Inside looked like a futuristic hospital. It expanded away from them and to the right, running back along the full length of the corridor they had just walked down. There were hospital beds surrounded by equipment along the left wall, which reminded Jericho of the one he first woke up in. A glass partition formed a square room in the corner, filled with lab equipment. To the right of that, along the back wall, was an area made of opaque glass with a sign that announced it was an operating theater.

Grouped in the center of the large room were various workstations with an array of computers and paperwork on them. Each one was staffed by a man or woman wearing a white coat and protective glasses.

Josh led them right, toward the far end. A woman wearing a striped top, navy pencil skirt, and heels looked up from behind a desk as they approached.

She stood and moved around to greet them. She glanced

at Jericho but said nothing. "Mr. Winters," she said with a smile. "What can we do for you?"

Josh returned the smile. "Hey, Gloria, I need you to give Mr. Stone here a once-over. He underwent surgery last week to replace a damaged eye, and he took the bandage off today and experienced—"

"It hurt like hell, ma'am," Jericho said, stepping forward.

She smiled sympathetically. "I'm sure it did, Mr. Stone. I'm Dr. Gloria Phillips, a senior consultant for GlobaTech's medical research division. If you don't mind, I'd like to take a closer look at your new eye..."

She turned and walked back to her desk, picking up a penlight. Without much hesitation, Jericho followed her.

"Just take a seat on the edge of the desk," she said, turning back around.

Jericho did, and Gloria moved in front of him, leaning close and clicking the light on. He tried to relax and ignore what his instincts were telling him about being there. He found himself thinking back to earlier that morning, when Julie was doing much the same thing.

"Just stare straight ahead and take some deep breaths," Gloria instructed.

He did, and she shined the light into his right eye, examining the reactions professionally. After a moment, she moved away again and clicked her light off, placing it on the desk before turning to face Josh. "Okay, the good news is the eye has taken—the surgery was a complete success, and it will function perfectly... once it's adjusted. This, however, takes time, and the bad news is you removed the bandage sooner than we would've liked. There's some damage to the lens because it wasn't strong enough to deal with the light. It's not permanent, but it will set your recovery back a couple of weeks."

Jericho nodded. "So, I'm not going to go blind or need it removed?"

Gloria smiled, shaking her head. "Not at all. Think of it as if it's first thing in the morning and sunny outside. You can't open your eyes straight away because they haven't been used in a few hours and will be sore when the light hits them. Same thing here, except your eye hasn't been used *ever*, so it'll take a bit longer for it to get used to the natural light." She moved around her desk, opened one of the drawers, and took out an eyepatch. She handed it to Jericho. "Wear this for a couple of weeks, then start taking it off every two hours for thirty minutes the following week. Then you should be good to go."

Jericho took it reluctantly, regarding it in his hand before looking first at Julie, then at Josh before addressing Gloria. "Can't I just wear sunglasses?" he asked.

She shook her head. "Even the most expensive sunglasses you can buy won't stop enough of the UV radiation the sun emits to actually be effective. You need total blackout for two weeks. Otherwise, you *do* risk more severe, longer-lasting damage."

Jericho looked at Josh, who shrugged back at him. "Doctor's orders," he said. "So, suck it up. Two weeks is nothing to rock the Nick Fury look, and you'll be back to normal."

Jericho frowned. "Who? Anyway, it's easy for you to say that. You're not the one walking around without the ability to judge distances properly. And I wouldn't be in this position if it wasn't for you, violating my human rights by giving me this eye in the first place without my consent."

Gloria averted her gaze and cleared her throat. "Mr. Winters, if you don't need me for anything else, I'll leave you to it."

Josh smiled and nodded. "Of course. Thanks for your help, Doc."

She exchanged silent pleasantries with everyone and excused herself.

Josh waited until she was out of earshot before replying. "Okay, technically... yeah, I suppose we did 'violate your human rights', as you keep putting it, and I'm sorry about that. But no offense, big guy—it's time you cracked open a can of *Man Up* juice and got over it. We're at war here, okay? And you're a high-ranking target on the enemy's shit list. We did what was necessary to save your life, and we took an opportunity to do you a favor at the same time in the hope that once you were back to your full strength, you'd maybe do something for us in return."

Jericho took a deep breath, standing to his full height and width as he fought to bury the flash of anger that just surfaced inside him. He didn't always care for Josh's tone, but he could see the man had a point. While he was still trying to piece together everything he had been told in the last twenty-four hours, he knew enough to understand that he would need help if he were to stay alive long-term. He was very aware of how the CIA could operate, if need be.

He let out a sigh. "I'm sorry, all right? It's been a long couple of days, and I've had a lot to deal with. I know you stuck your neck out for me, and I'm grateful for it."

"Forget about it—you have every right to be angry. That's the only reason we handled you leaving the way we did: so you had space to calm down and think things through, get the answers on your own. You should go easy on Julie as well, all right?"

Jericho looked across at her and smiled. "You *are* pretty badass. I'll give you that."

Julie smiled back sheepishly. "You have no idea. But

we're good." She held her fist out, which Jericho bumped—the universal gesture of camaraderie among soldiers.

The three of them huddled together in silence for a moment as Jericho put on the leather patch with its hardened outer surface. He adjusted it for comfort, more aware of it than he had been with the bandage. He cracked his neck and looked around, getting used to the sensation of it covering his eye.

"So, here's the pitch," said Josh. "All cards on the table. The coming days and weeks are going to be hard. The CIA is unofficially dedicating practically all of their resources to finding Adrian. And now they know *you're* alive, they'll be coming for you too. Whether you like it or not, Jericho, the president of the United States, with the CIA director's help, orchestrated a terrorist attack on the entire world, covering it up and framing someone else beautifully. Adrian has all the evidence implicating them, which is why he's a target. He's working on a plan, but he needs our help running interference to buy him some time."

Jericho paced away, resting again on the edge of a nearby table and crossing his arms. After speaking with Julius Jones and having had CIA operatives come after him already, he was inclined to believe what Josh was telling him, no matter how difficult it might be.

"How can I help?" he asked.

Josh took a step forward, standing next to Julie. "There's a lot of work to be done," he said. "Obviously, GlobaTech as a company is doing... well, *everything*, to help the people and the countries affected. We're doing that publicly and with President Cunningham's official blessing—for what *that's* worth. He hasn't authorized foreign aid of any kind to assist our efforts. He's simply playing the savior and saying the U.S. has the best resources, meaning us. Behind closed doors, however, we're launching our own investigation into what *El Presidente* is doing in the aftermath of all this and how he intends to capitalize on his grand scheme coming to fruition. Whatever he's got up his sleeve, I doubt we're going to like it all that much, and the more we know, the better our chances of stopping him. That's where you come in."

"You want me to help investigate the president?" he asked.

Josh shook his head. "My plan is to put together a small team of exceptional soldiers, operating... quietly, shall we say, whose sole purpose is to stop any attempts the president makes to do whatever it is he's trying to do."

Jericho nodded. "That's a bold move. If what you say is right, there's no way he won't know you're behind it."

"You're probably right," admitted Josh. "But I'm hoping the fact he's publicly endorsed us will buy us a little leeway. If we're smart, we can piss him off just enough that he doesn't feel the need to risk exposure by retaliating."

Jericho stroked his chin for a moment. "Okay, but if I agree to help you, we do it my way, understand? I'm in command of the unit on the ground. What I say goes. I don't want my decisions questioned. You've been asking me to trust you since I woke up. Now I'm here, I expect that to work both ways."

Josh flashed a quick look at Julie, who shrugged her indifference. He nodded and looked at Jericho. "Okay, then it's settled. But I will say this, Jericho. I'm happy for you to run the unit, but you work for me—you need to remember that. You're not a soldier anymore. You're not a CIA asset, you're not in charge of the D.E.A.D. unit, and you're not a member of the U.S. Armed Forces. Are we clear? You're now an independent contractor. You don't answer to anyone except Ryan Schultz and me. You're a GlobaTech employee, and we're a company, not an army. The sooner you realize that, the better off we'll be, all right?"

Jericho nodded. He'd been a soldier of some kind his whole life. He had always thought the private sector was for people who either couldn't make it or had retired. But looking around, listening to Josh, seeing what the world had become... GlobaTech was more than just a private military contractor. They were keeping the planet together and were the only ones in a position to protect innocent people from what was coming—whatever that might be. How could he not want to be a part of that?

"When do we start, sir?" he asked before smiling and correcting himself. "Sorry... *Josh*."

"Right now," he replied. He stepped to one side, nodding to Julie. "Meet the other member of the team—Julie Fisher."

She smiled, and Jericho nodded once. "Figures. Who else?"

"There's another guy en route," said Josh. "You'll like him. For now, it'll just be the three of you. I'll be providing support from here while I can, but that's it. I'm not exactly advertising the fact we're doing this to our board of directors. Like you, there aren't all that many people I trust at the moment. The smaller and more discreet we keep this, the better." He glanced at Julie. "Would you be so kind as to show Mr. Stone to his quarters?" He turned back to Jericho. "You can stay on base for now, if that suits?"

Jericho nodded. "Works for me. I don't have a permanent residential address anyway. I stayed on base with D.E.A.D., and before that, I moved around different Army bases ever since I was a kid, so I've never needed one."

"Perfect. Now, if you'll excuse me, I have a meeting with Schultz. I'll leave you both to it." Josh flashed a smile at Julie as he left the room.

Julie watched him leave and then turned to Jericho. "So, do you wanna buy me a drink?"

He frowned. "It's not even lunchtime..."

She shook her head and laughed. "What's your point?"

He thought for a moment and then shrugged. "No point, I guess. But I think after everything, you owe *me* at least one beer!"

She laughed. "Dream on, big guy. The first round's on you." She poked his shoulder and then walked off, leaving him standing alone in the room.

He looked around for a moment and shook his head, smiling to himself. "I hope you know what you're doing..." he whispered.

He headed out the door and along the corridor, catching up with Julie as they reached the elevator.

11

Jericho and Julie went to a local bar a half-mile east of the base, just before the gas station they had stopped at the day before, during their staged escape. She had told him The Call to Arms was a regular haunt for many GlobaTech employees, given it was the only option for miles if they lived on base and wanted a drink.

The place itself wasn't anything fancy. The bar area was a large, square, open-plan space filled with uneven tables and uncomfortable chairs. A dull, threadbare carpet lined the floor, stained in patches from decades of spilt drinks. The entrance was against the right wall and brought you in to the left of the bar counter. Booths lined the near wall, across from the pool table, over in the far corner.

They were sitting opposite each other in one of the booths, both with half-empty glasses of beer. There hadn't been much conversation since they arrived, and Jericho was staring absently with his uncovered eye at the scratched surface of the table, cradling his drink in one hand.

Julie took a sip of her drink and cleared her throat

loudly. "I'd say *a penny for your thoughts*, but I'd rather give you ten bucks to stop being so goddamn miserable."

Jericho looked up at her, startled. "Huh? Sorry, I was... distracted."

"No kidding..." she said. "You need to lighten up. You're in a bar with a hot chick. What's the matter with you?"

He saw the grin on her face and could tell she was messing with him. He smiled. "Yeah... sorry. This is the first time I've been able to relax in a while. In a *long* while. Still taking it all in, y'know?"

She nodded. "I can imagine. So, are you over the whole 'violation of my rights' thing now?"

She put on an exaggerated deep voice as she said it, mocking Jericho. He raised an eyebrow and shook his head, feigning offense. "Yeah, I guess. I still can't believe everything that's happened, though. The 4/17 attack, this... conspiracy involving the White House. I mean, how did no one see this coming?"

She took another gulp of her beer. "Are you kidding? Pretty hard to predict something like this when everyone's intel is coming from the people behind it, don't you think?"

"True. I just can't figure out why the president would even want to do something like this. The money he made this country by legalizing cocaine and prostitution—sorry, *companionship*—it's not only dug everyone out of a recession, but it's kick-started the first economic boom since the early nineties. He was fixing the country anyway."

Julie shrugged. "Yeah, I guess. But the bottom line is he's a man in power who simply wants more power. He'll want for the world what he's given to America, and he figures the best way to do that is to make everyone else do what he says."

"The guy's a traitor."

"He is. I'm sure Adrian *Hell* is going to fix it though..."

Jericho picked up on the hint of sarcasm in her voice. "Don't you approve of the boss's call to trust him?"

She thought about it for a moment. "I trust Josh and Mr. Schultz. If they think he can get it done and that he's our best option, I'll support it. One hundred percent."

"But?"

She smiled. "But... the guy's a hired killer. What's he gonna do, assassinate the president of the United States?"

"Christ—imagine that."

She nodded to his glass. "You ready for another, big guy?"

He finished his drink and got to his feet. "Yeah, I'll get these. Same again?"

"Yeah, but put them on my tab. I don't want you spending your stolen drug-dealer money in my favorite bar."

Jericho smiled and headed for the bar. He returned to his seat a couple of minutes later with two more beers. He passed one across the table, which she took with a gracious nod.

He regarded her silently for a moment, watching as she took a healthy gulp, and then asked, "So, why GlobaTech? I've seen you in action—I'm guessing you were military before this? What made you go private?"

Julie shrugged. "Better money, better benefits... I know it ain't exactly patriotic, but whether people like to admit it or not, money makes the world go 'round. Especially nowadays. Back home, my mom got sick, and we had medical bills that needed paying. Even with all the special allowances, military pay isn't the greatest. Plus, I had to leave her for weeks, sometimes months at a time to risk my life... and for what? Turns out our way of life is founded on bullshit anyway. At least here, I earn five times what I used to, which is some consolation."

Jericho nodded, understanding completely where she was coming from. Back when he was military, before he joined the CIA, he knew plenty of men and women in similar situations, and many of them had taken private security jobs on the side to make ends meet.

"Still," she continued, "forgetting the financial benefits for a second, we're in an incredible position to help people here. We're more than just a private army and a bunch of glorified guns-for-hire."

He took a deep breath. "Yeah, I guess you're right. I know I had my doubts—and maybe I still do, to an extent—but I agree that GlobaTech is as close as you can get to the good guys at the moment."

She tipped the neck of her bottle toward him. "Exactly."

"So, what happened?" he asked delicately. "With your mom..."

Julie gave a taut smile. "She passed away a few years ago."

"I'm sorry," he said genuinely.

"Don't be—you didn't give her cancer." She smiled, warmer this time, to lighten the mood. "My dad took it hard. His health hasn't been great since, but he's coping. We both are. So, come on. What's your story?"

Jericho shrugged. "Not much of a story, really. I was a captain in the Army, then about seven years ago, I was recruited by a guy called Julius Jones to join the D.E.A.D. unit. If it wasn't for the last couple of weeks, I'd probably still be there, oblivious to the damage I was causing."

Julie looked at him for a moment, studying his face. She could see the guilt, the shame, and the anger, in his eyes.

She leaned forward, resting on her elbows. "Listen, Jericho. None of this is your fault. You know that, right?"

He looked away for a second before speaking. "I was being used by the people behind all this. Whether I knew about it or not doesn't change the fact my actions have contributed to how bad things are."

"You can't know that..."

He nodded stubbornly. "I can. The things my unit did... When I look back, there's no way we weren't being played. Adrian had it right—we were nothing more than a clean-up crew for the bastards behind all this, and that makes me just as guilty as they are."

Julie took another sip of her beer. "Okay, you wanna know what I think? I think you're too damn proud to see through all the bullshit here. I know they say things are always clearer in hindsight, but you were doing your job, nothing more. You didn't know what was going on behind the scenes—no one in your position ever would—but now you do, you've turned your back on them so that you can help the people working to stop them from hurting anyone else. Forget what's happened before. This is the right move, and you should seek comfort in that. So, take all that guilt and whatever else you're using to beat yourself up with, and use it to fight back."

Jericho didn't know what to say. He wanted to argue his point, to justify how he was feeling in some way, but he couldn't. He chuckled. "Damn... Are you, like, a therapist or something in your spare time?"

She shook her head and smiled sheepishly. "No, I'm a woman. We're good at this sort of thing." She stood and stretched at the side of their table. She was wearing a tight-fitting black vest top and cargo pants, with her brown hair in a ponytail. She cracked her knuckles and looked at him. "Wanna shoot some pool?"

He shrugged. "Sure. As long as you don't mind getting your ass kicked..."

Julie grabbed her drink and walked backward away from him, pointing her finger. "Oh, it's *on*, big guy!" she said before turning and strolling over to the vacant table opposite. She racked up and picked the nearest cue from the stand on the wall. "My break."

She stood close to him and nudged him out of the way using her hips. He stepped back and arched an eyebrow. "Are you always such a pain in the ass?"

She leaned forward, bending over the table and lining up her shot. Jericho stared at her legs for a brief moment, impressed. She turned and winked at him, seemingly oblivious to his gaze, and then hit the white ball into the pack, scattering them and sinking three. "Yeah. Better get used to it, *boss*."

Jericho shook his head and smiled as she continued clearing the table. He took a deep swig of his beer and glanced around the bar, letting out a heavy sigh and allowing himself to relax. He was feeling almost human again, after everything that had happened to him recently. It felt good to unwind for once, to not worry about being in charge or being responsible for anyone.

12

The hours passed by quickly, and the bar got busier as day turned to evening, though it was still far from full. The two of them drank and shot pool, pausing briefly for some food late afternoon.

Jericho stood up straight after taking a shot, pausing to assess the table and apply some more chalk to his cue.

"Head's up," said Julie, appearing next to him and distracting him from his thoughts.

"What?" he asked.

Julie gestured with a discreet nod at three guys who had just walked in and congregated at the bar. One of them distracted the barmaid while the other two shared a joke.

"These three assholes work for our internal security," she explained. "Everywhere they go, they cause trouble—either hitting on women or starting fights or something. They give our company a bad name."

Jericho looked over as the group of surly-looking men in tight-fitting T-shirts and combat pants laughed raucously among themselves. He could see the barmaid smiling politely at their comments but doing her best to get on with her job of serving them.

Despite the last day or so being evidence to the contrary, Jericho still prided himself on being a good judge of character based on first impressions, and he had no doubts about the three security guys.

"Pricks," he replied with a shake of his head. "This is supposed to be like a regular job, right? Can't they just discipline them or fire them?"

Julie shrugged. "No one will rat them out—they're too afraid. The internal security team is a close group. You get your schoolyard bullies everywhere, I guess. But they could make your life hell, given half a chance."

"Huh, and here's me thinking I'd signed up to help protect the world. Turns out we *are* just like everyone else."

"Come on, ignore those douchebags," she said, leaning over to take her shot and potting the black ball to win the game. "Rack 'em up, bitch!"

He shook his head and smiled, moving back over to the table and setting it up for another round. He looked over as he heard the doors open again and saw another man walk in, wearing an impossibly bad Hawaiian shirt and Aviator sunglasses. He headed over to the bar, standing next to the three security guys. He signaled the barmaid, and Jericho could see quite clearly, even from where he was standing, how her eyes lit up when she saw him. There was no music playing, and the rabble of conversation around him was low, so he could just about hear the conversation.

"Hey, sweetheart," the man said in a gravelly Irish accent. "Can I grab a beer from ya?"

"Sure, you can," replied the barmaid excitedly. "First one's on me."

"Ah, you're somethin' else, darlin'. Ya really are."

Jericho rolled his eyes at the man's transparent charm.

"Hey, you shooting pool or checking out the customers?" asked Julie, distracting him.

Jericho leaned forward to line up his shot. He looked down the table at the triangle of balls. Julie was standing in his eye line, one hand on her hip. He smiled to himself, determined not to be put off by her. He took aim and slammed the cue into the white ball, scattering the triangle and sinking five balls.

"Can't I do both?" he asked as he stood up and smiled at her.

She shook her head and laughed. "Nice."

They continued playing pool for another ten minutes before the sound of raised voices at the bar distracted them.

"Hey, asshole," shouted one of the security guys, looking over at the Irishman in the Hawaiian shirt. "You honestly think you got a shot with *her*?"

Jericho and Julie looked over to see him gesturing to the barmaid.

The Irish guy turned and stared at him. "With Jess here? Oh, me and Jess go way back." He glanced at her and smiled. "Don't we, darlin'?"

She smiled back, her cheeks flushing red.

He looked back at the security guy. "Now if ya could do me a favor and leave me ya sister's phone number before ya piss off, that'd be grand."

Jericho smiled to himself. "He's a brave sonofabitch. I'll give him that."

"Or stupid…" countered Julie.

He shrugged. "In my experience, it's a pretty thin line between the two."

They stood transfixed, along with the few other people

in the bar. The Irishman appeared unaware of the attention, and the security men didn't seem to care.

"What did you say?" the guy replied, leaning in close and getting in his face.

The Irishman turned away from him. "Ya heard me. Now piss off, would ya? I'm tryin' to appreciate a well-earned drink here."

Another security guy stepped forward, tapping his friend on the shoulder. "Hey, I know this guy," he said. "This is Ray Collins. The loud-mouthed, womanizing drunk with a gambling problem. Typical Irish prick. You're a disgrace, Collins!"

In a flash, Collins was on his feet, knocking his stool over in the process. He pointed his finger at the man who spoke. "Hey! I resent that. I am *not* a drunk. I'm a... social consumer, all right?"

Jericho smiled as he placed his cue down on the table, then folded his arms across his chest.

Julie looked at him. "What are you doing?"

He shook his head. "Nothing. Just watching."

Collins stood his ground, keeping his right hand raised. "Now back... the hell...off. Walk away right now, the lot of ya."

The three men formed a line in front of him and spread out. The first guy who spoke took a step forward. "Or what?"

Collins looked along the line and sighed. "Ah, bollocks..."

He stepped forward, dropping his shoulders and whipping his head toward the nearest man to him. The head-butt connected, his forehead smashing into the guy's nose, splattering blood across both their faces.

Over by the pool table, Julie nudged Jericho. "Imagine if *you* did that?" she said quietly. "You'd kill someone."

"Huh... yeah, I must remember that," he replied without looking away from the ensuing bar fight.

The remaining two men rushed Collins, each grabbing an arm and pinning him against the bar. The recipient of the head-butt scrambled to his feet and stood in front of him. He unleashed four big punches to Collins's ribs and sides, alternating left, then right with each one.

Jericho tensed his arms and took a deep breath, trying to stay calm and talk himself out of intervening.

Julie turned her back on the proceedings and placed a hand on his forearm. "You look like you're fixing to do something stupid," she whispered.

Jericho looked at her with a humorless smile. "Or something brave..."

She shook her head and smiled. "Is this that line you were talking about?"

"It could well be, yeah."

Suddenly, Collins pushed himself off the bar, breaking free of the grip they had on his arms. He shoved the guy to his left, putting a little distance between them, and then turned and threw a left body shot to the guy on his right, catching him in the stomach. Finally, he launched a hard kick at the guy in front of him, connecting with his balls, causing him to double over.

It looked for a moment as if he might be getting the upper hand, but the guy on his left recovered and jumped him, slipping a chokehold on him from behind and holding him steady. The other two men recovered and took turns launching horrendous shots to Collins's body and face.

He had no chance.

"That's it," said Jericho, pushing past Julie. "Wait here."

He strode over toward the bar, his gaze fixed on the nearest of the two men punching Collins. As he approached, he threw a straight right hand of his own, connecting flush with the guy's already busted nose. The impact knocked him backward and over a table, sending him, along with the table and surrounding chairs, crashing to the floor.

"What the—" managed the other guy throwing punches before Jericho grabbed him by the throat, heaving him effortlessly over the bar and sending him flying into a stack of dirty glasses. The guy grunted as they shattered on impact, and Jericho watched as he rolled to the floor, bleeding from several tiny wounds along his arms and face.

He looked at Collins, who met his gaze and raised his eyebrows in silent thanks. Suddenly, he bent his knees, dropping his weight and freeing himself from the choke hold. He lashed his right elbow back, hitting the remaining guy in his stomach. He turned as the guy keeled over and delivered a strong knee to his face, sending him sprawling backward. He leaned forward, resting his hands on his knees, catching his breath.

"You all right?" asked Jericho.

"Aye... I'm grand," replied Collins, standing up straight and extending his hand. "I'm Ray." He nodded at Jericho's eyepatch. "And you must be Blackbeard?"

"It's Jericho," he replied, shaking his hand and ignoring the attempt at humor. "I've gotta hand it to you, Ray—you can really take a beating."

Collins shrugged. "I can dish 'em out even better. It's just these limp-wristed dick-bags travel in packs. Shouldn't have let 'em get the jump on me."

"Anyone ever told you that mouth of yours is gonna get you killed one day?"

Collins laughed. "All the time, matey, but they ain't been right yet."

"Are you boys gonna make out now or what?"

They both turned to see Julie standing there, her arms folded across her chest and her eyebrow raised.

Collins smiled, instantly forgetting everything that had just happened. "I've seen ya around, but I've not had the pleasure..."

Julie playfully patted his face with her palm. "That's because I'm *way* out of your league," she replied, stepping past him and standing in front of Jericho, her head level with his chest as she looked up at him, smiling. "Wanna get out of here, big guy?"

Jericho looked over her head and raised an eyebrow at Collins, who laughed and shrugged back. He looked down at her, staring into her brown eyes. "Lead the way."

She headed for the door. Jericho set off after her, stopping when he was level with Collins.

"You gonna be all right?" he asked.

"I'll be fine," he replied. "Thanks for the save. Ya better watch ya back though..." He nodded over to the door, where Julie was stood waiting. "I think you're about to have a rougher time than I just did!"

"Yeah, maybe," Jericho replied, patting him on the shoulder and smiling before following Julie outside.

They stood side by side, both taking in a breath of cool air as they looked up at the dark orange sky. Dusk was giving way to nightfall, and the temperature was dropping to a more manageable level than it was during the day.

They set off walking back to the GlobaTech compound. After a couple of minutes of peaceful silence, Julie said, "Just so we're clear, you absolutely are *not* getting laid tonight."

Jericho smiled but didn't look at her. "It hadn't crossed my mind."

They made their way back to the base and headed for

the tenement buildings that housed the live-in employees, which were situated in the far corner, close by the perimeter fence, in the shadow of the mountain range beyond. There were three large tower blocks in total. Jericho was in the nearest one to them as they approached, on the third floor.

"This is me," he said, ambling to a stop.

Julie didn't slow down or even turn around. "What do you want? A parade?" she called back, raising her hand and waving it casually. "See you tomorrow, big guy."

She carried on toward the building farthest away from his. Jericho watched her, convinced she was putting an extra sway in her hips to wind him up. He shook his head and smiled. "Sonofabitch..."

13

April 21, 2017

Jericho was woken by a persistent knocking on his apartment door. He opened his left eye slowly, rubbing it to remove the grit accumulated during the five hours of broken sleep he had managed. As per the doctor's instruction, he had left his eyepatch in place.

He swung his legs out of bed and stood slowly, stretching and grimacing through the cacophony of aches and cracks. Wearing nothing except his boxer shorts, he padded slowly over to the door, opening it without a second thought.

Julie was standing in the corridor, leaning on his doorframe. She looked wide awake and fresh-faced. Her hair was tied up, and she was wearing a similar outfit as the previous day, though her vest top was a different color.

"Hey, Sleeping Beauty," she said with a smile, looking him up and down. "Get your shit together—we've got a meeting to go to."

"Who with?" asked Jericho, still half-asleep.

"Josh and Schultz. C'mon, let's go."

"What time is it?"

"Just after six. Why?"

Jericho sighed and shook his head. "No reason—I've just not re-adjusted to military mornings yet."

Julie looked at him with mock sympathy, pouting. "Poor baby. Come on, move your ass."

He frowned. "I thought I was in charge?"

She smiled and stuck her tongue out playfully before turning on the spot and walking back down the corridor. He raised an eyebrow and smiled before ducking back inside and closing the door. He grabbed a quick shower and threw some clothes on before leaving his apartment and following her out of the building.

The pale sun was climbing into another cloudless, blue sky. Jericho navigated his way across the base, which was already alive with activity. He caught up with Julie as they neared the office building in the Southwest corner of the compound. The base was so large that it took them nearly ten minutes to walk there from the apartments.

The meeting was on the fourth floor. They rode the elevator up and walked side by side along the corridor toward the conference room. As they entered, Jericho realized it was the same room he had met with Josh and Ryan Schultz in a couple of days ago. He looked at the large display screen mounted on the wall, noting someone had replaced the one he had smashed.

Josh and Schultz were standing at the far end of the table, and they both looked over when Jericho and Julie walked in.

"Thanks for coming so quickly, guys," said Josh. "Take a seat."

He gestured to two chairs facing the door, backs to the window.

Julie was the first to sit down, leaning back on her chair and resting one leg on the table. Jericho took a seat next to her and looked around, noting the tense look on Schultz's face.

"Has something happened?" he asked.

"Nothing bad," said Josh before Schultz could say anything. "We just have news. And a mission for you. We're just waiting for one more. He should be here—"

"Sorry I'm late," said a voice from over by the doorway.

Everyone looked over to see Ray Collins standing there, smiling as his gaze rested on Jericho and Julie.

"Blackbeard!" he said, laughing.

"You all... know each other?" asked Josh, surprised.

Collins waved his hand dismissively as he stepped into the room and took a seat opposite Jericho. "Aye, we go way back! The big guy here saved my ass from a beatin' last night in the bar." He nodded at Julie. "And Sarah Connor over there just can't control herself around me..."

"You wish!" she scoffed, giving him the finger.

He smiled and nodded to her raised middle digit. "*You* wish, sweetheart!"

Jericho chuckled, which prompted Julie to glare at him and punch his arm. "Don't *you* start..."

Jericho shrugged. "Hey, what have I done?"

"All right, knock it off," said Schultz. He looked to his left. "Julie Fisher, Jericho Stone... this is Ray Collins. He's one of our best, believe it or not." He turned to Collins. "These two are your new teammates, so play nice." He sat back down at the head of the table, clasping his hands in front of him and leaning forward in his seat. "Okay, ladies, listen up. Individually, the three of you are impressive soldiers. Julie, Ray... you've both served GlobaTech for many years in some capacity, and you've proven time and again to be reliable assets. Jericho, you're a decorated soldier with a history of commanding a black-ops unit. But right now, in this room... *this* is the big leagues, understand?"

"Okay," said Josh, taking his cue. "You've all been briefed on what's happening and why you're here. We're putting together a small team, whose purpose will be to *quietly* conduct our own investigation into the CIA, with regard to the recent attacks. Also, we need to know how the president factors into all this."

He took out a remote from his pocket and aimed it at the TV on the wall opposite. He clicked it, and an image flickered onto the screen, showing a file photo on the left and information on the right, bullet-pointed.

"Our first client, so to speak," he continued. "We've been contacted by one of our employees—an engineer who worked on the Cerberus satellite. In light of the recent terrorist attack and our internal revelation about who's responsible, he's come to realize that he has information about the work he did that actually serves to implicate the president in what happened."

"Christ..." said Collins. "Who is he?"

"His name's Daniel Vincent. He's hiding out in Prague, staying in a low-key hotel. He's concerned the CIA might be on to him, so we need to get to him first and bring both him and his information home safely."

"Sounds easy enough," commented Jericho.

"Things like this always *sound* easy. But remember, you're not military anymore, okay? You're an everyday citizen with a nine-to-five job, so watch yourself. If things get messy or go wrong in any way, you could be arrested, and there's nothing we can do to help you. The government has the advantage here, so play it smart."

Jericho nodded. "Understood."

"I want you all to prepare for this. Get yourselves kitted out and ready to move on a moment's notice. Let me be clear, guys and girls—if we can get more evidence to back up what Adrian Hell's carrying around with him, we're one step closer to bringing the bad guys down... publicly. Which is safer for all concerned. I suggest you head over to the armory now and prepare. Questions?"

Collins raised his hand tentatively, as if unsure whether he should or not. "I might be a little behind the times on a few things here, but did you say Adrian Hell has the evidence against the CIA?"

Josh nodded. "That's right. He's public enemy number one right now, and that intel is the only thing keeping him alive."

"Jesus..." He turned to address the others. "Let me tell ya, I helped that guy get over the Ukrainian border and into Pripyat last week. He's tough as all hell and a whole other kind of crazy." He looked back at Josh. "How did he do over there, anyway? Did he get his girl back?"

Josh nodded and smiled. "He did, yeah. And he's eternally grateful to you for your help."

Collins shrugged as if it were no big deal. "How did it go down?"

"He stole a tank, blew up most of an abandoned research facility, went underground and took out over twenty guys, and then walked his lady friend right out the front door."

The few moments of stunned silence in the room that followed was eventually broken by Collins, who clapped his hands and cheered. "See, *that's* what I'm talkin' about! Good for him!"

Josh smiled again. "Indeed."

Jericho had to admit he was impressed. What he remembered of his brief interaction with Adrian, back in Colombia, left him with the impression he was a capable guy. He let out a heavy sigh and went to speak but hesitated.

Josh noticed and nodded to him. "What is it?"

Jericho sighed again. "Look... I spoke to my old contact at the CIA, which I'm guessing is what put them onto me. If the agency is already on Vincent's trail, involving me will only increase the risk to him, surely?"

Josh shook his head. "The CIA's involvement with regards to both Daniel Vincent and you was inevitable. Yes, it would've been ideal if we could've gone a little longer without them knowing you were still alive, but it doesn't matter. You needed to figure things out for yourself. I get that. And now you have, you're prepared for what comes next, which is a positive thing."

Jericho stood, which prompted Julie and Collins to do the same.

"Okay," he said, feeling an urge to take charge. "We'll get ourselves ready to move. I'm assuming transportation isn't an issue around here?"

Josh smiled, glancing out the window before answering. "Yeah, we've got most things covered."

Jericho smiled briefly. "I figured."

He turned and left the room, followed moments later by his new colleagues. He made his way to the elevator at the end of the corridor and held the doors for the others. Once inside, he pressed the button, and they rode it down to the lobby.

"So, where's the armory?" he asked.

"We've got a couple," said Julie. "One main storage unit and another for testing."

"Aye, this place is like Candyland, mate," added Collins with a mischievous grin.

The elevator dinged, and the doors opened.

"Can't wait," said Jericho quietly as he stepped out, allowing Julie to take the lead.

They walked across the compound to the North side, toward a long, low building next to a helipad. Julie nodded a professional greeting to a few people as they made their way over.

"This is the testing area," she explained, calling over her shoulder. "Probably a good idea to go here first. Some of our weapons and tech will be a little different to what you're used to."

"A gun's a gun," said Jericho casually.

Julie turned and exchanged a knowing smile with Collins before answering. "Spoken like a true soldier. But we're a good five years ahead of the military in terms of technological advancement, so open your mind a little, big boy."

She strode on ahead with a casual, confident swagger. Collins turned to Jericho. "She's quite a character, ain't she?"

Jericho laughed. "Yeah, I'm getting that impression." He nudged Collins's arm with his elbow. "I think she likes you, brother."

Collins laughed. "And who could blame her, right? She's got eyes..." He immediately fell silent and smiled nervously. "Ah... shit. Sorry, Jerry. I didn't mean no offense. Y'know, what with that eyepatch and everything..."

Jericho shook his head. "You didn't offend me."

Collins rolled his eyes and let out a sigh of relief. "Oh,

thank God for that! Believe it or not, I can sometimes let my mouth run away with me."

"Really?"

He put his hand to his chest and nodded solemnly. "On my mother's life. When I meet new people, I just like to make sure we all know where we stand with one another, y'know? Dot the I's and cross the T's and all that." He looked away and cursed to himself. "Ah, bollocks. I've gone and done it again, Jerry! Sorry, I didn't mean dot *your* eyes, I meant—"

Jericho put a hand on his shoulder. "Ray, I couldn't give a damn about my eyepatch. I'm not offended by references to it, but in the interest of knowing where we stand with each other, if you keep making jokes about it, I'm gonna knock your teeth straight out of your ass. Are we clear?"

Collins nodded and chuckled nervously. "Bloody hell... you're a scary bastard, ain't ya? I'm glad you're on my side!"

Jericho smiled to himself as they followed Julie inside the building. The entrance was a large, spacious foyer with gunmetal gray paneling on the walls, giving the place an almost futuristic feel. Multiple corridors branched off in five different directions. Large, stenciled white lettering was on the adjacent wall, advising what lay at the end of each one.

Julie was just turning out of sight down the second corridor on the left, which was marked as leading to a weapons testing range. Jericho and Collins hurried after her, following the corridor as it doglegged right and opened out into a large hangar, divided into various sections by a mixture of wooden and glass partitions. The corridor terminated on a walkway, roughly twenty-five feet up, which stretched all along the side of the area. A metal staircase descended just to the left of them.

They made their way down, catching up with Julie as

she approached a black man dressed in fatigues and wearing a cap, which he had on backward.

"Fisher," said the man loudly. "What brings you here, girl?"

"Hey, Dev. Just giving the newbie a tour," she said, gesturing to Jericho with her thumb. She turned. "Jericho, this is Devon Green. He's our resident weapons expert."

Green looked over and then up at Jericho's massive frame, which dwarfed him by almost a foot. "Holy crap!" he said, laughing before extending his hand. "Call me Dev."

Jericho smiled politely and shook it. "Good to meet you."

Dev turned to Collins and gave him a curt nod. "And how you keepin', Ray?"

They shook hands. "Ya know me, Dev—I'm doing just fine."

Dev laughed. "You're right. I *do* know you—that's why I'm asking!" He pointed to the bruising on Collins's face. "Was *that* over a woman, by any chance?"

Collins touched his face. "Oh, *this*? Nah—that was just a misunderstanding."

"Uh-huh. You tend to have a lot of misunderstandings."

Collins smiled. "Keeps life interesting."

"Mr. Winters sent us to gear up," said Julie, changing the subject. "We're heading out soon, so..."

"Say no more, girl," Devon replied. He picked up a handgun from the workstation beside him, hooked his finger through the trigger guard, and flipped it around, presenting the butt to her. "We call this *The Negotiator*. The barrel's larger than normal pistols and has a separate, smaller barrel underneath the chamber, with space in front of the trigger guard for a miniaturized magazine. The grip's bigger too but shaped ergonomically to fit comfortably in the palm of your hand."

Julie racked the slide back and examined the weapon admiringly as Jericho and Collins looked on.

Dev pointed to the grip. "The one you're holding is a prototype, but on the real thing, there's a thumb print scanner next to the trigger. The weapon is tailored to a single user. If it ain't your gun, the trigger won't depress. Same story if your thumb ain't on the scanner too. That's your safety—just adjust your grip when you're ready to shoot. The gun fires standard nine mil parabellums from the main mag but can also fire specialist rounds from an additional, smaller magazine attached to the secondary barrel. So far, we've got two types: a modified high-explosive incendiary/armor-piercing round and a developmental bullet that emits a low-level EMP on impact—useful for taking down security systems."

"Impressive," nodded Julie.

She handed it to Jericho, who took it without hesitation. His father has served in the military, and it always felt like a genetic inevitability to him that he would develop an affiliation for soldiering and combat. He believed that being a soldier was like any other trade—to be the best at it, you had to understand the tools you would be using.

At a young age, he taught himself how to take apart, clean, and reassemble pretty much every type of gun. Then he trained religiously, during both active duty and in his spare time, on how to use one effectively. He was probably one of the most accurate shooters ever to serve.

He looked up at Dev. "Very nice. Can I have one?"

Dev laughed, turned, and opened a large box that was sitting on another table top behind him. Inside, resting in compartments cut into the foam lining, were three more *Negotiators*. He picked up the box and presented it to the trio, grinning. "Mr. Winters said you all might be interested."

Julie and Collins exchanged an excited look. Jericho placed the one he was holding on the table and smiled calmly as they were each handed their own, personalized version. He noticed the small pad on the grip lit up blue when he gripped it.

"That'll turn red for anyone besides you," said Dev, not needing to be asked.

Julie stepped forward, checked her weapon, and found just a standard magazine was loaded. She chambered a round and looked at Jericho. "How good of a shot are you?" she asked him. "I'm not working for someone who can't shoot straight."

"That'll be a first," smirked Collins.

Julie shot him a look. "I'm holding a loaded gun, asshole..."

Collins held his hands up, feigning shock. "Jerry, ya won't let her shoot me, will ya?"

"Keep me outta this," he replied. There was a twenty-yard shooting range next to them. A target sheet was pinned to the end, showing the silhouetted outline of a man's torso. Jericho looked at Julie. "Take your shot."

She shrugged. "Okay."

He nodded at the range. "Down there, not at Ray."

She pouted. "Spoilsport."

Collins rolled his eyes as she took her aim and fired, hitting just left and slightly higher than dead center.

"Not bad," said Jericho.

He picked up a standard mag from the table next to him, taking a step forward as he slid it into his own weapon and worked the slide to chamber a round. Like lightning, he raised his right hand and fired once, shooting from the hip with no obvious preparation. Even with one eye, his bullet hit the target in the center, dead on, just to the right of Julie's shot.

"Whoa!" said Collins. "Nice shootin', Tex!"

Jericho turned and smiled at Julie. "Straight enough for you?"

Dev and Collins laughed. Julie simply continued to smile at him, an impressed look on her face.

"I've got one more thing for each of you," said Dev, pushing past Jericho and walking to another workbench just to the left of them. He held up a piece of material and ceremoniously handed it to Julie. He then picked up two more, one for each of the guys. "These are Tech Sleeves. You'll notice a hard surface stitched into the lining on one side, with the face of it showing, and a bracelet stitched onto the wrist. Slide them over your forearm, with the plate on the inside."

They all inspected them dubiously before doing as he asked. It reached almost to their elbows without restricting the bend of their arms. It was made into a fingerless glove at the bottom end, which covered the palm and knuckles with a hole cut out for the thumb. Jericho tapped the dark gray, plastic surface that was molded to the shape of his arm curiously.

Positioned around his wrist was a bracelet, which had numerous tiny holes in a semi-circle around the edge of the circumference on the inside of his arm. It had a watch face on it, set to the right time, and a single button on the outside edge.

"Press it," said Dev, watching Jericho admire the technology.

He did as the others looked on, intrigued. The small holes flashed into life, and the image of a touchscreen device was suddenly projected onto the hard surface. It looked, for all intents and purposes, like a fully-functioning tablet.

"Nice," said Jericho, distracted.

The others followed suit, equally stunned when their own Tech Sleeve did the same thing.

"That," explained Dev, "is a state-of-the-art, portable projection computer. Inside the wristband is a transmitter and a two-terabyte server chip. It piggybacks the nearest cell tower signal, giving you encrypted access to all of GlobaTech's networks while you're out in the field."

"These are great," said Julie. "Thanks, Dev."

"Yeah, appreciate the upgrades," agreed Jericho. "And it was good to meet you."

Dev smiled. "I'm sure we'll be seeing a lot of each other in the future."

The three of them turned and headed out of the armory, back up the stairs and down the long corridor. Julie walked on ahead as Jericho lingered, fiddling with the interface on his arm like a child with a new toy on Christmas morning.

Collins appeared next to him.

"Hey, Jerry, d'ya think this thing can get porn?" he asked quietly.

Jericho closed his eyes with disbelief and laughed but didn't dignify the question with an answer. They quickly caught up with Julie, just as she was stepping outside. They looked across the compound and saw Josh walking hurriedly toward them.

"All kitted out?" he asked as they approached.

"We certainly are," said Jericho.

"This technology is awesome," added Julie.

Josh shrugged. "Only the best for my new team. Now you'll have plenty of time to figure out how to use it in the air. Your flight leaves in..." He paused momentarily to check his watch. "...four minutes." On cue, a transport vehicle arrived on the road alongside them. "Jump in. Everything you need is on the plane."

"Blimey... we're not hangin' around, are we?" observed Collins.

Josh shook his head. "Time is of the essence. Now ordinarily, you would be in GlobaTech fatigues, but given the sensitive nature of your mission and the current climate, it's best you blend in as much as possible. So, discretion is mandatory. Be part of the crowd, and secure Mr. Vincent and his intel as quickly and as quietly as possible. Understood?"

They each nodded their understanding.

Josh saluted them casually. "Good luck, boys and girls."

The three of them climbed aboard, and the driver set off. Ten minutes later, they were in the air, en route to Prague.

14

April 22, 2017

The three of them sat in their anonymous black sedan, parked by the side of the road in Wenceslas Square, facing the museum. The sun was rising, casting a picturesque glow over the skyline from behind the spattering of gray cloud.

They had landed in Prague a couple of hours earlier, and their body clocks hadn't yet adjusted to the massive time difference. They had stopped off for some food as they made their way from the airfield.

They all managed to get some rest on the flight over, and Jericho was feeling more like his old self. The seemingly endless uncertainty and paranoia had made way for more familiar feelings—purpose, self-belief, and a sense of duty.

He looked around, watching the people go about their lives. Already the streets were filling up. Prague was closer than most to the atrocity that was 4/17, with their northern neighbors, Poland, absorbing a sizeable percentage of the overall damage. Jericho was reminded of the atmosphere in

New York in the days that followed 9/11. People were carrying on as normal, but everything was respectfully slower and quieter.

Behind him, Collins was sitting in the middle of the rear seat, resting his head back and staring at the roof with a cigarette between his lips. He blew out a thin stream of smoke with a heavy sigh.

"Do you have to do that in here?" asked Julie, glancing over her shoulder at him from the passenger seat.

"I really, really do, sweetheart," he replied as he fought the onset of jetlag. He lifted his head, catching Jericho's eye in the rearview mirror. "So, where the hell is this guy?"

All three of them were wearing their Tech Sleeves. Jericho glanced down at his forearm, pressed a few buttons, and brought up some information on the display. He looked around as he examined it. "He's in the hotel at the back of this row of stores," he announced, pointing in front of them.

"So, what's the plan?" asked Julie.

"I'll make the approach," said Jericho. "Ray, you follow me inside, but keep your distance. Watch for anything out of the ordinary. Julie, wait outside by the car. Watch the street —you're driving when we come out."

Collins sucked in an uncertain breath. "Don't take this the wrong way or anything, mate, but I reckon *I'm* better making the approach."

Jericho looked over his shoulder, raising his eyebrow and silently questioning his logic.

Collins continued. "It's just... ya know... you're really big and scary!"

Julie rolled her eyes. Jericho frowned.

Collins sighed, quickly tiring of trying to be polite. "I just mean, if this guy's on edge anyway, what's he gonna think when a seven-foot pirate with the physical dimensions of a tank and a scar across his head like Frankenstein walks toward him, holding a gun? I'm a people person. Let me go in, talk to him, make him see we're here to help, and then walk him out, all civil-like."

Jericho stared out the window, resting his elbow on the doorframe and absently tapping his eyepatch with his index finger, thinking about what Collins had just said. Daniel Vincent was GlobaTech, so all he would need to see is some ID, and problem solved. But he wasn't naïve enough to not see Collins had a point. He felt conflicted and wasn't sure of the best move.

Julie watched him staring blankly ahead, his internal debate visible on his face.

"Jericho, can I say something?" she asked.

He turned to her. "Shoot."

"You're overthinking things. This doesn't have to be a complicated, tactical rescue mission. Daniel Vincent is just a guy sitting in a hotel bar. I hate to say it, but maybe Ray has a point. There's no denying the importance of why we're here, but we should approach him informally, as friends."

A brief, tense silence descended before Jericho let out a long sigh. "Fine. Ray, you make the approach. Julie, you back him up inside. I'll cover the area out here."

Julie smiled. "Good call."

Jericho nodded once, trying to swallow his pride. "Everyone on comms?"

The three of them put their earpieces in.

"Check," said Julie.

"Check," said Collins.

"Check," said Jericho.

There was a crackle of static and then another voice sounded out.

"Everybody set?" asked Josh.

"We're good," confirmed Jericho. "Ray and Julie will make the approach. I'm on damage control."

"Good. Listen, we've been monitoring Vincent since you left here. He's made no attempt to contact anyone, but keep your eyes open. Given how badly the world has gone to shit recently, there's no way you're the only ones after him. We don't want to cause a scene."

From the backseat, Collins tapped Jericho on the shoulder. "Hey, Jerry, ya hear that? We gotta keep our *eyes* open! Ha! You're screwed!"

Jericho shook his head, glancing at Julie, who was doing her best to suppress a smile. "Hey, Ray, you hear *that*?" he replied.

Collins frowned and shook his head. "What?"

"The sound of you getting your ass handed to you by three glorified security guards."

Julie laughed out loud, and even Josh's sly chuckle could be heard on comms.

Collins frowned. "Well, it's good to know I'm never livin' *that* down..."

"Not as long as you keep making jokes about the eyepatch."

"All right—focus, children," interrupted Josh. "I'll be tracking your progress from here. I've got a real-time satellite feed on you, and I'll offer support where I can."

"Copy that," said Julie.

Everyone stepped out of the car and took a moment to look around casually. Jericho made sure his weapon was concealed under his top. They had all dressed in civilian clothes, changing on the plane just before it landed. He was wearing loose-fitting jeans and a hooded sweater.

Collins set off down the narrow side street that led to the hotel. He had opted for a more conventional plain white T-shirt with dark jeans, instead of another of his trademark Hawaiian shirts.

A few moments later, Julie followed him. Jericho couldn't help but cast an appraising eye over her as she walked away. Since ditching her nurse's uniform and dropping the innocent act, Julie's true beauty had very much shone through. Her figure was slender but toned—not overly muscular, retaining her femininity. Her shoulder-length brown hair was tied back, and she was dressed in fitted black leggings, with light brown, low-heeled, calf-length boots. Her top was loose-fitting and concealed her gun easily. She had sunglasses on, and she looked amazing.

"Stay alert, okay?" said Jericho on comms. "Like Josh says, we might not be the only ones here. Watch your six."

"Hey, Jules," said Collins. "I'll watch ya six for ya, if ya want?"

She sighed. "Screw you, Ray."

"Heh... promises, promises."

Jericho shook his head and smiled to himself. He paced idly back and forth in front of the car, scanning the crowds of people shuffling around Wenceslas Square—a place that had historically proven to be popular with tourists. Groups of women moved from store to store on either side of the boulevard that ran through the center. In the middle, he saw a large crowd of Japanese tourists posing awkwardly in front of the large monument, which stood proudly between the two roads.

"Okay, I'm inside," said Collins over the comms. "It looks clear. I have eyes on Vincent now. He's sitting alone, eating breakfast. He's got a briefcase with him."

"Copy that," replied Josh. "Sit tight, let him finish his meal. If he gets spooked and decides to run, we could lose him and that information forever."

Jericho scanned the crowd expertly as he listened to Josh's instructions. He had a tremendous height advantage over almost everyone around him, but the place was so busy that even looking down at the sea of people, he knew he would struggle to pick out anyone who was trying to stay hidden.

Just then, however, something caught his eye. Maybe six hundred yards away, at his ten o'clock. He snapped back, narrowing his eye as he focused on the crowd, trying to pinpoint what he had just glimpsed—a split-second image of something that triggered a subconscious familiarity.

"Was that..." Jericho whispered to himself.

He saw it again, clearer this time. A mohawk haircut, poking up out of the masses.

"Shit." He pressed his comms. "Guys, listen up. We've got company."

"Who?" asked Josh. "I don't see anything..."

"Damien Baker," Jericho explained, strolling casually back toward the car and leaning against it, keeping his eye on the alley. "He's a member of my old D.E.A.D. unit. Damn it. If he's here, the rest of them are too, which means whatever Vincent has in his briefcase, it's important enough to warrant sending the best *they've* got to secure it."

Jericho thought how Baker had always been a good, loyal soldier to work with, back when he was leading them. He shook his head as he struggled to grasp that it was only a fortnight ago when they were part of a close-knit unit on the CIA's unofficial payroll.

"What's your call, Jericho?" asked Josh.

"I'm thinking..." He cursed himself as he remembered Julie's words from earlier. He paused, took a deep breath, and listened to his gut. "All right, change of plan. Ray, make the approach now. Be delicate, but understand we don't have much time. Julie, watch his back."

"Copy that," she acknowledged.

Jericho scanned the square again. He still had a fix on Baker, who had taken up position across from him, maybe a couple of hundred feet farther down.

"There's no way he's not made me," whispered Jericho.

"All right, sit tight and wait for the others," replied Josh. "Can you see if he's with anyone?"

"Negative. But the rest of them have to be here somewhere. I'll find them."

"I'm scanning the area now via satellite," said Josh.

Jericho looked back over, but Baker had disappeared. He quickly scanned the immediate area but saw nothing that raised a red flag to him.

"Shit... I lost him," he said.

"Never mind. I might have something," replied Josh. "Across the street, on the roof of the hotel at your one o'clock."

Jericho directed his gaze where Josh had instructed, looking to the sky. The rooftop had a large, decorative stone barrier along the edge, with small spaces between the waist-high pillars.

"I can't see anything," he said.

"We've got a sniper," confirmed Josh. "Lying prone and staring in your direction."

Jericho sighed. "Charlotte LaSharde—it has to be." He looked away casually. He knew she wouldn't shoot without reason as she would need to retain cover until Vincent was in play. "Ray, whatever you're doing, do it faster, would you? I've got a sniper marking me. Julie, how's it looking?"

"Still clear on my side," she said.

"You know these people, Jericho," said Josh. "What's the play?"

Jericho let out a taut breath. "These guys are pros. They won't break cover until they need to, and they'll be swift and effective when they do. We need to be better, simple as that."

Jericho touched the gun at his back subconsciously before looking back up at LaSharde for a moment. He took a deep breath, turned away, and headed down the alleyway after the others.

"Julie, I'm coming to you," he said.

Inside the hotel, Collins rested casually against the bar in the restaurant area to the left of the entrance, listening to the chatter on comms. He spotted Daniel Vincent almost straight away, sitting alone at a table, sipping a glass of water with an empty plate in front of him.

He quickly scanned the room, dismissing the notion of any immediate threat. Besides Vincent, there was a family of three away to his right and two young women sitting directly ahead.

He tapped his gun through his top, ensuring it was accessible on a moment's notice, should he need it, and headed over toward Vincent. The man had thick, short hair, a full beard, and thin-framed glasses. He wore a sweater vest over a shirt, with a tie fastened loosely around an open top button. He was sitting at an angle to the table, with his legs crossed and his briefcase visible, resting by his feet. He looked up as Collins approached the table, visibly tensing as they made eye contact.

Collins held a hand up to him when he spotted the change in body language. "Daniel Vincent?" he asked.

Vincent nodded, straightening up and tensing.

"Danny Boy, my name's Ray—Ray Collins. I'm from GlobaTech, and I'm here to get ya home safely, all right?"

Vincent frowned, shifting nervously in his seat. "H-how do I know you are who you say you are?" he asked.

Collins made slow, deliberate gestures with his hands. "I'm gonna reach into my back pocket and take out my ID, all right? Be cool."

As his hand disappeared behind him, the unmistakable sound of automatic gunfire rang out. Instinctively, he scrambled over to Vincent, dragging him to the floor.

"Shit!" he yelled, taking out his *Negotiator* and positioning his thumb to enable it. He looked over to the entrance to see a man disappearing behind a nearby wall for cover. Collins fired three rounds in his general direction.

"Hostile!" he shouted over the comms as more bullets sounded out around him. "Danny Boy, stay on the floor, all right? Under the table, face-down. I'll handle this."

Collins rolled away and pushed himself up, resting on one knee. His weapon ready in front of him, he scanned the area. There was no sign of the shooter. He figured there was only one, but he wasn't sure.

He looked over at the family cowering behind their table. He placed a finger to his lips. "Just stay down," he said, looking at the man, whom he assumed was the husband and father. He had his arm around the woman, who, in turn, was shielding the young child in hers. "I'll get ya outta here, I promise."

He glanced over at the doorway and caught a glimpse of the man who shot at him as he peeked around the corner. He was a good height, with dark hair and stubble.

"Jerry, where are ya, matey?" he asked, quickly looking back to check on Vincent.

"Coming to you," he replied. "Sit tight."

"Julie, I don't like people shooting at me! Where are ya, sweetheart?"

"Quit whining," she said, sounding out of breath. "I'm looping around the hotel to enter the restaurant from the other side. I'll be right with you."

More gunfire sounded, and Collins hit the floor again as bullets flew past his ear. "Shit! That was close!" He slid a mag of high explosive rounds into the secondary breech of his gun. "Let's see what ya can do..." he muttered.

He waited until the hostile paused to reload, then leapt to his feet, taking aim and firing a single shot. The impact was deafening, and the subsequent explosion destroyed the doorway and surrounding walls, punching a hole straight through to the street. The recoil almost knocked him off his feet.

"Holy shit!" he yelled, laughing.

He saw movement to his right and spun around to see Julie enter the room, gun raised.

She glanced past Collins at the damage before looking at him questioningly.

He shrugged and turned to Vincent. "Danny Boy, the brunette's with me," he said, pointing to Julie. "Go with her. She'll get you to safety."

"Wh-what are you going to do?" he asked.

Collins glanced around the room. "I need to get the rest of these people outta here. She'll protect ya, and we have another guy outside who'll help, okay? Just do what she says."

He nodded uncertainly and hurried over to her. Without a word, she grabbed his arm and dragged him back the way she had come, through the opposite doors and out into the hotel.

He turned back just as the hostile re-appeared in the doorway to the restaurant, his assault rifle raised. The man smiled for a moment as time seemed to freeze. Collins looked on as he leveled his weapon. Time resumed its normal pace a moment later, and he ran to his right, diving over the top of the bar for cover as a cacophony of stuttering death was unleashed toward him.

He heard screams as he landed. Bullets splintered the counter above him, shattering the glasses stacked up behind.

After a few moments, it went silent. He chanced a look over the bar and saw the guy had gone. He stood, gun raised, and quickly scanned the room. The two young women were sprawled across their table, a river of blood at their feet.

"Bollocks," he muttered, looking over at the family, who, thankfully, were still hiding behind their table. "Jerry, I've got two civvies dead in here. Hostile's gone, possibly comin' your way."

Outside, Jericho had taken up position against the opposite wall, halfway along the alley. The rear entrance to the hotel was facing him, and the street was away to his right. He watched through the doors for any movement.

"Copy that," he said. "I'm here, Ray..." A ripple of commotion prompted him to turn and look back down the alley, toward their car. He saw movement at the other end—people running, scattering in all directions. "But I think we're about to have incoming. Julie, what's your position?"

"Heading out the back entrance and around the

building now, coming to you," said Julie. "No sign of our hostile."

Jericho moved farther along the wall, closer to the street. He alternated between glancing over his shoulder, waiting for Julie to appear with Vincent, and looking down the alley in case Baker or anyone else decided to engage.

Julie and Vincent appeared next to him a few moments later. He paused for a moment to eye Vincent up and down and nod a curt greeting.

"On me," he said to them, turning and heading back down the alley. "Watch for the sniper," he called over his shoulder. "On your one o-clock as you exit the alleyway."

"Roger that," shouted Julie.

They made their way quickly along and emerged onto the street, prompting more screams and panic from everyone nearby who saw their guns. Jericho scanned the crowds, struggling to focus amid the chaos. He couldn't see Baker but figured he had to be nearby. LaSharde was likely still in place as well, which complicated matters further. Knowing the remaining member of the unit, Rick Santiago, usually occupied the same role Josh was covering for them, he could only assume the one Collins was chasing was Chris Black. He wrinkled his face in a moment of anger and then let it pass. He knew it wasn't the time for vengeance.

They moved over to the car. Julie was behind Vincent with a hand on his shoulder.

"In the back," she said to him. "Stay down."

As he gripped the door handle, Jericho happened to glance down at the road, still wet following a recent downpour. There were a few shallow puddles around, but it was mostly damp. The thin film of moisture allowed the sunlight to reflect, enhancing its glare. He could see the wavy outline of a blinking light beneath their car. Straight away, he knew what it meant.

"Get back!" he yelled to Julie, running into the center of the square, away from the car. He looked around frantically at the crowds. "Everybody, move!"

He raised his gun and fired twice into the air, causing more screams and chaos as people stampeded away from them in every direction.

Julie and Vincent drew level with him just as the car exploded.

15

The blast was violent and loud, and the shockwave sent the three of them flying forward. They landed heavily and awkwardly on the other side of the boulevard. Piercing screams sounded out as people close to the explosion were burned.

Jericho tried to sit up but felt dizzy and disoriented. A loud ringing in his ears drowned out all extraneous noise. He blinked rapidly, struggling to focus, his vision blurry and his expression vacant and confused. "Shit..."

Next to him, Vincent was lying face-down, with Julie sprawled on top of him. She pushed herself up and held her gun out in front of her, doing her best to keep her aim steady. She patted Vincent on the back of his head. "Are you okay?" she shouted.

He let out a low groan but couldn't form the words to respond.

"Good enough," she said before looking over at Jericho. "What about you? Still with me?"

Jericho could hear her voice despite it sounding hollow

and distant. He nodded vacantly and placed a finger to his ear. "Ray? Ray! Do you... copy?"

On the other side of the flaming wreckage, in an adjacent alley, Collins was running after the hostile from inside the hotel, whom he could see just ahead of him. He didn't have a clear shot and had paused momentarily when he heard the blast.

"I'm here, Jerry!" he yelled. "What the hell was that?"

"Our ride!" Jericho shouted back.

"Bollocks! Everyone all right?"

"We're alive. Where are you?"

"Just comin' out of the next alley over, chasin' the bastard who shot at me."

Collins picked up the pace, exiting the alley at full speed, skidding to the ground instinctively as automatic gunfire erupted to his left. He fired blind as he rolled into the road, shielding his face from the heat of the burning car nearby.

He yelled a guttural roar, clambering to his feet and heading over to the others, all the while trying not to hit any innocent civilians on the way.

Suddenly, more gunfire sounded out in front of him—slow, deliberate shots, which Collins identified immediately as sniper rounds. He dove to the ground, sliding to a stop a few feet away from the rest of his team, his right arm bleeding from the friction.

"You all right?" shouted Jericho.

"I'll be honest with ya—I'm a little pissed off!" replied Collins, shuffling over to them while keeping as low as he could. "This managed to go south *real* quick, didn't it?"

They were taking cover behind a bench on the island in the center of the boulevard that ran the length of Wenceslas Square. Collins looked around at the crowds running in all directions and then his eyes settled on something. "Ah, crap... Jerry, head's up."

He nodded toward the charred wreckage of their vehicle, which was still burning fiercely. Chris Black stepped into view next to it, holding an assault rifle loosely in his hands. Jericho looked over, and their eyes met. Despite the distance, the mixture of shock and hatred on Black's face was clear to see.

Jericho lurched forward, his instincts taking over, guiding him to his feet so that he could run at the man who left him for dead days before. As he got to one knee, he felt a hand on his shoulder. He snapped his head around and saw Julie staring at him.

"Don't be an asshole," she said. "This isn't the time or the place, and you know it."

He held her gaze, breathing deep to subdue the adrenaline. After a moment, he nodded and sat back down next to Vincent. Over to their right, on their three o'clock, they knew Damien Baker was among the crowd somewhere, so they couldn't head in that direction without endangering more innocent lives. And behind them, on the rooftop, looking down, was Charlotte LaSharde and her sniper rifle, keeping them in check.

Jericho tried to listen to the voice of logic and reason in his head, to start figuring out a way to get everyone out of there alive. But he couldn't. The only thing he could think of was wrapping his hands around Black's throat.

He shook his head and pulled his arm free of her grip. "Stay here."

"Jericho!" she yelled, but it was too late. He got to his feet and ran toward Black, who turned and disappeared back down the alley, heading for the hotel.

Collins tapped her arm. "Where's he going?"

Before she could answer, Josh's voice came over comms. "He's going after the man who betrayed him and left him for dead. Now listen. The sniper's moved, so you're clear behind you. I need you two to get Vincent out of there alive. Do you understand me?"

Julie touched her ear. "Copy that. We'll get out of the square, secure a vehicle, and head back to the airport."

"What about Jerry?" asked Collins.

Julie fixed him with a hard stare. "Right now, he's on his own. Our mission is Vincent, not revenge."

"Ah, I don't like it, Jules. We can't leave him."

"What choice do we have? Do you really want to jeopardize this information to go after him?"

"No, but I don't want to leave him, either. We should—"

Gunfire ricocheted around them, cutting their conversation short. Vincent cried out in fear as Julie put her body in front of him and took aim in the direction the shots came from, though she couldn't see anything.

Collins scrambled to his feet and looked across the Square. The stampeding crowd parted, and he saw a man with a mohawk standing before him, holding a handgun by his side.

"Piece of shit..." he muttered. "Josh, I've got eyes on one of them, and I haven't got him pegged as the sniper."

"That'll be Damien Baker, then," he replied. "Do not engage, Ray. You're surrounded by civilians and have your GlobaTech ID on you. You need to protect Vincent and get him out of there.

"Yeah, I know that, but this guy's fixin' to engage me, whether I like it or not."

The two men stood staring at each other amid the chaos. Collins felt as if he were in an old western, in a standoff with the enemy.

Behind him, Julie shouted, "Ray, try to lure him away from here."

Without looking around, he replied, "No point, Jules. He's here for Vincent's information. He ain't goin' anywhere."

In a flash, Baker raised his weapon and started firing. Collins immediately did the same. They broke into a sprint, quickly zig-zagging toward each other, desperate to avoid the other's bullets. They met in the middle as both weapons clicked empty. Collins dropped his shoulder and tackled the taller Baker, wrestling him to the ground. Straight away, he felt elbows rain down on his back. He pushed off and rolled to the side, quickly getting to his feet.

Baker was on him in a heartbeat, stepping in close and throwing multiple short punches to the head and body. Collins did his best to weather the storm, keeping his guard up and moving his torso back and forth, ducking and weaving like a boxer. He saw an opening and unleashed a torrent of his own, catching Baker under the right arm, on the side of his ribcage. He knew the bones there were like matchsticks. Baker staggered back, hunching over slightly. Collins paused to catch his breath.

"Just hand Vincent over," said Baker. "This isn't your fight."

Collins smiled. "Sure, it is. Ya see, Danny Boy's one of us, and we're here to take him home. Him *and* his briefcase."

Baker grimaced and spat blood on the ground beside him. "You have no idea what you're involved in here. No idea who we are..."

Collins laughed. "Ya know we've got ya old boss on our side, right? We know exactly who ya are. And as we speak, I reckon Jerry's beating the holy hell out of ya new leader. Now I can't let ya keep runnin' around shooting ya gun near all these civvies, so stand down, or I'll put ya down, ya goofy, Sonic-the-Hedgehog-lookin' *Sons of Anarchy* reject."

Baker said nothing. He just straightened up as best he could and smiled.

Collins frowned. That wasn't the reaction he was expecting. But then he felt the cold barrel of a gun rest against the back of his head, and he immediately understood why Baker looked so relaxed.

"Ah, bollocks..." he said.

"Drop your gun, asshole," ordered Charlotte LaSharde from behind him.

Collins sighed and tossed his weapon aside before slowly turning around to face her. As he did, he was taken aback by how attractive she was. Her smooth, dark skin shined in the morning sun. Her eyes were dark, free from the shackles of emotion and conscience, and her arm was straight, holding the gun with unwavering calm.

He circled idly around, away from Baker, as if he were retreating. LaSharde tracked him slowly, following his movements. After a minute, he had subtly managed to turn her around, so she had her back to Baker.

He winked at her. "Hey there, lady. What say we both set our differences aside and go grab ourselves a drink?"

She glared at him. "Are you being serious?"

Collins laughed. "For once, no, I'm not. No offense, but ya ain't my type, sweetheart. I have a strict policy against dating psychopaths. I was just distracting ya, so *my* friend can sneak up on *your* friend and put a gun to *his* head."

LaSharde's eyes flickered with anger. She quickly stepped back and to the side, so she could keep her gun trained on Collins but also see behind her.

Julie was standing behind Baker, pointing her gun at him, smiling at her. "As much as I sympathize with you wanting to shoot him," she said, nodding at Collins, "I need you to put your weapon down, right now."

No one moved, locked in a lethal stalemate. The noise of people screaming and rushing around them was suddenly accompanied by the sound of distant sirens. Julie and Collins exchanged a glance, knowing they didn't have much time.

"Ah, screw it," muttered Collins.

He grabbed LaSharde's wrist, thrusting her arm upward as she fired a shot. He turned his hands, twisting her arm away from him. She crouched in an effort to relieve the pressure on her arm. He raised his fist, aiming for her exposed jaw, but hesitated.

"Shit!" he said.

"What is it?" shouted Julie.

"I can't hit her... she's a woman."

Julie rolled her eyes. "Are you kidding me?"

Collins threw her a look. "What? It's not my fault! I like women—I've never had cause to hit one before. It's not an easy thing to wrap my head around, y'know?"

LaSharde looked up at him and sneered despite her face being contorted with discomfort in his grip. "Didn't figure you for a pussy. I bet I've got a bigger pair than you, you—"

She stopped abruptly as she hit the ground, out cold. Collins looked down at her, shaking his hand to remove the stinging pain in his knuckles.

Baker tensed his body and went to take a step toward Collins, but Julie tapped the barrel of her gun against his head, reminding him she was still there. Reluctantly, he relaxed again, holding his arms out slightly to the sides in compliance.

Satisfied, Julie looked over at Collins. "What happened to not being able to hit a woman?"

Collins thought about it for a moment and then shrugged. "After careful consideration, and given she shot at me and insulted me, I decided she doesn't count."

Julie shrugged. "Fair enough."

In a swift and brutal movement, she pushed her leg down on the back of Baker's knee, causing him to buckle and drop to the ground. As he did, she slammed the butt of her gun into the base of his skull, knocking him out.

"Come on," she said. "Let's get Vincent and go and find Jericho."

They both dashed back over to the bench, which Vincent was propped up against. He was sitting on the ground, hugging his knees, with his briefcase trapped between his legs and his body. He looked up as they approached.

"Oh, thank God!" he said.

Collins smiled. "Thank Jules, more like. Come on, buddy, we need to—"

Police cars and fire engines arrived in waves at the scene, the wail of their sirens deafening over the chaos.

Collins and Julie looked at each other and shrugged.

"Now what?" she asked.

"Put your weapons away," said Josh's voice on comms. "Ditch your earpieces and flash your ID badges. They won't like it, but you were doing your jobs: protecting your client. You don't know who attacked you, and you want to be taken to the U.S. Embassy immediately. Got it?"

"Copy that," said Julie, taking her comms out and tossing it away to her left. Collins did the same.

A few moments later, a group of six armed officers approached them, fanning out and raising their weapons. "*Stop! Nehýbejte se!*" said one of them, glaring at the group.

They both had a basic grasp of the language and knew

that roughly translated as "Stop! Nobody move!" They raised their hands slowly in compliance. Vincent got to his feet and raised his right hand, his left still clutching the briefcase as if his life depended on it.

"I hope Jerry's all right," whispered Collins, "because he's on his own now."

16

Jericho entered the hotel via the rear entrance, sliding to a
stop with his gun held low in front of him. He knew Black
had to have come the same way, but there was no sign of
him. Slowly, he moved forward, past the maintenance area
and through a set of swing doors, into the lobby. To his left
was an entrance to the restaurant area, and directly ahead
was the hole in the wall Collins had created earlier. The
front desk was on his right, with a set of stairs just beyond,
leading to the second floor.

He moved toward the restaurant, figuring he would do a
quick sweep before heading upstairs. He kept to the wall,
checking his angles as he approached the doorway. He
dropped to a crouch and peered inside, but the bar
obscured his view. From what he could see, the room looked
like a warzone, and there was a pool of blood disappearing
out of sight.

He sighed and slowly stood, quickly scanning the room.
He could see the blood was coming from a table with two
young women slumped lifelessly over it. The bar itself was

torn to shreds from gunfire, and there was broken glass everywhere.

But the thing that drew his attention was Chris Black. He was standing in the opposite corner of the room, smiling. At his feet was the body of a man. Jericho could see he was still breathing, but he was unconscious. Knelt over him was a woman, sobbing hysterically. In front of Black was a little girl, no older than eight. His hand was on her shoulder, and his gun was resting against her head. She was crying but stood still, like a statue, likely frozen in fear.

Jericho snapped his gun up and aimed at his former second-in-command. "Chris, let the girl go. This has nothing to do with her."

"You're goddamn right it doesn't, Jericho," yelled Black. "But all this... it has nothing to do with you either. Just hand over Daniel Vincent, and all this goes away."

"Not gonna happen."

"I swear to God, I'll kill her, Jericho!"

Jericho gambled and shook his head. "No, you won't. Forget what happened in the past. I know you. You're a soldier. A damn good one, if I'm honest. You're a patriot, not a murderer. You wouldn't harm her."

"Don't think you know me, Jericho. You don't know anything about me! All those years, I followed your lead. All those years, I had to nod and smile and watch you play things safe, by the book, like a good little doggy. You were the perfect soldier, weren't you? Jones's golden boy. I don't know what happened back in Colombia, Jericho. Maybe you went soft. But getting all friendly with that assassin? That was a mistake! I couldn't believe my luck when Director Matthews gave me the kill order. Finally, it was *my* time!"

Jericho clenched his jaw hard, suppressing his instinctual

anger, trying not to let Black's words affect him. He opted to do what he figured Collins would—antagonize. "And how are you enjoying running my old unit, Chris? I bet you were employee of the month after I told Jones I was still alive. I wonder how pissed off he was, knowing his new puppet couldn't even take someone out from ten feet away when they weren't even looking. Wasn't exactly a strong start, was it?"

Black snapped, gesturing angrily at him with his gun. "Go to hell, Jericho! You were lucky you survived the first time, but you're not leaving here alive. You're right—Jones was pissed at me, but he knows I'm still the best option he has. My orders are to kill Vincent and retrieve his briefcase. But I know if I return with your corpse in a bodybag, all will be forgiven."

Jericho didn't listen to what Black said. He was too busy planning his shot. His risk had paid off. Black was no longer pointing his gun at the girl, which was all he was worried about. He took a deep breath, adjusting his aim a fraction, and fired. The bullet struck Black just below his neck, ploughing straight through his clavicle. As he fell backward, his muscles went into spasm, and he fired a shot. The bullet hit nothing. Jericho breathed a sigh of relief. He dashed across and held out a hand to the girl.

"Come on, it's okay," he said to her.

She ran to him, and he scooped her up effortlessly with his arm. He walked over to her parents and placed her beside her mother, who hugged her tightly.

Jericho smiled to himself for a moment, glad the girl was safe. He looked at the mother. "You should get her out of here."

"W-what about my husband?" she sobbed.

"I'll make sure he's safe here and get him out when I'm finished, I promise. But the man I just shot is still alive and very dangerous. You need to get your daughter to safety right away."

The woman nodded, reluctantly getting to her feet. She paused to look down at her husband and then grabbed her daughter's hand before running for the exit.

Jericho watched them leave and then focused his attention on Black. He was conscious, lying on the floor with blood pooling around him. The shot wasn't fatal—Jericho had made sure of that—but it would hurt like hell.

As he neared him, Jericho kicked Black's gun away before tucking his own back in his waistband behind him. He crouched beside Black and pressed two fingers into the bullet wound.

Black screamed with agony. "You sonofabitch!"

Jericho gritted his teeth as he pressed harder. "Does that hurt, Chris? Huh? Is that painful? Try getting shot in the goddamn head!" He withdrew his fingers, balled his hand into a fist the size of a wrecking ball, and smashed it into Black's face. "The biggest mistake you ever made was not killing me."

Black snarled through the agony; spittle formed on his lips. "Cut the shit, Jericho. You won't kill me. You're a glorified boy scout now, aren't you? Working with GlobaTech, you need to be a good little soldier. No more sanctioned kills for you. No more down and dirty missions that don't exist. No more anything. You're a dead man, Jericho. Jones will send everyone he has to come after you. There's nowhere you can hide!"

Josh's voice sounded over the comms. "Jericho, if you can hear me, Julie and Ray have been detained by Czech authorities. They've taken out the rest of Black's team and secured both Vincent and his information. They're off comms. You're on your own, but you need to get out of there. The area's being cordoned off as we speak. Their next stop will be inside the hotel. They can't find you. Understand?"

Jericho regarded his former subordinate, keeping an impassive expression as he listened discreetly to Josh's words. Finally, he smiled. "Julius Jones has enough to worry about. He doesn't need to add me to his list of problems."

Black frowned. "What do you mean?"

"Oh, didn't you know? It turns out the CIA is being used by the president to mastermind a global conspiracy that was responsible for 4/17. *Your* D.E.A.D. unit are puppets whose only purpose is to clean up after their mess."

"What are you talking about?" he scoffed. "You've lost your mind, Jericho. Maybe my bullet damaged more than just your eye."

"Do you remember Adrian Hell? Well, that laptop he stole contained proof of everything I just said. So does Daniel Vincent's briefcase. We've got it all, and my team has taken out Baker and LaSharde. So, while GlobaTech is gonna continue fighting the good fight and supporting those who need help, Adrian's going to bring it all crashing down around the president's ears." He grabbed Black by the throat and leaned in close. "And I'm going to help him do it."

He squeezed tightly. Black's eyes grew wide with panic as his hands grabbed at Jericho's wrist. But his flailing was futile. Jericho's massive frame and frightening strength was too much for him to deal with. He was lying on his back, which prevented him from gaining any leverage, and his left arm was useless due to the bullet wound above his shoulder. Jericho could see the realization in his eyes—the exact moment when he knew he was going to die.

Jericho continued to squeeze until he crushed the esophagus, killing Black where he lay. He took some deep breaths and allowed his adrenaline to subside before getting to his feet. He placed a finger to his ear. "Copy that, Josh. I'm done here."

There was a hiss of static before he heard Josh's voice. "Did you find Black?"

"Yeah."

"And?"

"He's dead."

Josh paused. "I'm guessing he wasn't like that when you found him?"

Jericho walked over to the man whose family was waiting outside. "Do you really want to know?" he asked.

There was another pause. "Not really. Head for the embassy. You'll find the rest of your team there."

"Copy that."

Jericho bent down and scooped the man up, placing an arm over his shoulder and holding him upright around the waist. He slowly headed outside, so he could reunite him with his wife and daughter.

17

The door opened to General Matthews's office. His secretary walked in, standing uncomfortably in front of his desk, keeping a respectful silence. He looked up from the report he was reading, eyeing her up and down before speaking. "Yes?"

She said, "Sir, there's a call for you. It's—"

"Tell them I'm busy," he replied, waving his hand dismissively and cutting her off.

"But sir, it's... it's the president."

Matthews raised his eyebrows, unable to hide his surprise. He placed the report down on his desk and straightened the jacket of his military suit, taking a deep breath to compose himself. He nodded to her. "Put him through."

The secretary nodded and made a hasty exit from the room. A moment later, his desk phone rang. "Mr. President, good morning," said the CIA director as he answered.

"Is it, Tom?" asked President Cunningham, his voice full of frustration. "You clearly haven't seen the news."

Matthews frowned. "No, sir. What news?"

"Turn on the TV. It doesn't matter which channel..."

Matthews's heart rate increased as he fumbled for the remote to the TV in his office, which was mounted on the wall to the right of his desk. He clicked it on to see a news report showing live video footage from Prague. According to the caption, a shootout had taken place there earlier in the day, both inside a hotel and outside in Wenceslas Square.

"What is this?" he asked absently, turning up the volume.

"Just watch..." said the president patiently.

A news reporter on the TV was in the middle of speaking. "...local authorities arrived on the scene, prompting two gunmen to flee. Three people were taken in for questioning but were later released to the U.S. Embassy. They were employees of GlobaTech Industries, the military contractor currently providing almost all the foreign aid to nations affected by 4/17. A spokesman for the company released an official statement just over an hour ago, explaining they were protecting a client from a suspected kidnapping attempt, and they did everything they could to minimize the number of casualties. Local security footage that has been made available to the press certainly seems to back that up.

"Over thirty people were injured by the initial blast from the car bomb, with at least a hundred more sustaining minor injuries in the rush to leave the area. There are currently seven confirmed fatalities, but reports suggest that number could rise..."

Matthews turned off the TV. He felt the color draining from his face. "Mr. President," he began. "Sir, I don't know—"

"What to say?" offered Cunningham. "I wouldn't say anything if I were you. Jericho Stone was one of those three GlobaTech employees, in case you were wondering. Your

D.E.A.D. unit were the people fleeing the scene. The information Daniel Vincent has is now in the hands of the only people capable of preventing the next stage of the plan from going ahead."

Matthews swallowed hard. "Sir, I understand you're upset..."

"To say I'm upset would be an understatement."

"Of course. Leave this to me. I'll—"

"You won't do anything, Tom. I've already told you to take a backseat. But you better make damn sure you get your house in order. Am I clear?"

"Yes, sir, Mr. President."

"I'm going to make life very difficult for GlobaTech Industries, Tom. Nothing can stand in the way of what's coming next. Not now."

The phone clicked off, leaving Director Matthews standing behind his desk, sweating and feeling genuinely nervous for the first time in his life. He took a few moments to compose himself and then stormed out of his office, his face a picture of anger. He made his way down the hall and left, bursting through the door to Julius Jones's office without knocking.

Jones was sitting behind his desk, watching his own TV. He looked up as Matthews entered. "I was wondering when I'd see you, Tom."

Matthews's fury boiled over. "I'm the goddamn director of the CIA, and you will stand when I walk in the room!" he bellowed.

Jones raised an eyebrow before slowly getting to his feet.

Matthews continued with his tirade, pointing to the TV. "That is a goddamn nightmare—for the president, for me, and for this agency! Your D.E.A.D. unit caused that shitstorm, Julius, and it's unacceptable!"

Jones took a deep breath, raising his hands and gesturing for the director to calm down. "Sir—you need to take a moment to relax." He knew the president would have been on the phone to him, and he could guess how that conversation would have gone.

"Don't tell me to relax, you arrogant bastard! All this is your fault!"

Jones frowned, taking exception. "Hey, wait a damn minute, *Tom*. I get that Black and his team screwed up, but the fact they were even there was *your* call. Which you made with the president's backing. I'm not saying this isn't a shit-storm—I agree with you on that—but barging in here and pointing the finger at me simply because the president likely just tore you a new one and you need to feel better about yourself isn't going to make things right!"

Matthews took in deep, adrenaline-fueled breaths, staring Jones right in the eye. After a few moments, he calmed down enough to see sense.

"Shit!" he hissed, turning to pace around the office and clear his head.

"We just need to think of a way to spin this so that it tarnishes GlobaTech's reputation," offered Jones. "If we sow the seeds to damage their credibility now, it will serve to immediately discredit any information they may or may not come forward with."

Matthews waved his hand dismissively. "That ship's sailed, Julius. It's already on the news that Jericho Stone and his new friends were innocent bystanders, simply doing their job... blah, blah, blah."

Jones sighed. He had an idea what the next step was, and he wasn't happy about it. "So, what do you want to do?"

Matthews stopped and looked at him. "The D.E.A.D. unit is gone, effective immediately. Do you understand? Any records are destroyed. Your funding is cut and will be re-distributed accordingly. Your entire program is dead and buried. Whoever is left is no longer in any way linked to this agency. We cannot afford to let our reputation take a hit like this, not now. Not with Adrian Hell still on the loose with his stolen intel. Are you listening to me, Julius?"

Jones was staring blankly at the surface of his desk, hearing every word but unable to express how he felt about them. The D.E.A.D. program had been his brainchild, his baby, for over twenty years. It began with Adrian Hell. He thought it ironic how it's with him, albeit indirectly, that it ends.

He nodded, sitting down heavily in his chair.

Matthews regarded him quietly for a moment. "Get it done, Julius. This isn't the time for sentiment."

He turned and left, slamming the door closed behind him.

Jones sat for a while, silently. He was angry at the decision, but he was angrier that his trust in Chris Black to manage the unit in place of Jericho had apparently been misplaced.

He snapped out of his trance and picked up the phone. He had preparations to make.

18

After a couple of tense hours in the U.S. Embassy, Jericho, Julie, and Ray were allowed to return to the States. With Vincent in tow, they flew back to California and touched down on GlobaTech's airstrip several hours later. They were met on the runway by a transport vehicle, which drove them to the main office building. They made their way to the fourth-floor conference room, where Josh and Schultz were waiting for them.

As everyone else took their seats, Daniel Vincent stood awkwardly by the door, hugging his briefcase to his chest. Josh stood and walked over to him. "I'm glad you're able to join us, Daniel," he said formally before nodding to the case. "Would you mind if I take a look at that?"

Vincent reluctantly handed it over, and Josh slid it across the table to Schultz, who was sitting at the far end. He nodded, and Josh placed an arm around Vincent's shoulder, walking him to the door. "Daniel, do me a favor? Head on down to the front desk and speak to one of the girls there. They're expecting you, and they'll arrange for one of our medical teams to give you a once-over, okay?"

He nodded vacantly and turned to walk out of the room. He paused at the door and looked back over his shoulder. "Th-thank you," he said. "To all of you, for everything you did for me."

Julie smiled at him. "It's no problem. You were pretty badass yourself, you know that?"

He smiled weakly and headed out of the room.

Josh shut the door behind him and then turned to face the three returning members of his new team. He glared at each one of them in turn, his calm, friendly demeanor quickly changing to one of anger and frustration.

"So, would anyone care to tell me *exactly* how that whole thing got turned into the nightmare that's currently on every news station in the world?" he shouted.

Collins went to speak, but Josh cut him off. "That was rhetorical! I'll tell you how—you acted like a bunch of amateurs!" He pointed to Collins. "Ray, what part of discreet don't you understand?"

Collins frowned. "What? I thought I was very discreet," he said defensively. "I made the approach perfectly fine. It wasn't my fault Jerry's old unit decided to show up..."

"No, it wasn't—but it *was* your decision to blow a hole in the side of the bloody hotel!"

"Oh yeah... *that*. I just wanted to see what'd happen, if I'm honest. Sure as hell stopped that guy shootin' at me anyway!"

He looked around, chuckling, but both Jericho and Julie shook their heads at him, signaling for him to stay quiet. He fell silent and stared at the surface of the table, feeling as if he were back in high school, waiting outside the principal's office.

Josh paced across the room and stood beside Schultz, using both hands to rub his eyes and forehead with frustration. "Guys, come on... you're meant to be professionals. You are civilians now, and you represent this company in everything you do. You know what we're up against at the moment. The last thing we need is any bad press."

"Josh, with respect, we did the best we could," said Julie. "We did everything right, and yeah, once Jericho's old unit showed up, things went to shit, but—"

"Yes, things really did go to shit, Julie!" He looked at Jericho. "You left your team and your mission to run off on some Rambo-style quest for revenge, which resulted in you killing one of the CIA's top assets."

Jericho said nothing.

Josh sighed. "Jesus Christ, Jericho. I thought you were smarter than that. I really did. I understand why you did it —don't get me wrong—but you didn't consider the consequences of your actions, of which there are several."

"Josh, we did our best to save the innocent people in the hotel," interjected Julie. "We protected Vincent and his information *and* got out of there alive."

"Plus, they struck first," added Collins. "They blew up our vehicle. That crazy sniper bitch had us pinned down. Oh, and that Hell's Angel wannabe was in the crowd too. I'm guessing *he* was the one who planted the bomb in the first place? And as for that fella Jerry killed... well, good riddance, if ya ask me."

The room fell silent as the three of them watched Josh pace back and forth, his hands clasped behind his back. He exchanged a glance with Schultz and then stopped in front of everyone.

"Okay," he said finally. "One massive pain in the ass at a time. I guess we have a PR department with millions of dollars at their disposal for a reason. Ryan, what's in the case?"

Schultz clicked the briefcase open. He took out a handful of documents and a flash drive, resting them on the table before putting the case on the floor next to him. He quickly scanned the papers as everyone looked on.

"Sonofabitch..." he murmured eventually.

"What is it?" asked Jericho, speaking for the first time since they entered the office.

"Whatever it is, it'd best be worth the shit we went through to get it," added Collins.

Schultz slid the papers across the table. "Documents detailing the hidden extras that were added to the Cerberus satellite post-production," he said. "Signed off on by Cunningham himself."

"Holy crap," said Josh. "This is perfect. This intel alone is enough to at least get a Senate hearing. This *proves* the president knew what the satellite was really capable of. And if he knew, it's not much of a stretch to link him to the attacks that utilized those capabilities." He looked at everyone in turn. "Guys, this is amazing."

Schultz slid the flash drive across the table to him. "See what's on that too."

"Will do," Josh said, picking it up. "I think I've got a call to make."

He turned and left the room in a hurry.

Jericho looked at Schultz. "Where's he going?"

"I imagine he'll be getting Adrian on the line to tell him the good news."

Julie cleared her throat. "Mr. Schultz, Josh said something about consequences..."

Schultz cleared his throat as he pushed the briefcase away from him. "The three of you were a goddamn disgrace out there. You shined a spotlight on this company that we didn't need. You know the importance of what we're doing, and we can't lose the trust this world has in us. Not now."

"We understand that," nodded Julie.

"But your problems don't end with some bad press. The bottom line is you neutralized Jericho's old unit. They were the CIA's main weapon in this conspiracy, and them being out of action will be a major blow to their side."

"Surely, that's a good thing?" said Collins.

"Oh, it is," agreed Schultz. "But you can bet your bottom dollar the president doesn't think so. Or the CIA. Or anyone else our commander-in-chief decides to include. The dirty truth is this: you three, along with Adrian Hell, are now unofficially the most wanted people on this planet. We can't risk having you associated with GlobaTech anymore."

Julie shot to her feet and slammed her palms down on the desk. "You're *firing* us?"

"Ah, this is bollocks," added Collins, gesturing with his arms.

Schultz held up his hand. "I don't care if you don't like it. It's for your own good and the good of this company. What's going on here is bigger than the three of you. We can't fight a war with the CIA because you decided to turn Prague into a goddamn shooting gallery."

Julie sat back down. "You can't do this to us. After everything we went through..."

Jericho put a hand on her arm and leaned forward. He nodded to her and to Collins before turning to Schultz. "It's my fault we're in this position."

"No arguments there, son," replied Schultz. "But taking the blame doesn't change a goddamn thing."

Jericho nodded. "I know. I didn't expect it to. We'll all leave quietly on one condition."

Schultz narrowed his eyes. "And that is?"

"Let us stay and help until this thing is over. We've been through too much to walk away now. The whole point of putting us together was to fly under the radar, right? I get that we had a bad start, but if you didn't think we were the best, we wouldn't be sitting here. We'll keep our heads down, do what needs to be done, help where we can, and when all this is over... when Adrian Hell's done whatever he's planning to do... we'll all leave and disappear. You won't hear from us again. If you need to go public with anything, you can spin it that we were rogue operatives or something —put all the blame on us and keep GlobaTech's name clean."

"I think that's a great idea," said Josh, who had reappeared in the doorway.

Schultz coughed. "I'm not sure—"

"Ryan, it's fine," he said, cutting him off. He looked at Jericho. "I'm sorry I gave you such a hard time before. I've just had a conversation with Adrian, who is the grand master of reckless vengeance. Speaking to him tends to put things in perspective, y'know? I get why you did what you did, and I hope you got what you needed from it."

Jericho nodded. "I did."

"Good. Bottom line, Adrian's gonna be making his move in a few days, and the information we secured in Prague is invaluable to his efforts. He asked me to pass on his gratitude, by the way. But we're gonna need all the help we can get in the coming days and weeks. You're right, Jericho. Long-term, you can't be associated with this company. Not anymore, not after yesterday. But until you have to leave, I'll gladly have you here."

Jericho stood, prompting Julie and Collins to do the same.

"I appreciate that. Thank you," he said. "But I do have one request."

Schultz rolled his eyes. "Jesus Christ... you're making demands now?"

Jericho ignored his understandable frustrations, focusing on Josh. "I don't want to lead this unit."

Josh's eyes narrowed. "Okay..."

"Prague went down the way it did because I couldn't focus on being in command. I can't risk that happening again. I've done my time in charge. I just want to help."

Josh held his gaze for a long moment before nodding. "Fair enough."

Jericho looked around the room. "I would, however, like to recommend Julie to take my place." He felt her gaze on him, but he ignored it. "She's a hell of a soldier and a million times smarter than I will ever be. I'd follow her into battle without question. And I'm sure Ray would agree."

Josh turned to Collins, who shrugged and nodded silently. His gaze then fell to Julie. "So, what do you say, Miss Fisher? Up for a promotion?"

She stood straight and tall, taking a deep breath. "Yes, sir. Thank you." She turned to Jericho. "And thank *you*."

He smiled at her. "Don't mention it. *Ma'am*."

She rolled her eyes but said nothing.

Jericho extended his hand to Josh. "Thanks. For everything. You're a good man."

Josh shook it. "No problem." He looked at the others. "Now enough with the sentimental crap, all right? We've got work to do."

Everyone smiled, feeling fresh and motivated with renewed purpose. The three of them left the room and headed for the elevator at the end of the corridor. As they stood waiting for it, Collins turned to Julie and Jericho. "So, this is it, then? Once Adrian does his thing, we're out of here?"

"Looks like it," said Julie.

"What are ya both gonna do when this is over?"

Julie shrugged. "No idea. What about you, Jericho?"

The doors opened with a ding, and they all stepped inside. Jericho pressed the button for the first floor, and the doors slid shut again. As they descended, he looked at the two of them. "I don't know, but whatever we do, I think we should do it together. Agreed?"

Julie and Collins exchanged a glance and smiled. "Agreed," she said.

The doors opened, and they stepped out into the lobby.

"So, what now?" asked Collins.

"Drink?" offered Julie.

Jericho shrugged. "Sure thing, boss."

Collins clapped his hands together and stepped between them, placing an arm around each of their shoulders. "Jules, Jerry... this could be the start of a beautiful friendship!"

They walked outside into the California sun, laughing together as they headed to the bar just a half-mile down the road.

19

April 23, 2017

Baker was driving the Jeep, with LaSharde beside him. They had returned from Prague a little over an hour ago and were en route to their base. The sun was already high despite the early hour, and he wore sunglasses to shield his eyes from the pale glare.

The mood was low and tense. Not only had they been unsuccessful in their attempt to get the information from Daniel Vincent, but they had run into a team of GlobaTech operatives, who had already secured their target. And what made matters worse was that one of them was Jericho Stone.

They had traveled back mostly in silence. Black was dead. LaSharde was struggling to come to terms with it, which Baker understood. He had figured words weren't necessary right now.

He pressed a button on the vehicle's console, and the barrier guarding the base entrance slowly lifted. He drove through, checking his rearview to make sure it descended automatically behind them. He guided the vehicle over to the motor pool, next to the armory, and came to a stop.

"What now?" he asked LaSharde.

After a moment's silence, she took a deep breath and looked at him. "You go and get rid of Santiago's body. I should contact Jones and find out what the hell happened back there."

Baker nodded and headed over to the armory, where they had left Santiago bleeding out from the stab wound Black had given him before they left. LaSharde began emptying the trunk.

She moved without thinking, operating in a daze as the events of the last twenty-four hours began to replay in her mind. Jericho had killed Black. The people with him from GlobaTech were good, and they took her and Baker out before securing Daniel Vincent and his briefcase. Their unit was in tatters, and they had failed their mission. She knew Jones wasn't going to be happy.

Hurried footsteps sounded on the gravel, distracting her. She looked around the vehicle to see Baker running toward her, visibly shaken.

"What is it?" she asked, concerned.

"It's Rick," he replied, trying to catch his breath. "He's gone."

"What?" LaSharde pushed past him and walked quickly toward the armory. She looked around but saw nothing except a dried pool of blood on the ground. There weren't any visible tracks leading away from where the body had been left. She looked around frantically, but there was no sign of Santiago. She turned to face Baker, who had appeared behind her.

"Where the hell is he?"

"I don't know," he said. "I'll check the security feeds and see if there's any footage of what happened."

She nodded. "Good idea. I'll be right with you."

"What are you gonna do?" he asked.

She sighed. "Make the hardest phone call of my life."

She took out her cell and paced begrudgingly away back toward the vehicle, punching in a number from memory. It was answered immediately. She took a deep breath. "Jones, it's LaSharde."

"Where are you?" replied Julius Jones, uncharacteristically flustered. "And what in the blue hell happened in Prague?"

"We've just arrived back in Granada. Julius... Jericho was there. He was working with GlobaTech and—"

"I know he was!" interrupted Jones. "You know how I know? Because it's being broadcast on a loop on every goddamn news channel in the country! Am I right in assuming Daniel Vincent's intel is not in your possession?"

She sighed. "No, GlobaTech got to him before we could. Jericho's new team got the drop on us. We had to back off once the local authorities arrived so as not to risk the exposure."

"Risk the expos—Jesus Christ! You were already exposed! I can't begin to tell you how pissed off both the director and the president are right now. My ass is in the firing line, and you better believe yours is too! Our local monitoring station saw everything. You were sloppy, and you were loud. Now put Black on the phone."

She bit her lip to control a flood of emotion, angry at herself for even allowing her feelings to surface. "Chris is dead, Julius. Jericho killed him."

There was a heavy sigh on the line, followed by silence.

"I'm sorry," said Jones eventually. "I know you were close. Are you sure it was—"

"I saw the body. We managed to sneak into the hotel during the chaos, looking for him. He had been shot, and his throat was crushed."

There was more silence before Jones spoke again.

"All right. The way things are right now, especially for the agency, we can't afford this kind of publicity." He paused. "Effective immediately, the D.E.A.D. program is no more. I want you and Baker to cleanse the Granada base and move out. You'll be contacted in due course. Until then, you drop off the grid and keep your heads down."

Her anger surfaced, and she spoke, forgetting her place. "You can't do that! Jericho killed him! You have to give us a chance to take out Jericho and get that intel back. We'll—"

"It's done. The order came directly from the Oval Office. Do you understand me? Clear up and move out. I'll be in touch."

"Julius? Julius!" The line was dead. She threw her phone to the ground. "Damn it!"

LaSharde took a moment to compose herself and then strode over to the main building. She headed through the entrance and left, to the communications room, where Baker was sitting in front of the computer, staring blankly at the screen.

"Please tell me you have something..." she said.

Baker sighed loudly, pressing a button to begin playback of the security feed. "Yeah. *This.*"

She leaned on the desk and watched the high-definition, black and white feed on the monitor from approximately twelve hours ago.

Santiago was lying motionless on the ground. Then he started to twitch. Just his legs at first, then his right hand.

After a few minutes, he managed to take his cell phone out, fumbling with it before placing it to his ear. He dragged himself to his feet, talking as he hunched over, clutching his stomach wound. He staggered awkwardly toward the armory and disappeared out of sight of the camera as he entered.

"What the hell is he doing?" muttered LaSharde. "And who is he talking to?"

"Just keep watching," replied Baker.

Santiago reappeared ten minutes later, just as another man hurried into view and ran across the courtyard. The unknown male moved to Santiago's side, gently lifting his arm over his shoulder to support his weight. They walked side by side across the screen. The feed was triggered by motion sensors. The video switched to another feed, and she continued watching as the two figures walked toward an unregistered sports car parked near the barrier. They couldn't see the face of Santiago's friend. He helped him into the passenger seat and then climbed in behind the wheel before driving away in a hurry.

"Seriously, who the hell was that?" she asked, knowing there was no answer.

"The better question is," replied Baker, "what was he doing in the armory for ten minutes?"

They stared at each other for a long moment, arriving at the same conclusion at the same time. They turned in unison and sprinted out of the building, back over to the armory. They ran inside, frantically searching for something they both hoped they wouldn't find.

But Baker found it.

"My God..." he said, stunned.

LaSharde joined him and followed his gaze. At their feet, in front of a crate of ammunition, were three blocks of C-4 taped to a gasoline can. There was a timer counting down, and it had a little under eight minutes left.

"Oh, shit!" she exclaimed. "Can you defuse it?"

He shook his head. "Santiago was the explosives expert," he conceded. "I probably could but not in the time that's left."

LaSharde took a breath to calm herself. "Okay, we've got plenty of time. Grab any personal effects and meet at the Jeep. I'll load the trunk with weapons. We're moving out, right now."

They both moved swiftly and efficiently, and just over seven minutes later, they were clear of the barrier and heading down the dirt track toward the coast. Baker was driving, and after a minute or so, he slammed the brakes on, turning to look behind him as they stopped. LaSharde did the same, and after a few tense moments of silence, a deafening explosion rang out, shaking the vehicle and the ground beneath them. Smoke and flames billowed to the sky, and despite the distance, the smells of fire and gas and gunpowder still stung their nostrils.

"Holy crap!" said Baker, breathing a heavy sigh of relief before turning to LaSharde. "What now? What did Jones say?"

She swallowed hard, taking a few quick, deep breaths to subdue a surge of adrenaline. "He said that because of Prague, the president has ordered our unit to be shut down, effective immediately. We're to separate, drop off the grid, and await further instructions."

"Can they do that?"

She shrugged. "It's the president—he can do what he likes. But there's no way they'll contact us again. Not after we failed to get that intel from Vincent. And not with Jericho still alive. Chances are, we're going to be hunted down and killed. We're a goddamn liability now, and they'll need someone to blame for all this."

"So, we've been disavowed?" asked Baker. "This ain't right. Well, screw separating. You ask me, Charlie, we're better off together."

She nodded. "I agree."

"So, what's the plan?"

She took another deep breath. "The way I see it, we're on our own now. The CIA will want us silenced, but that's not going to happen. There's only one reason we're in this position, and that's Jericho. As far as I'm concerned, nothing matters now except putting that bastard in the ground. We've got weapons and money. If we bury him, maybe the CIA will let us back in. Or at the very least, they will let us walk away without us having to look over our shoulders for the rest of our lives."

Baker stared ahead, processing their situation. The dirt road before him stretched away into the jungle. He nodded slowly. "Yeah... I reckon you're right. Payback's the only option now."

He stepped on the gas, speeding away from the flaming remains of their base. He glanced in his rearview at the blackening sky.

"So, where do you wanna go?" he asked after a moment.

LaSharde rested one foot up on the dash and her arm against the window of his door. "Guatemala," she replied. "Jericho's working with GlobaTech. The CIA is probably coming after us. We need to disappear until we can find some allies of our own."

20

The room bustled with urgent activity, filled with the loud rabble of commotion and conversation. People were studying reports, talking animatedly on phones, and huddling in small groups around desks, desperately trying to find resolutions to an ever-growing list of problems. News of the explosion at the base in Nicaragua had arrived a couple of hours previous, and everyone had been on high alert since. Satellite footage of the incident was displayed on a large monitor mounted on the left wall, playing on a loop.

Julius Jones stood in the center of the operations room, staring intently at a bank of computer screens, oblivious to the noise around him. He had removed his tie and unfastened his top button, trying to feel more comfortable and relaxed, but it was having little effect under the circumstances. He took a sip of his coffee, which had long since cooled, and let out a frustrated sigh. It was after two in the morning, and he knew that sleep wasn't a luxury he would be afforded any time soon.

His team was scouring the globe for the remaining members of the now-defunct D.E.A.D. unit, and he had been transfixed on their progress from the minute he walked in. He had explained finding them was a matter of national security, and there would be no rest until they had been located. That was why, despite the hour, he was surrounded by so many people, all looking more alert than he felt.

His frustrations were rooted in the anger he felt toward himself. In his last conversation with LaSharde, he had told her to cleanse the site, which he knew was explicit in its definition—wipe all hard drives and computer systems, remove all weapons, and leave no trace of their presence. It did not, under any circumstances, mean he wanted the base destroyed. At first, he felt he had underestimated LaSharde's state of mind. She was clearly upset about Black's demise at the hands of Jericho. But upon reviewing the satellite footage, it was clear that LaSharde and Baker weren't leaving; they were fleeing. Which meant they weren't the ones who blew up the compound.

This left him with another problem. Not only did he have to find them, he had to figure out who was behind the explosion. The location of the base was classified, which immediately narrowed the list of suspects. His first thought was Jericho, but his instincts were telling him this wasn't his style. Plus, with his new affiliation with GlobaTech Industries, his movements would be limited.

He took another deep, tired breath and sipped his coffee. The taste finally seemed to register, and he pulled his face as he looked down at his mug.

"Can somebody get me some goddamn hot coffee?" he shouted to no one in particular.

Barely a minute passed, and a young analyst wearing a headset appeared beside him holding a fresh cup of steaming hot caffeine. Jones took it gratefully, nodding his thanks, and turned his attention back to the screens.

The unenviable task of tracking their D.E.A.D. unit down had been delegated to him by Director Matthews, who thought it best he distanced himself from the whole operation. Reading between the lines, Jones knew Matthews was out of favor with the president, and passing this over to him was his way of staying off the White House's radar while Cunningham's plan unfolded. He wasn't in the president's inner circle himself, but he had seen enough classified information to know that whatever was coming was big, and the CIA was to play a major part in its success. Anything that jeopardized that would be swiftly removed, and right now, he was the best person to ensure that happened.

Manning the plethora of screens before him were two men, sitting side by side, working feverishly at their individual consoles. Jones moved behind them and rested his hands gently on the backs of their chairs.

The man to his left was his top analyst, Simon Cross. He was in his early forties, which was relatively young for a man in his position. He had been with the agency for over a decade and was justifiably fast-tracked to the top of his field. Jones had recruited him personally, seeing the potential in him from the start. He was well-liked and well-respected, with a natural suspicion of everything, which made him perfect for deciphering any intercepted communications from potential threats.

The other man was Major Samuel Drake, one of the most experienced drone pilots in the U.S. Air Force. A few years older than Cross, he had over one hundred and fifty UAV combat missions on his record. He was a family man, with a wife and two sons back home. He was also a patriot and career military. He obeyed orders without question, which made him perfect for the current mission.

Jones looked on as Drake expertly piloted a surveillance drone, currently flying at fifty thousand feet over the El Salvador/Guatemalan border. It was an RQ-4 Global Hawk —one of the few drone programs still used in the United States that wasn't designed by GlobaTech Industries. Having reached what was left of the compound a little over twenty minutes ago, they were tracking the most likely destinations LaSharde and Baker would be heading to, based on the direction they left.

"Anything?" asked Jones openly.

"Nothing yet, sir," replied Drake, his voice monotonous with concentration.

He nodded to himself and patted the back of the other chair. "Cross, have you been able to make contact with our local operatives in Guatemala City yet?"

"I have, Mr. Jones," said Cross confidently. "There have been no reported sightings of either operative. I'm running a search at the moment on the D.E.A.D. unit's mission logs from the past three years, cross-referencing them for any locations within a hundred miles of the city."

Jones frowned. "What are you looking for?"

"Well, I believe their ultimate goal will be to head State-side. I've yet to determine their intent, but they will be in survival mode right now, and it'll be too risky for them to approach any known safe house or supply drop we have in the region. I think there's a chance they may have their own contacts there, and they will use this time to drop off the grid and travel to the U.S. quietly."

Jones raised an eyebrow. "Black never showed me anywhere near the level of competency required to support that theory. I wonder if the same can be said for his unit."

"Well, they were Jericho Stone's unit first, Mr. Jones."

"Hmm, good point. Well, you're better at this sort of thing than I ever was, so I'll leave it with you. Keep me posted."

Cross nodded, suppressing a swell of pride. "Will do, sir."

Jones paused and took one last look at the monitors before pacing away and sitting down heavily in the chair at the head of the long conference table in the middle of the room. He leaned back and rubbed a hand over his head, clenching his jaw muscles as he thought about everything and nothing all at once. He felt the onset of fatigue as well as the pressure of knowing he had to produce results... and soon.

"Sir, I think we have something," called Drake from across the room a moment later.

Jones strode quickly over to him. "What is it, Major?"

Cross leaned over and pointed to the screen. "This is the Port of San Jose, on the Guatemalan coast. Approximately two hours ago, a seaplane landed there. We did a fly-by, and by all accounts, it's a chartered flight that originated from La Boquita—a coastal resort in Nicaragua, just under eighty klicks from Granada."

Jones frowned. "And you think they were on it?"

"I do, yes. There was no manifest logged, but I've tracked back through archived satellite footage, and you can definitely see two people approaching the take-off site on foot, a little over ninety minutes after the explosion at the base. It ties in with the flight time, so I believe right now, Charlotte LaSharde and Damien Baker are in Guatemala."

Jones nodded. "Just like we thought. Have you been able to track them since?"

"It's been difficult because they know how to hide, but I

think they're heading..." He paused to lean forward and point to Drake's monitor. "Here."

Jones leaned in between the two seats and squinted at the screen. "Cuyuta? Never heard of it. Is there anything there?"

Cross shook his head. "I don't know. Our only presence in the country is in Guatemala City. But this is the most likely destination, based on where they arrived and how they left, and it ties in with the idea they may have their own network of contacts outside of the agency."

"This is good work," said Jones. He placed a hand gently on Drake's shoulder. "Major, this is a reconnaissance mission. As soon as you have a visual, you tag them and call it in. Our job is to find them, not take them out. Understand?"

Drake didn't move but said, "Copy that, sir."

Jones walked away and sat down at the conference table. He slumped slightly in his seat and stroked his chin thoughtfully. He knew this needed to be handled quietly, but any attempt to terminate would be expected, which would result in more mess to clear up.

He remained there for over ten minutes before jolting upright in his chair.

He had an idea.

21

The ringing was loud in the silence of his bedroom and was accompanied by the noise of the phone vibrating across the surface of the bedside table. Josh Winters lay on his front, his face buried in his pillow. He fumbled blindly for his cell but failed to reach it before the ringing stopped.

He groaned and pushed himself up, propping himself on his side using his elbow. He clicked his lamp on and checked his watch. It was just before six a.m.

"Whoever that was better have been female and hot," he muttered as he dialed into his voicemail.

His eyes grew wide as he listened to the message, and he stared absently into space for a few minutes after it had finished.

"Huh..."

He jumped out of bed, dressed quickly, and headed out. His apartment was on the top floor, in the same building as Julie's. He rode the elevator all the way down and walked hurriedly outside. The sun was beginning to rise, though the moon was still faintly visible. He made his way across the compound, which was already busy for the time of day. He put his cell to his ear and said, "Ryan Schultz."

The voice-activation called the number, but there was no answer.

"Bollocks," he muttered to himself.

He entered the main office building and headed to his office. Once inside, he shut the door and returned the call he had missed earlier. It was answered on the second ring.

"Didn't wake you, did I?" asked Julius Jones.

Josh sat heavily in his chair and swiveled to look out the window. "You did, actually. I've not decided if I forgive you yet."

"Did you get my message?"

"Yeah."

"And?"

"And... I'm taking a huge risk just talking to you. With everything that's going on, you must have some balls to contact me, of all people. What does your boss think about it?"

"My boss doesn't know. No one does. What about you?"

"For now, this is between us."

"Probably for the best, all things considered."

"Seriously, Julius, are you out of your mind? How do you expect me to trust a single word that comes out of your mouth after what you did to Jericho?"

"I don't. But for the record, I didn't do anything to Jericho."

"Maybe not directly, but don't start arguing over semantics with me. He went through what he did because of you and who you work for."

Jones sighed. "I know, Josh, and that's partly the reason I got in touch. To make amends with everyone."

"You don't need to. I wasn't the one shot in the head, and

Jericho's fine now he's working with me. I think the safest thing you can do is walk away."

"I didn't call looking for a fight."

"I know why you called. Problem is, I think you're full of crap."

"Which is understandable, given our current predicament. But Josh, you and I... we go way back. I'm not here to get into a discussion about who's doing what and where. This is about making things right with Jericho."

"Really? And why would you want to do that?"

Jones paused momentarily. "Honestly? Because I know him well enough to know I don't want him coming after me."

Josh smiled to himself. "Bullshit."

"I don't—"

"Bullshit."

"No, it's—"

"Bullshit! Seriously, how can you concentrate on this conversation with the pungent odor of manure spewing from your mouth? Don't patronize me by thinking I'll buy any line you feed me, Julius. You say you know Jericho well enough, but you know me better than most. And vice versa. So, cut the crap and tell me why we're talking."

Jones sighed. "Fine. Charlotte LaSharde and Damien Baker have been disavowed, and the D.E.A.D. program has been shut down, effective immediately—an order from President Cunningham himself. I've been tasked with bringing them in..."

"You mean killing them?" interrupted Josh.

Jones cleared his throat. "Yes. I know roughly where they are, but frankly, I don't want my name anywhere near this operation. So, yes, there are selfish reasons behind my calling you, but they're not the only reasons. I meant it when I said I want to make things right with Jericho. The order to take him out didn't come from me personally, and I don't like the fact he got caught up in all this. I know the kind of man he is, and I'm sure knowing two members of the unit that betrayed him are still out there is tearing him up inside. I'm offering to outsource the mission of tracking them down to your company."

Josh nodded thoughtfully. "In exchange for..."

"Anonymity. You take them out for me, you get to take the credit for bringing down the people ultimately responsible for the attack in Prague. Meanwhile, I get to put a little distance between me and whatever Matthews is caught up in with Cunningham. Everybody wins."

Josh fell silent, staring out the window at the mountain range, which cast its large and impressive shadow over the GlobaTech compound. He knew Schultz would flip if he found out GlobaTech was carrying out work for the CIA on the side. Especially with everything that was happening.

That said, he also knew Jones had a point about Jericho. Even with Black dead, he wasn't completely convinced Jericho could forgive and forget the rest of his old unit. He wanted the best out of his new recruit, and if he removed any potential, nagging thirst for vengeance, he would be a better operative for it.

He took a deep breath. "Let's say I agree. How would we do this?"

"Simple," replied Jones. "I'll send you the exact coordinates of the last sighting we have of LaSharde and Baker. You can verify them and take whatever action you see fit."

"And you don't want anything except your name kept out of this?"

"That's right."

Josh knew from experience that when something

seemed too good to be true, it usually was. But his spider sense was quiet, and the upside to this far outweighed any potential reprimanding from Schultz.

He sighed. "Screw it. Send me the details. *My* D.E.A.D. unit will nail the bastard."

He clicked the phone off and put it on his desk. He stood and paced back and forth behind his desk. "I hope you know what you're doing..." he said to himself.

Julie Fisher grunted from the exertion as she completed her thirtieth rep. Having already done three miles on the treadmill, she had begun work on her shoulders and back. She was using the wide-angle grip on the bar, pulling herself up and alternating between leaning forward, so the bar touched the back of her shoulders, and leaning back, so it touched the top of her chest. Her legs were bent at the knees, her ankles crossed behind her as she hung for a moment in the deserted gym before dropping to the floor. She had struggled to sleep and was making herself angry just lying in bed, staring at the ceiling, so she decided to get an early start on her morning routine.

She picked up her water bottle and took a healthy swig, breathing heavily from the workout. Her light gray vest was stained dark with sweat. She wore black yoga pants with a white stripe running down the outside of each leg and white running shoes. Her hair was tied back in a ponytail, and her face glistened from the exercise.

Julie had always been disciplined, and she thrived off routine. Each morning, usually around six a.m., she would hit the gym for an hour before clocking in. She was a naturally strong woman, both in physique and personality.

Consequently, she had never felt the need to prove herself to anyone, and the fact she excelled in what was still typically a male-dominated job only served as a testament to her hard work and dedication.

That said, she was beginning to feel the pressure of having to maintain the level of success she had reached now she was in charge of Josh's new D.E.A.D. project. But this only motivated her further. She knew... she *believed* she could handle any situation, and it was that belief that gave her the drive to get her where she was today.

Her mind wandered while she rested, thinking of her new teammates. Collins was a great soldier—fearless, loyal, highly-skilled. Any shortcomings in his personality were really more defining than detrimental, and while she would never admit it to him, she was grateful to have him with her.

She caught herself smiling as she thought about Jericho. The man was a mountain and a highly-decorated soldier. He was clinical and regimented, almost to a fault, but he was intelligent and a force of nature out in the field. Julie knew that—on paper at least—he was far better suited to her role than she was. But after everything that had happened to him, he didn't want the responsibility anymore. He was forging a new path for himself, and she thought his vulnerability simply added to his charm.

She shook her head, took another sip of water, and then moved to the next machine, positioning herself in the seat and adjusting the weight. She glanced around as she prepared herself for the next routine in her workout.

"Early start?"

The voice from behind startled her. She jumped up and turned to see Josh standing there, smiling.

She breathed a heavy sigh of relief and smiled back. "Couldn't sleep. What's your excuse?"

"I had a phone call about an hour ago."

She raised an eyebrow. "I bet you were thrilled."

"Yeah, I could barely contain myself. Now, listen, we've... ah... we've got a thing. It could be big. Gather your boys, okay?"

"Is everything all right?"

He shrugged. "I honestly don't know. Look, get yourself freshened up and wake the others. I'll explain everything in my office. Say... thirty minutes?"

"Yeah... you got it, boss."

He took a step closer and leaned in slightly, lowering his voice. "And do me a favor, would you? Keep an eye on Jericho. He might not like what I'm gonna say, and I need him thinking straight."

She frowned and nodded slowly. "Sure thing, Mr. Winters. Whatever you need."

He stood up straight again. "Thanks."

He turned and walked away, leaving her sitting on the seat of the weight machine, staring at the floor, wondering what it could be that had Josh so worried about Jericho's reaction.

Jericho frowned as the faint knocking gradually grew louder. It took a few moments for him to realize it wasn't in his head, and there was actually a knocking. It took another few moments for him to realize there was someone at his door.

He groaned as he stirred, consciousness fighting hard to take over. He tried to swallow, but it felt like his throat was packed full, preventing him from doing so. He rolled over and smacked his head against the side of his bed.

"Damn it..." he muttered.

He tried to open his good eye, but it was stuck together with grit. He sat up, fumbling blindly for anything to grab a hold of, but was hit by a wave of nausea and dizziness that left him with no choice but to lie back down.

"Oh my God..."

The knocking persisted, which was adding to his already significant headache. He stretched out in a futile attempt to reach the door. "What?" he shouted.

The door opened, and Julie stepped into his apartment. She had showered and changed and was wearing skinny jeans and tan boots, with a T-shirt that said 'Bullet Babe' on the front of it. Her hair was still wet and tied back.

"Your door was open," she said, staring down at him. "Why are you on the floor? And why are you naked?"

He frowned. "Huh? What?"

He shot upright and sprung to his feet but managed one step before falling sideways. Luckily, he landed on his bed, but he was still unable to open his eye. Panicking, he simply rolled across it and dropped off the other side, landing heavily on the floor.

Julie failed to suppress a smile. "Okay, I'm sorry—you're not naked, really. But that was funny! I take it you and Ray stayed and had a few too many last night?"

Jericho's hand appeared over the side of the bed and gave her the thumbs up.

She shook her head. "Well, unfortunately, we don't have time to truly savor this moment, so get your ass up and dressed, big guy. Josh wants us in his office in fifteen minutes."

Jericho's hand made the 'okay' gesture.

Julie turned to leave but paused and looked back over

her shoulder. "Please understand that there will be absolutely no living this down."

Jericho gave the thumbs down gesture, and a moment later, he heard the door shut.

A little over fifteen minutes later, the door to Josh's office opened, and the three members of his D.E.A.D. unit walked in. Julie was first, looking alert and professional. She stood at ease in front of the desk and nodded a curt greeting to him. Collins followed her and stood to her right. He also looked alert, though not as much as his superior. He had black bags beneath his eyes and stifled a yawn as he cracked his neck. Jericho was last in, and he closed the door behind him. He moved slowly to Julie's left, also nodding a courteous greeting.

Josh smiled. "You look like shit, Jericho. Everything okay?"

Jericho shook his head. "When the room stops spinning, I'm going to punch Ray really hard."

Collins chuckled. "Not my fault ya can't handle ya drink in ya old age, Jerry."

Jericho went to reply but realized there was nothing he could say. Collins had a point.

Josh stood and walked around his desk, moving to the window that overlooked the compound and pausing for a moment to take in the view. He took a deep breath and turned to face his unit. "Okay, so here's the thing. Someone at the CIA made contact with me this morning."

Everyone exchanged a glance of concern before Julie asked, "Who?"

Josh cast a quick look at Jericho before saying, "Julius Jones."

Hearing the name felt like a punch in the gut to Jericho, which did little to help his current mood. But the soldier inside him awakened. He sat on the edge of Josh's desk and took a deep breath. His years of military experience focused his mind, temporarily wiping away his hangover.

"What did he want?" he asked.

"He wanted to make things right with you," replied Josh.

Julie and Collins looked at Jericho, watching him struggle to hide his emotions beneath his mask of professional disassociation. Finally, he said, "He can't. He betrayed me. If I see him again, I'll rip his heart out."

No one said anything. They all knew that wasn't a threat. It was a very real, literal promise. After a few moments of silence, Josh stepped toward him. "He told me they know where the rest of your old unit is hiding out."

Jericho leapt to his feet. "What? Where?"

"Take it easy, Jericho," said Julie, moving toward him and placing a hand on his chest. She turned to Josh. "You can't possibly trust this guy?"

Josh shook his head. "Good God, no. But he sent me the intel he has, and he *does* know exactly where they are, so he's not lying about that."

Collins moved beside him and leaned back on the window. "Okay, wait a minute. This is the CIA guy who oversaw the D.E.A.D. unit, right?" He looked at Jericho. "How well do you know him?"

Jericho shrugged. "As well as I needed to."

"Well, he sounds like a grade one piece of shit to me. Why would he even care about making it right with ya?"

Josh nodded. "Valid point. As far as we're concerned, he's working with the enemy. That's a fact. And I absolutely do not trust him. But... he said he's been given the job of *retiring* what's left of Jericho's old unit because of how badly they screwed up in Prague. He doesn't know what Cunningham and Matthews are planning, but he knows it's big, and he doesn't want his name linked to any of it. He's offering us the intel, so we can take them out, in exchange for not mentioning to anyone how we found them."

Jericho took a step forward, but Julie stood her ground, keeping a hand on his chest. She looked up at him. "Take it easy," she whispered before looked around at Josh. "You can't possibly be considering this?"

Josh walked back over to his desk and sat down in his chair. "Forget about Jones and the CIA for a moment, okay? Let's focus on the potential targets. They all tried to take the three of you out in Prague, and it was a pretty good attempt, by all accounts. Jericho, you took Black out of commission, but these other two—LaSharde and Baker—you know how dangerous they can be. They're wanted by the CIA. They've gone to ground... for now. You tell me, what are they gonna do next? What's their move?"

Jericho paced away, thinking about it. He tried to forget everything that had happened, all the violent thoughts running through his mind, and pretend he was still in charge of the CIA's D.E.A.D. unit. He knew them all as well as anyone. He trained them. The better question here was what would *he* do in their position?

He turned to face Josh and the others. "Wherever they are, they'll be planning revenge for Prague. Either against the CIA or against us."

Josh nodded. "I agree. These two pose a genuine threat. We know that. But now they're desperate and have very little left to lose, which makes them an even bigger threat we can't afford to ignore."

"Now hang on a minute," said Collins. "We're all pretty bad-ass. How tough do ya think they are? We handled them in Prague easily enough."

Jericho shot him a serious look. "That's because Black was reckless, and it was a public skirmish. I recruited these people, Ray. I know them. They're very resourceful and extremely capable in the field. I know that because I trained them to be." He turned back to Josh. "Odds are they won't go after the agency. If they've been disavowed, they will understand Jones will be going after them, and that's not a fight you win—doesn't matter how pissed you are."

Josh smiled. "Don't let Adrian hear you say that."

Jericho shrugged. "I don't care what *he* thinks. I'm telling you right now, these two won't pick a fight unless they believe they can win. Which means they're coming for us."

"But they ain't gonna win that fight either," added Collins.

Jericho nodded. "Damn right. But they won't agree. Theoretically, I'm a much easier target to go after than Jones is."

Julie stepped back and looked at Jericho. "So, what are you saying? You wanna take the fight to them?"

Jericho shrugged and looked at Josh. "I ain't doing the agency's dirty work. I'm done with that."

Josh laughed. "I know. Now you do *my* dirty work! But seriously, I think this is an opportunity. End of the day, we're not doing it for Jones or the CIA or Cunningham. We're doing it for us. It doesn't matter where the intel came from."

"But we wouldn't have been going after them otherwise, would we?" offered Julie.

"No, we wouldn't—you're right. But like I said, this is an opportunity to stop a potential threat before it knocks on our front door. This way, we won't be caught with our pants down. Plus..." He pointed at Jericho. "It probably won't do Thor over here any harm putting that part of his life to rest once and for all." He looked at him. "Am I right?"

Jericho said nothing.

Josh smiled. "I know a thing or two about seeing people I work with battle their demons, okay? Trust me, Jericho, if you have the option to slay one of yours, take it. I want the best from my team. I don't want your old unit hanging over your head forever."

Jericho looked at Julie and Collins in turn. They both shrugged and gestured to him that it was his call. He nodded and turned back to Josh. "I'm not doing this for the agency."

Josh held his hands up. "I know."

Jericho took a deep breath. "Okay, then. Where are the bastards?"

22

The tree line on either side of the road was a continuous green blur as the open-top Jeep sped along the CA-9A toward Cuyuta. Baker was behind the wheel, silent and focused. He had spent the last eighteen hours glued to a laptop and a phone, reaching out to every contact he had ever made, calling in favors across the world. They had chartered a seaplane from a guy he knew in Nicaragua who made some money on the side transporting drugs across the border. Baker knew their journey wouldn't be logged in any books, and he was confident they could disappear once they landed in Guatemala.

LaSharde was sitting next to him, leaning back in her seat, relishing the cool breeze as they travelled. She stared absently at the morning sky, streaked with pink as the sun began its daily climb. She had mostly remained silent since leaving what remained of their base. While Baker had kept himself occupied, she had found herself faced with an unfamiliar feeling.

For the first time in her life, she was scared. She knew they had dropped the ball in Prague, and she fully understood the severity of the situation they were now in. She had been with the agency long enough to know that, if they decide it was time you retired, there was no escape. With the agency after them and Jericho working for GlobaTech, she knew they had no option but to take the fight to them.

"We're nearly there," announced Baker. "It's just a couple more klicks up ahead."

LaSharde turned to him. "So, who is this guy again?"

Baker didn't take his eyes off the road. "His name's Travis. I know him from when I served—we did two tours of Afghanistan together. He stayed on for a third when I left to join the agency."

"What's he doing way out here?"

"He's been running a team of mercs for the last few years, mostly out of South America and parts of Africa. He took to ground in a village around here after 4/17, just until the dust settles, y'know? But he's well-connected. He'll be able to help."

"Good. We need all the help we can get right now."

The small village was located just outside of Cuyuta, roughly two kilometers along a beaten track that cut through the thick forest. If you didn't know to turn off the main road, you would never see it. Each bump in the road rattled the weapons lying across the backseat. A handful of handguns and rifles, some ammunition, and a secure laptop was all they could salvage from their base before it was blown to pieces.

Baker eased the Jeep to a stop as the track opened out into a clearing. There was a large space in the middle, with three defined paths that branched off to the left, the right, and straight ahead, deeper into the trees. Each one led to a small settlement of wooden buildings and looked too narrow for a vehicle. He saw a handful of 4×4s over to his right, so he drove slowly toward them and parked nearby, spinning the Jeep around so that it faced the exit. Just in case.

They both stepped out and looked around. There were a few people wandering absently across the clearing, but no one really paid them any attention. They huddled together. Baker reached into the back and retrieved an assault rifle, which he slung over his shoulder, adjusting the strap for comfort.

"Okay, let me do the talking," he said to LaSharde.

LaSharde tucked a handgun into the back of her cargo pants, then looked at him, frowning. "I thought you said you knew this guy?"

Baker nodded. "I do."

"Then why are you being so cautious?"

"Because I don't know the people he has with him."

LaSharde rolled her eyes and muttered, "Great..."

They walked across the clearing, maintaining an easy pace. As they reached the path, two men appeared from inside a small hut on the right, moving in front of him, blocking his way. They were both tall; each had a couple of inches on Baker. He stopped and regarded them in turn but said nothing.

"We don't know you," said the man on Baker's left. His skin was dark, like coal, and his voice was low and gravelly, his English broken. "Turn around and go."

Baker shook his head. "I'm here to see Travis."

The men exchanged a glance and then the man on the right said, "Nobody here by that name. You're in the wrong place, asshole." He had a lighter complexion but still had a natural tan. His accent was European, though his grasp of the language was much better than his friend's.

Baker stood his ground. "No, I'm not. Now look... I'm not

here to cause trouble, all right? Travis is an old friend, and I need his help. I don't have time for senseless posturing, so either take me to him or step aside, so I can find him myself."

The man on the left smiled back, revealing his yellow teeth. "Last warning... you and your pretty friend get back in your Jeep and leave, or we will bury you here. Understand?"

With an almost impossible speed, LaSharde drew her weapon, whipped it around, and leveled it at the man's head with unwavering precision. She stepped forward and rested the barrel between the man's eyes.

"Understand this—I get you're just doing your job, but you have no idea who I am or what I'm capable of. My beef isn't with you, but I can still spare a bullet if I need to. In fact, I could flatten this whole village, and there's nothing you could do about it. Now where's Travis?"

Baker closed his eyes for a second and shook his head, cursing how quickly the situation devolved.

Seconds later, a third man appeared from inside the hut, wearing jungle fatigues and a backwards baseball cap. He had dark stubble on his face and smiled a handsome, politician's smile.

"Damien? I thought that was you," said Travis.

The two men stepped aside, allowing him to move in front of Baker. His smile grew as he examined LaSharde. "Don't be pissed at these fellas, sweetheart. They're just thorough."

She waited a moment to make a point before lowering her weapon.

"Fair enough." She tucked the gun back in her waistband before glaring at Travis. "But you call me *sweetheart* again, I'll kick your balls up behind your ears."

He chuckled, which prompted the men standing behind him to do the same. "Fair enough."

Baker hadn't seen Travis in years, but he looked exactly how he remembered him. He extended his hand, eager to intervene and defuse any tension. LaSharde was a wild card at the best of times, but he had no doubt she would go on a rampage at the slightest thing.

"How've you been, man?"

Travis shook his hand. "Keeping busy, y'know? Tough times all around at the moment. What about you?"

"The same," he replied dismissively. "Listen, is there some place we can talk?"

"Sure." He gestured to the hut behind him. "Step into my office."

He moved aside, and Baker walked past him, followed a second later by LaSharde. Travis followed them inside the hut. The layout was basic. The floor was comprised of dirty wooden planks laid unceremoniously next to each other. There was a small, round table in the middle of the room with three chairs around it. In the back corner was a small, rusted stove with a kettle resting on one of the hobs.

Travis moved around and sat down in the chair facing the entrance. His two men stood in the doorway with their backs to the room. He gestured to one of the chairs next to him. "Take a seat, please."

Baker did, nodding at LaSharde to take the other one.

"So, how can I help you, old friend?" asked Travis.

Baker leaned forward, resting his arms on the table. He took a deep breath and proceeded to explain everything that had happened in the last two weeks.

A heavy silence had fallen inside the hut. Travis was leaning back in his chair, balancing on the back two legs, trying to process in his mind everything Baker had just spent twenty minutes telling him.

"I need a drink," he said finally.

Baker smiled faintly. "Welcome to our world."

"I mean... that's a whole lot of shit you're in, old friend. How exactly do you want me to help you?"

Baker stood and paced slowly back and forth for a moment before stopping to look at Travis. "I want to get back into the United States, kill Jericho Stone, and destroy GlobaTech Industries."

Travis laughed. "And I want to wake up next to Monica Bellucci every morning, but that's not gonna happen either!"

"I'm being serious."

"So am I! Have you seen her?"

"Travis..."

His smile faded, and he nodded slowly. "All right, gimme a sec." He went quiet as he ran his hand along his stubble, feeling the coarse hair grate on his palm, thinking about his friend's request. "Okay, you must know that what you're asking is a lot, right?"

Baker nodded. "I'd owe you."

"Damn right, you would. Now getting you Stateside isn't a major issue. The hard part is getting to your old boss. GlobaTech is everywhere, and they're being featured on almost every news outlet in the world. Irrespective of any beef you might have with them personally, you can't deny they're doing a lot of good for this world right now."

Baker shrugged. "I don't care about any of that. Not anymore. Bottom line, our president and the agency had a mission that I was a major part of, and now half of my team is either dead or missing, and I'm on the run because of those assholes. If we put an end to them, we all get back in the good graces of our commander-in-chief."

Travis nodded. "Okay, let's look at this another way. What's in it for me?"

LaSharde slammed her palm down on the table. "Are you kidding me? After what we just told you, you're seriously—"

"Easy, Charlie," said Baker before looking at Travis. "You'd be doing me a favor. And I'm a good person to have owe you one."

"I'm sure you are, but favors don't pay the bills. I run a large team of very skilled, highly sought-after independent contractors. I can't ask them all to do you a favor for nothing in return. This is business. Dangerous business. You want me to risk my men to help you, you have to make it worth our while. I'm sorry, man, but that's how it is."

Baker thought for a moment. "Okay, name your price."

Travis smiled. "For what? Getting you across the border, helping you kill this Jericho guy, or for taking down the largest military contractor and private security firm in the world? Jesus, Damien. God Himself couldn't afford all that!"

Baker fell silent and began pacing absently around the hut. He knew he wouldn't be able to do anything without Travis's help, but he also knew his old comrade was right. He couldn't afford to pay him, and he had nothing to offer that he would want. Except maybe...

He turned to look at Travis. "How about a job?"

"What do you mean?" he replied.

"Yeah, what *do* you mean?" asked LaSharde, her brow furrowed as she turned to glare at Baker with an expression of confusion and concern.

"I mean," he said to both of them, "if we do this, there's no way the CIA doesn't take us back, right? Cunningham's got big plans for our country that our unit will have a key role in. It wouldn't be a problem for me to convince the agency to hire you and your outfit to help us. That's a regular, guaranteed payday for you and all your men. Plus, you'd get to be front and center on the winning side when the world changes."

Travis frowned. "What do you mean? What's the president planning?"

"Honestly? I don't know. I suspect very few people do. But I've worked for the government long enough to know that when the CIA director gets involved in covert missions personally, there's more going on than what's in the briefing. After 4/17, the winds of change are blowing, and I'd bet the last dime in my pocket the United States is working the fan. You know what I'm saying?"

Travis thought about it for a moment, then said, "Okay, I'm interested. Do you have a plan?"

Baker shrugged. "Maybe. What are the chances of you getting us across the border near El Paso?"

"Texas?"

"Unless you know another one?"

Travis let out a long sigh. "It's possible. Why El Paso?"

Baker took a deep breath. "I lived there from the age of six. I grew up there, and I only left to join the Army. I had no parents or family. I was raised on the streets, and when I turned fourteen, I joined up with a gang of bikers. I rode with them until the day I left. It's a brotherhood, y'know."

LaSharde raised an eyebrow. "I never knew that. How did you get accepted into the forces—or the CIA, for that matter—if you were affiliated with a gang?"

Baker shrugged. "I was never arrested for anything. I think they looked at me as the baby brother of the outfit, if I'm honest. They always tried to keep me away from the questionable side of things. But let me tell you, they're the real deal. Guns, drugs—they've got deals with other gangs from Mexico, all the way to Florida."

"How many men?"

"After all these years, I have no idea, but they have chapters all along the border and the East coast. Could be hundreds; could be thousands."

Travis nodded. "Do you still have a way in with them?"

"Like I say, it's a brotherhood, man. You're never out, even if you leave. Sometimes that can be a bad thing. Other times, it can be quite useful."

"Do you think they would help us?"

"I can make the call. As good as I'm sure your contacts in the States are, Travis, you still only have, what? Fifteen people? Doesn't matter how good they are. This is a number's game, right? The CIA and GlobaTech are both worldwide entities with unlimited resources. Once we're back on home soil, we'll need more than that."

Travis thought about it and nodded once. "Okay, get in touch, set up a meeting, then co-ordinate with me, so I can arrange with my contacts to meet us at the border nearby."

LaSharde turned to Baker. "What's the name of your biker gang?"

Baker smiled. "The Dogs of Lucifer."

She rolled her eyes as her lips betrayed a small smile.

"Now check this out," continued Baker. "Santa Fe, New Mexico is a straight, five-hour run down I-25 from El Paso."

LaSharde shrugged, frowning. "So what? I thought once we make it to El Paso, we were going after Jericho?"

Baker nodded. "We will be. But El Paso is just the beginning. We can't just storm the gates of GlobaTech's main compound, even with a thousand bikers backing us up. They will see us from a mile away and take us out before we even caught sight of the gates. No... we need to bring them to us. Specifically, Jericho and his new friends."

"And we can do that in Santa Fe?" asked Travis, his curiosity piqued.

"GlobaTech Industries has a small research facility there. It's low-key but high-tech. They're working with the CDC to develop medicines for all the countries affected by 4/17, and they intend to ship them out as part of their role as U.N. Peacekeepers."

LaSharde frowned. "How do you know all that?"

He smiled. "I swear to God, I Googled it on the plane over here."

She laughed with disbelief. "No shit?"

"Crazy, right? I figure, if we hit that facility, it'll trigger a response. And if they know it's us, all the private security in the world won't be able to stop Jericho coming here."

"So, we use ourselves as bait?" asked Travis. "That might work... but it's risky."

"I know, but it's the only way. They won't be expecting our small army, and we can wipe them out in one strike. We'll deliver Jericho's head to Langley ourselves, and we're back in business."

"But if they're tracking you, like you think they will be, won't they notice a few hundred bikers behind our truck?"

"If they scrutinize the surrounding area, they will soon notice that large motorcycle movement is common, so they won't associate it with us. Plus, Jericho has no idea of my history with the Dogs of Lucifer. We need to be careful, obviously, but I think we can ambush them."

"And then what?" asked LaSharde.

"What do you mean?" shrugged Baker.

"Let's say this all goes down like we plan. We all take out

Jericho and his team. What then? We'll have GlobaTech on our asses."

Baker nodded. "We will, but we only have to outrun them until we make it to Langley. Once we meet with Jones, we get back in their good graces for taking out Jericho, and Travis..." He turned to his old friend. "You'll be gainfully employed by the CIA, meaning you never have to worry about looking over your shoulder, fearing retribution from GlobaTech."

Travis raised a quizzical eyebrow. "Really?"

"There's no way they will openly attack an agency asset. They have too much to lose."

Travis thought for a moment before getting to his feet, temporarily filling the small hut with the sound of his chair scraping across the wooden floor.

"Sounds like you got it all figured out," he said to Baker. "I'll tell my people what's happening. You two should rest up while you can. We'll move as soon as you've made the arrangements with your old friends."

He strode from the hut, leaving Baker and LaSharde alone at the table. They regarded each other for a moment.

"You okay?" asked Baker finally.

LaSharde nodded. "Yeah, I guess. So, this plan of yours... this is it, right? Our final stand. Our one shot at redemption. At revenge."

"I reckon so."

"Do you think it'll work?"

Baker thought long and hard before answering. "I believe it has to. I'm not naïve to the risks. To all the things that could go wrong. But you said it yourself. This is our one chance at clearing our names and getting revenge for Chris."

"Well," she said, getting to her feet, "let's hope your

friend, Travis, comes through and can get us to El Paso. Otherwise, all your Googling will count for nothing."

She walked past him, placing a hand on his shoulder as she drew level. Then she headed outside, leaving Baker to stare at the scarred surface of the table, wondering if he even believed his words himself.

23

Josh had spent the last hour talking his D.E.A.D. unit through the intel Jones had provided him. He stood near the wall facing his desk, pointing to the big screen opposite, which currently displayed a topographical map of South America, specifically highlighting Guatemala.

"So, we know roughly where they are and how they got there," he said, "even if we don't know why they're there or what they're planning next."

Collins and Jericho were sitting in the two chairs in front of the desk, which they had turned around to face the screen. Julie was resting against the edge of the desk itself, between them.

"There's a CIA safe house and ops center in Guatemala City," said Jericho, shaking his head. 'It's not like either of them to take that kind of risk."

"Desperate times…" offered Josh. "You're sure you don't know of any old contacts in the area?"

"I had a source I used for intel gathering in Belize, but that was off the books. No one knew about it except me, and that was the only one. Unless Baker or LaSharde had their own network of people I didn't know about, I can't think why else they would be there."

"That has to be it," said Julie. "They must know someone there whom they think can help them."

"Help them do what?" asked Collins. "I can't see how either of them could even fart right now without the CIA knowing about it, so how do they expect to get into the country and start their campaign of revenge?"

Josh moved toward them. "Here's what I'm thinking. The way I see it, there's no urgency until they make it into the U.S.—assuming that's what they intend to do. We get our own people on it, monitor the area, and watch for any movement that's likely to be them. We have our own analysts—and Jericho, I want you working with them on this—so we'll use the data we get to predict any and all potential scenarios. Then I want us to work on contingencies for anything they come up with. Julie, Ray—that's what you two will be doing. Questions?"

Julie sighed heavily. "I don't like it. I don't know what it is, but there's something about this that just—"

The door to the room burst open before she could finish her sentence. Josh's secretary, Kim Mitchell, appeared, looking flustered and slightly out of breath. She was in her late forties but looked younger, with bleached blonde hair and a borderline-respectable amount of make-up on. She had worked for Josh since his first day with the company, and he would freely admit he would be lost without her to organize his life for him.

Josh turned to look at her, immediately noting the urgency and panic in her expression and sensing something was amiss. "Kim, what is it?"

She paused for a moment, collecting herself. "They broke through the security barrier. We... we have them surrounded, but... one of them is armed." She paused and turned to Jericho. "They're asking for you."

Everyone exchanged glances, a mixture of surprise and concern. Without another word, Josh bolted from the room, followed moments later by the others. They headed out of the building and across the compound toward the entrance. They saw three trucks ahead of them, parked in a loose triangle, surrounding a fourth vehicle. There were at least twenty GlobaTech personnel standing with their weapons trained unwaveringly on a convertible sports car, which they saw in the middle as they neared the scene.

The four of them stopped just outside the circle of operatives. Josh and Jericho pushed their way through and stood beside the hood. The driver was wearing sunglasses and staring straight ahead. He gripped the wheel tightly enough that the color had drained slightly from his knuckles. His breathing was visibly heavy and rapid. Standing on the passenger seat, resting a gun on the top of the windshield for balance while clutching an obvious and bloody stomach wound, was Rick Santiago.

"Holy shit..." said Jericho, mostly to himself.

Josh turned to him. "You know these guys?"

Jericho nodded at Santiago. "I know him." He took a step forward. He wasn't angry. He felt no animosity toward him. But as far as he was concerned, anyone who worked for the agency was still the enemy. "Rick, you've got some balls showing up here after what went down in Colombia. What's going on?"

Santiago looked at his former leader, his eyes glazing over. "A little... help... boss?"

He lowered his gun and fell sideways onto the driver's lap. Jericho rushed toward them. Josh moved around the circle, gesturing with his arms for everyone to lower their weapons.

"Everybody, stand down," he shouted. "Give us some room." He called over his shoulder, "Julie, get a medical team out here ASAP."

Jericho yanked the driver's door open, and the man sitting there carefully climbed out, lowering Santiago's head onto the seat as he did. Jericho looked at him. "Who the hell are you?"

He took his sunglasses off with shaking hands. He was Hispanic, like Santiago. A little taller, a little heavier, but they looked similar, like they could be related.

"I'm... ah... I'm Rick's cousin. He called me after he..." He looked down and pointed to the wound on Santiago's stomach. "...after *that* happened. I got him outta there."

Jericho frowned. "Out of where?"

"Nicaragua, man. My boy got left for dead by his friends."

Jericho turned and locked eyes with Josh. "He needs help! We need to—"

Josh held his hand up. "Already taken care of."

Jericho moved away and stood with the others as a medical team pushed their way through the crowd, moving with practiced efficiency as they tended to Santiago's wound and loaded him onto a stretcher.

Collins, who had kept his distance while the chaos unfolded, moved to Jericho's side and put a hand on his shoulder. "Ya doing okay, big fella?"

He shook his head. "Black did this to him. He may have already got what was coming to him, but Baker and LaSharde? If you ask me, they are just as culpable, and they're going to pay for this. For everything. Do you understand me?"

Julie moved beside him and placed her hand on his other shoulder. "Bet your ass they are."

Sometime later, Jericho was sitting opposite Josh on a chair that felt as if it would buckle under his massive frame at any moment. They had been stationed outside Santiago's recovery room ever since he came out of surgery, a little over an hour ago. There was a palpable tension in the air, but it wasn't bred from animosity. Jericho simply didn't know what to do, which made him restless.

Josh regarded him silently. He thought to himself how, over the last two weeks, he had seen many changes in Jericho. The man had gone from someone who was essentially afraid, who felt alone in a new world and couldn't bring himself to trust anyone, to a humble, effective, critical member of his new team. He had bonded immediately with Collins and Julie. Especially Julie. Josh suppressed a smile as he recalled all the times he had witnessed their awkward interactions. Conversations that couldn't quite bring themselves to be flirtatious.

He looked on as Jericho absently ran his fingers over the eyepatch he still had to wear. He had been through a lot, and Santiago showing up earlier that day seemed a catalyst of sorts, sending him into a trance where he could go either way—back to not knowing where to turn and who to trust or cementing his allegiances further with GlobaTech Industries.

"You okay?" he asked eventually.

Jericho looked up, tearing his gaze away from the light gray tiling that covered the floor. He nodded once but said nothing.

"Okay, so here's my plan." Josh gestured with his thumb to the door next to him, which led to the room where Santiago was sleeping. "I intend to go in there and have a conversation with your old friend to help me figure out if he's a bad guy or not. Assuming he's here to help—or, at the very least, not still working with the CIA or what's left of your old unit—I'm going to fill him in on everything that's happened, where we're up to now, and what we plan on doing next. Hopefully, he'll feel inclined to give us a hand. The more people we have on our side, the better. So, if you know anything or have any concerns about any of that, now is the time to speak up."

Jericho was leaning forward, resting his elbows on his knees, transfixed once again with the floor. He looked up momentarily when he heard the clacking of footfalls away to his right and saw two men walking past the far end of the corridor. When he looked back, he stared at Josh, setting his jaw and taking a deep breath.

"Rick Santiago is a good man," he said. "He's smart, he's loyal, and he made something out of his life from the crap hand he was dealt. I've got nothing but respect for him."

Josh raised an eyebrow. "I'm sensing a *but*..."

Jericho flashed a smile. "*But*... how can I possibly trust him after everything that's happened? How do I know he's not still with them?"

Josh leaned forward, matching Jericho's body language and posture. "You don't. That's why I'm going in there—to find out. You can talk to him if you want, if it'd make you feel better. I just assumed you'd feel like... well... like you do, so figured you might not want to."

Jericho was silent for a moment. "How long's he been out?"

Josh checked his watch. "Just over an hour. Our medical

team said the surgery went well. Whoever patched him up initially did a pretty good job, so he should make a full recovery. There was no damage to anything important. He was lucky."

Jericho smiled. "Yeah, lucky Chris Black sucked at trying to kill people he used to work with."

Josh laughed. "You should get badges made for the two of you or something." He drew a small circle with his finger over his left breast. "I *almost* got killed by an asshole."

Jericho laughed too and relaxed back in his seat. "Yeah... Chris Black—the world's worst murderer."

The mood lightened as their laughter settled, and Jericho took a deep breath, sighing heavily. "All right, I'll talk to him. Will you come in with me, to back me up in case I do or say something stupid?"

Josh smiled and nodded. "Of course. I've had years of practice doing that."

Jericho arched his brow. "With Adrian, right?"

Josh nodded again but didn't reply.

"What's he like? Really."

Josh sat up straight and took a deep breath. "Honestly? He's a guy who..." He paused and stared at the ceiling, searching for the right words. "He's loyal, and he has a very passionate sense of what's right and wrong, sometimes to his own detriment. And he just happens to be incredibly good at a very bad thing. Like many of us, he's had it rough. But I think nowadays, he just wants the world to leave him alone."

Jericho listened intently, trying his best to ignore his first impressions of the man his new boss spoke so highly of. "You say that, and yet, he's out there right now, on his own, basically trying to save the world he's so desperate to hide from. Go figure."

Josh shrugged. "Like I said, sometimes to his own detriment."

"Do you think he can do it?"

"What? Save the world?" He shook his head. "No. But then, he's not really trying to."

"What do you mean? I thought that's why we're trying to help him? What are we doing, if not that?"

"Jericho, it's *our* job—GlobaTech's job—to look after the world. All Adrian's doing is trying to stop the asshole who's making it worse. And given the somewhat unique circumstances surrounding this particular shit show, that's a fight not many people can have. He's in the unenviable position of being one of the few who can, and I'm gonna do everything in my power to help him win."

Just then, the door opened. Josh looked around at the doctor standing in the doorway. He got to his feet. "What's the deal, Doc?"

The doctor was a short man, an inch or two below average height, with graying hair and a mustache. He was wearing a white coat that was too wide for his narrow frame, and the bottom rested level with his ankles. "He's fine. He's resting, but if you need to talk to him, it shouldn't be an issue, provided it's not for too long."

Josh nodded. "Thanks." He looked over at Jericho. "You coming?"

Jericho got to his feet and strode into the room. Josh followed and closed the door gently behind them.

Santiago lay motionless in a bed, surrounded by equipment and covered in tubes and bandages. He looked like hell, but the slow rise and fall of his chest signaled he was alive and managing any pain, which Jericho found himself relieved at.

He moved to the side of the bed and tapped Santiago's shoulder gently with the back of his hand.

"Quit milking it," he said. "I know you're awake."

Santiago opened his eyes slowly and grimaced as he tried to smile. "Hey... boss."

"How are you feeling, Rick?"

"Been better. You?" He paused and frowned as he stared up at Jericho. "What happened to your eye?"

Jericho absently stroked his patch with his finger. "That's a long story. The bullet Chris put in my head did some damage. I'm fine."

"How are you... still alive, homes?"

Jericho stepped to the side, revealing Josh, and gestured to him with his thumb. "Because of this guy."

Josh took his cue and stepped forward. "Mr. Santiago, I'm Josh Winters. I work for GlobaTech Industries and currently head up an elite unit that your friend here is an integral part of."

Santiago tried to lift a hand to wave but didn't make it very far. "Wassup, man."

"You know, it wasn't all that long ago I was in this exact position with him," he said, gesturing to Jericho with a slight nod. "I had this big speech worked out and everything. How we're helping repair the world. How we need his help. The full welcome brochure, y'know? But I don't need to do that with you, do I, Rick?"

Jericho took a step away, watching Josh do his job and gauging Santiago's reaction.

Santiago shook his head slowly, grimacing a little at the effort. "No, sir."

"I know you're banged up and sore, and you're welcome here for as long as you need. This is probably the safest place on Earth for you right now, truth be told. But I gotta ask, Rick. Where do you stand? Which side are you on?"

He flicked his gaze to Jericho, who looked on, impassive and stern. Curious. He took a deep breath and nodded respectfully to Josh.

"I think standing is a ways off, but I can tell you right here and now, I ain't with the agency. And I ain't with Chris and the others. What they did to Jericho was cold. Like ice, man. It didn't sit right with me. Not for a second. The days that came after Colombia, they were tough. Chris kinda lost it. I know he suspected me of being against him. Hence the hole in my gut."

Jericho approached the bed again. "Chris is dead."

Santiago held his gaze. "When? How?"

"In Prague," Jericho explained. "We secured Daniel Vincent and his intel. A firefight broke out. There were casualties. Baker and LaSharde escaped. Black didn't."

Santiago exchanged glances with Josh before replying. "Did you get him?"

Jericho took a breath and paused, looking over at Josh in silent apology.

"Yes," he said finally.

Santiago nodded, allowing himself a small smile. "The sonofabitch deserved it."

"That may be," interjected Josh. "But the focus now remains on what's left of your old unit. I'll de-brief you on the bigger picture when you have more of your strength back. You'll need it, trust me. But Baker and LaSharde are still active. We know they've been disavowed by the CIA. Julius Jones got in touch to tell me."

"Oh, shit! Really? Do you believe him?"

"I do. We have... history, me and him. I'd know if he were playing me. He's not. He offered them up on a silver platter.

We know roughly where they are and have eyes on the region. We're monitoring all movement in the area, and the moment they make their play to head Stateside, we'll intercept."

"Where are they?"

"Guatemala."

Santiago glanced away, his eyes flicking rapidly back and forth, lost in a moment of intense thought. After a moment, he looked back at Josh and said, "Near Cuyuta, right?"

Both Jericho and Josh stood tall, immediately alert and on edge.

"What do you know, Rick?" asked Jericho.

"There's only one reason I can think of for them to risk going to Guatemala," he explained. "Damien sometimes spoke of an old Army buddy who operated there. A guy named... Travis. Runs a group of mercs—or at least he did. They sometimes used Cuyuta village to lay low."

Josh looked over at Jericho. "If ever there was a time for mercenaries to lay low, it's now, right?"

Jericho nodded. "I would say so, yeah."

"We should give this to our analysts right away," said Josh. "Thank you, Mr. Santiago."

Jericho watched Josh walk toward the door, waiting for him to realize he hadn't followed.

"Jericho, we should probably..." he began.

"Actually, I'm gonna stay with Rick a spell, if you don't mind," replied Jericho. "Ray and Julie and your pet nerds can handle this new intel for a bit, right?"

Josh hesitated for a moment before smiling. "Sure. Take your time, big fella. I'll be sure to pass on your apologies for not attending to my pet nerds..."

Jericho and Santiago exchanged a laugh as Josh left them alone.

Jericho grabbed a chair and whipped it around effortlessly, placing it beside the bed and sitting gently.

"How are you holding up?" he asked. "Really?"

Santiago sighed heavily. "I thought I was gonna die, homie. For real."

"Nah. I trained you better than that."

"You gotta believe me, boss. I had nothing to do with what Chris did to you. None of us did. But the others, they just went along with it. Charlie, for obvious reasons, and Baker... I dunno. The guy's a sheep. Just a goddamn sheep. It never sat right with me, and I made sure he knew it."

"Which was stupid," said Jericho. "And I *know* I trained you better than *that*. I appreciate the gesture, Rick, but look where it got you. Always think of the long game. Think multiple moves ahead. Anticipate. If you had stayed on their good side, you could've influenced what went down in Prague. You could've made contact with the guys here at GlobaTech. It could've been so much different."

Santiago stared ahead, ashamed to admit his former superior had a point. After a while, he said, "What happened to you, boss? After Colombia. How are you alive?"

Jericho sat back in his chair, crossed his arms over his chest, and smiled. "You're gonna love this story."

24

The sky was a majestic blend of orange and pink as the sun began its descent. It was late in the afternoon, and the warm light shone through the windows of the fourth-floor briefing room. Josh strode in through the open door with purpose, pausing briefly to close it behind him. Collins and Julie were already there, sitting casually next to each other at the long table, patiently engaged in small talk. A GlobaTech analyst was sitting at the opposite end, working feverishly away on a laptop, the screen of which was mirrored on the large monitor mounted on the wall near the door.

The conversation faded as Josh entered.

"What's the latest with Jericho's old buddy?" asked Collins.

"He's recovering well after the surgery," replied Josh. "Jericho's sitting with him for a little while. I think they have some catching up to do."

"Understandable," said Julie. "Did he give us anything to go on?"

Josh nodded as he took his seat at the head of the table,

facing the big screen and putting the two members of his team on his left. "He did, actually. The name of someone Damien Baker used to know, based in Guatemala. A mercenary called Travis." He looked over at the analyst. "Hey, erm... ah..."

The analyst turned and stared at him with an emotionless expression. "Paul."

Josh clicked his fingers. "Yes, Paul. Sorry. Can you run a search for a guy named Travis? If he's a merc now, the chances are he served somewhere. Cross-reference all government and military databases. Public and... y'know... otherwise."

Paul nodded once and looked away with a heavy sigh. "No problem."

Josh felt bad forgetting the guy's name. He had done that job many times, and he knew how thankless it can feel. The people who ride the desks, who use the keyboards like an instrument, who work the intel—they're the unsung heroes. Without them, the people with guns wouldn't know where to shoot.

"Can we trust him?" asked Julie.

"Who? Santiago?" Josh thought for a moment. "Yes, I believe we can. He mentioned Guatemala to us without any prompting. In fact, he told us the exact location—naming the village that Jones's intel all but confirmed, as well as Baker's old friend. If he were working against us in any way, I doubt he would reveal his cards without knowing how much we did or didn't know beforehand. He gave me that information before he heard anything from me because he wanted to help."

Julie exchanged a brief look with Collins before nodding her own satisfaction. "Okay, then. So, what's the move?"

Josh sat back in his chair and let out a tired breath. "Well, we're slowly filling in the blanks here, but my guess is that Baker got in touch with his old buddy, hoping this Travis guy could get him and LaSharde back into the States unseen."

Collins sighed as he crossed his hands behind his head. "It makes sense, but I still can't see how they're gonna do it. I know South America was largely unaffected by 4/17—at least compared to everywhere else—but that doesn't change the fact every street on the planet is crawling with local police, government suits, or military personnel... or our guys. Plus, their faces will be all over Interpol's Most Wanted after that shit-storm in Prague, right? Not to mention the fact they now know Jerry's alive and well and conquering the seven seas with his Blackbeard impression. Oh, and their old CIA bosses want their heads on a pike. They've got less chance than a snowball in a toaster of making it State-side in one piece."

Julie turned in her seat and regarded him with a raised eyebrow. "That was surprisingly logical."

Collins chuckled. "Heh... I'm not just a pretty face, love."

"Some may say, not even..."

"Ah, don't be shy, pet. Ya know ya want me."

She laughed humorlessly. "You didn't finish your sentence. What you meant to say was, you know you want me... to go and play on the freeway."

Josh cleared his throat. "All right, children. Can we focus?"

Julie sat forward again. "Sorry, sir."

He rolled his eyes before addressing the analyst again. "Paul, could you please pull up a map of South America on the big screen?"

Without a word, the analyst's fingers glided over the keys, tapping expertly until the map appeared.

Josh got to his feet and moved over to the screen. "You're right, Ray—South America *didn't* suffer to the same extent as everywhere else during 4/17. Hardly at all, in fact. Consequently, we only have a very small presence in the region—a handful of peacekeepers and some medical personnel in Texas, based mostly along the border. Plus, Jones said the CIA isn't actively pursuing either Baker or LaSharde, seeing as they've asked us to do it. Reading between the lines, I suspect they have more pressing matters to concern themselves with, given they're Cunningham's private army. But my point is that it might not be as hard as you would think to move unnoticed."

"That's still a lot of real estate to cover," observed Julie, pointing casually to the map. "There's no way we won't see a sizeable group of people and vehicles leaving Guatemala—which they must suspect. They'll know how this works. They'll know someone is watching their every move. They probably think it's the CIA and not us, but still. Are they going to risk it?"

Josh thought for a moment as he studied the screen, his eyes darting in all directions, considering all possibilities and outcomes.

"Okay," he said finally. "This is the way I see it playing out. They'll move by land, not by sea. To me, that's obvious. It'll be much easier to hide moving through towns, villages and jungles. If they're heading for the States, they'll travel west to Mexico City, then north to the border. If I had to guess, I'd say they'll keep west, but they won't go too far because I think Arizona puts them too close for comfort to us. They'll want to keep a low profile until they're ready to make their move against GlobaTech or Jericho—whichever comes first. Probably Jericho. Anyway... it makes sense to me for them to try their luck getting across the border here..."

He placed his finger gently on the screen.

"...in El Paso. It puts all of Arizona between us and them, which will feel more comfortable, but it's still close enough to operate without spreading themselves too thin over a long distance. Now, as you rightly pointed out, Julie—that's a lot of real estate. Close to two thousand miles, I'd say. They will feel time is against them, so they won't be driving. A chopper is too conspicuous, so my guess would be a private plane. If I were a betting man, I would say we're going to find out this Travis chap is well-established in the region, meaning he will have his own network of contacts. Probably not much of a stretch to get a small plane. If it were me, I would use the current global climate to my advantage, pose as refugees or aid workers, and shuffle across the border through one of the checkpoints—which, right now, are no doubt chaotic at best. Piece of cake. Hell..." He checked his watch. "Given the timeframe, they could already be in the U.S."

He took a deep breath as a long silence fell on the room, broken only by the sporadic keystrokes of Paul, the analyst.

Julie and Collins looked at each other, stunned speechless at the mini lecture they had just heard.

"That's..." Julie began. "That's a sound and impressive theory, but..."

"Did ya literally just come up with that?" asked Collins, butting in when he sensed Julie wasn't going to say anything more. "Like, right then, off the top of ya head... poof! Instant strategy."

Josh shrugged. "Well... yeah."

Collins shook his head and smiled. "Jesus! I'm starting to see why your boy, Adrian, was so good."

Josh looked away, feeling his cheeks flush a little at the compliment.

Julie got to her feet. "But how do you know? Like I said, it's a good theory, but—"

"If it were Adrian, that's what I'd tell him to do," explained Josh. "And that would be my thinking because that's how the CIA taught me to think."

Collins sat forward in his seat. "I'm sorry... what?"

Josh rolled his eyes. "Look, it's no big deal, but... Okay. The D.E.A.D. unit Jericho ran for the CIA? I used to be a part of it. In fact, back in the day, I was a founding member, and a certain violent, impulsive, sarcastic assassin who shall remain nameless ran it. That's how I know Julius Jones. He recruited Adrian, who, in turn, recruited me. That's how we met, and we've been like family ever since. But Jones oversaw the unit and the training that went along with it. It's the reason Adrian, me, and Jericho are as good as we are at what we do. And I'm telling you..." He gestured to the screen again. "This is the play we should prepare for."

"Does Jericho know?" asked Julie.

Josh smiled. "About my sordid past with the Central Intelligence Agency? Yes, he does. He doesn't seem to mind, so you two probably shouldn't either."

There was a knock at the door, and Jericho entered, nodding a short greeting to everyone.

"Where are we up to?" he asked.

"Mr. Winters was just telling us how he used to work for your old unit," said Collins, smiling. "Before your time though, which probably makes him quite old..."

"Young enough to still send you head-first through the window, sunshine," said Josh before turning to Jericho. "How's the patient?"

"He's doing okay," he replied as he took a seat beside the analyst. "Resting now, but I caught him up."

"So, can I add him to the payroll?" asked Josh.

"Honestly? I'm not sure. The impression I got was he would rather not be involved in any of it. When I told him about President Cunningham, the conspiracy, Cerberus, Adrian Hell, et cetera, he didn't seem completely surprised. It doesn't take a genius to see how screwed everything is at the moment. After everything he's been through, I can't say I blame him for wanting to put some distance between himself and whatever shit is about to hit the fan."

Josh shrugged. "Fair enough. We'll let him recuperate and see how he feels when he's back to a hundred percent."

Jericho nodded. "So, are we any closer to nailing Baker and LaSharde?"

"Well..." Josh gestured toward the analyst. "Paul here is currently running an algorithmic search for Baker's friend, Travis. And the three of us have just been working on possible scenarios for their plan of attack."

Julie looked at the screen for a moment, then at Jericho. "What do you think they're gonna do?"

Jericho took a deep breath. "We know they're currently holed up in a village near the South Coast, right? My guess is they're going to use this Travis asshole to sneak back into the States. It would make sense to charter a plane to the U.S.-Mexican border, which, presumably, Travis has the connections to do. No point attempting the sea—they'll be too exposed. So, the Texas border is still the most sensible point of entry for them. My guess would be somewhere west. Maybe El Paso? I dunno. It's far enough away from the chaos, I guess. The plane will land in Mexico, just south of the border. They'll likely try to sneak across at a checkpoint, maybe disguised as GlobaTech employees or relief workers or something."

Julie and Collins exchanged a look of disbelief before both staring at Josh, who was grinning.

"Told you," he said.

Jericho frowned. "What?"

"Nothing," said Josh. "I agree with you. We'll be tracking any and all suspicious movement out of Guatemala. They'll find it hard with such a large group, but it'll be necessary if they want to launch any kind of attack on you once they make it across the border."

"Erm... Mr. Winters?" interrupted Paul.

Josh turned to him. "You got something?"

He pressed a few keys, and the large display screen changed to show a file photo of Damien Baker's friend.

"This is Travis Dean," explained the analyst. "A former Green Beret who was dishonorably discharged in 2005 for assaulting his commanding officer. He worked for various private security firms before establishing his own mercenary operation in South America in 2009. Thirty-seven confirmed kills during his time with the Special Forces. I'll e-mail you a copy of his file, sir. But by all accounts, this guy was a force of nature."

"Sounds like a real piece of work," observed Collins.

"So, this guy and his team of mercs are gonna be escorting Baker and LaSharde Stateside?" added Julie. "Wonderful."

Josh shook his head. "Let's not start jumping to any conclusions just yet. We have no sign of movement from either of our primary targets or from Travis and his people. They're as smart as we are. Every potential issue we've identified, they will have thought of too. What they want to do is futile, but for them, it's necessary. I understand that. But that doesn't make it any easier. We've got the advantage here, okay? They're heading our way believing the CIA is after them and thinking they can get the drop on Jericho before things go to shit. But they don't know we're already onto them. We stay smart, we get the job done. Then we can go back to what matters, which is keeping GlobaTech on track with its worldwide effort to help everyone, as well as buying Adrian as much time as possible so that he can work his way down his naughty list. Questions?"

Everyone exchanged glances and shook their heads.

"Good. I'm going to put together a briefing on Travis Dean for you all. I suggest the three of you get some rest. I suspect you're going to need it."

The three of them thanked Josh for his time and took their leave. They walked side by side along the corridor toward the elevator.

Collins sighed as he looked at his teammates. "This is heavy, ain't it?"

Julie nodded. "It's probably going to get worse before it gets better, yeah."

"The bottom line is," said Jericho, "going after Baker, LaSharde, and now this Travis asshole is likely to be the last thing we do for GlobaTech as a unit. They're the last loose end—from Prague, from my old unit, from everything. We all agreed we wanted to stick around to help Adrian, and for the most part, I still do. But c'mon guys, really... how much help can we be to him? We can't jump down into the trenches with him. We can't do anything publicly because we're GlobaTech. And covertly, he already has every shred of intel and evidence he needs to legitimately shine a light on Cunningham and his administration for their part in 4/17."

The elevator dinged its arrival, and the doors slid open.

As Jericho stepped inside, he said, "The way I see it, going after my old unit is our final mission. So, let's finish strong. For Josh. We owe him."

"And for you," added Julie.

They bumped fists and exchanged a smile.

Collins pressed the button for the first floor.

"Well, that was very inspirational—cheers, Captain," he said, turning to look at them both. "So... drink?"

25

April 24, 2017

The first slivers of natural light crept across the dusty land-scape, peeking over the distant mountains as it broke through the horizon.

They had left Guatemala a little over five hours ago, flying under the cover of darkness in a chopper Travis had secured and re-painted with GlobaTech colors and brands. After Baker had arranged the meeting with the Dogs of Lucifer, they had turned to Travis to arrange the logistics. They landed just outside of Anapra, a small neighborhood in Cuidad Juárez, bordering the Rio Grande. A car was waiting for them with a trunk full of disguises and falsified documentation. Under the cover of charity workers returning from the Middle East, they took Route 498 across the border, knowing the GlobaTech checkpoint there was smaller and quieter than most.

Once across, they headed east on the I-10, following the river down into El Paso, where the four of them now sat in the parking lot opposite Southwest University Park. Baker had driven, with Travis riding beside him. They had discussed and fine-tuned their plan on the relatively short journey from the border.

LaSharde was in the backseat, slightly squashed beside the fourth man—one of Travis's most trusted mercenaries, Devoe. He was a mountain of a man in every dimension, with skin as black as night and a heart to match.

"I still think this is a mistake," said LaSharde. "What are the four of us going to do against Jericho and his new friends at GlobaTech? Seriously?"

Devoe turned to her. "You got a problem with how the boss is running things?"

His tone was firm without being confrontational. His voice was deep and roared like a NASCAR engine.

"Yeah, I got a problem. I'm here to pick a fight with the United States government and its largest defense contractor, and I'm sitting in a goddamn sedan with the three stooges!" Her hand subconsciously brushed against the handgun she had holstered to her right thigh. "And if you keep staring at me like that, I'm gonna add your corpse to all the goddamn dirt around here."

Both Baker and Travis shifted in their seats to face her.

"If you've got something you wanna say," said Baker, "now's the time, Charlie. Before the shooting starts."

She exchanged glances with all three men, hesitating momentarily before replying. "I don't understand why there's only four of us. We're supposed to be taking the fight to GlobaTech. To Jericho. What good are we going to do when we're outnumbered like this?"

"I already told you," said Travis, not giving Baker a chance to respond. "If the CIA are looking for you, there are very few places you can hide from their satellites and tracking technology. If we'd have travelled by road with my team of mercenaries, our convoy would've stood out like shit in a snowfall. They wouldn't even have swarmed us to take us out. Some asshole in some fancy office piloting a drone would've blown us to hell from thirty thousand feet up and three miles away. We wouldn't have seen it coming until we were burning. That's why. Travelling by chopper with small numbers is statistically the last thing your former employer will be looking for. You're welcome to your reservations about me, *sweetheart*, but understand I'm very good at what I do. Now what you two are trying to do here is, frankly, about as bat-shit crazy as just about anything I've ever heard of. But it's possible. Assuming Damien's contact checks out, we might just pull this off, but you gotta trust me. Hiding in plain sight is the safest play right now."

"He's right," added Baker. "This isn't gonna be easy. But if we do this right, we can bury Jericho and his new pals at the same time as saving our own asses and getting back in with the CIA." He looked over at Travis. "And get you some steady work!"

LaSharde exchanged heated glances with both of them before letting out a heavy sigh of resignation. "I still don't like it."

"Hey, nothing about this is perfect," said Baker, trying to offer some comfort. "But it's the only way."

"Whatever," she mumbled.

"When's your boy getting here?" asked Travis, eager to change the subject.

Baker looked at his watch. "Any minute."

It was a little after seven in the morning, and the daily rush of traffic was in its early stages. The roads weren't quiet but maintained a calm, steady flow in both directions. The parking lot was mostly empty, save for a couple of cars placed seemingly at random.

As if on cue, the stuttering roar of a motorcycle engine growled in the near distance.

"You three wait here," said Baker. "If it goes well, I'll give you a sign."

"And if it doesn't?" asked LaSharde.

"Well... I'll let you know that too."

He opened the door and stepped out, momentarily confused as he was simultaneously hit by stifling humidity and a refreshing breeze. He stretched before ensuring the T-shirt he wore as part of his charity worker disguise was pulled down enough to cover the handgun tucked into the back of his waistband.

The Dogs of Lucifer were a brotherhood, but he knew he couldn't rule out the possibility that being gone for so long would have consequences.

Baker turned a slow circle, taking in the scenery, familiarizing himself with his surroundings. He had parked with the baseball field to his right. He turned to face it, admiring the size without really appreciating what went on inside. Another ninety degrees and he was facing south, looking out across the freeway to the border beyond. The stark contrast was almost majestic. The definitive divide between the urbanized landscape of brick and blacktop on one side and the low-level horizon built on sand and struggle on the other. He turned west, staring at the featureless stretch of highway that disappeared into the distance, cutting through the barren desert all the way to Arizona.

As he turned once more to face north, a motorcycle rolled into the parking lot, looping slowly around before coming to a stop a few feet in front of him. The man straddling the impressive engine was dressed in black—denim and boots on the bottom, a T-shirt and leather waistcoat on the top. Dark sunglasses hid his eyes from the world. His long, reddish-brown beard rested on his chest, unkempt and distinctive.

He turned his back to Baker as he dismounted his bike, displaying the logo stitched to the back of his waistcoat. The large circle with *The Dogs of Lucifer* written inside it encompassed an image of a three-headed dog—each face snarling, displaying sharp teeth and saliva.

Baker smiled to himself, in part due to the wave of nostalgia he felt seeing the crest of his brethren for the first time in years but also at the irony that hadn't occurred to him until that moment. The image that adorned his friend's clothing was of Cerberus, the three-headed dog that stood guard at the gates of the Underworld.

He knew the man well. They had risen through the ranks together, from the days of their misspent youth through to manhood.

Baker stepped forward. "Floyd. It's been a long time."

The man turned to face him, standing motionless for a beat before slowly removing his sunglasses. His eyes narrowed as he looked Baker up and down.

Baker held his breath, on edge for a long moment, unsure of what would come next. Finally, his old friend's expression softened, a smile spread across his face, and his eyes lit up.

"Sonofabitch," said Floyd, extending his hand. "It's good to see you, brother."

Instead of shaking hands, they clasped each other's forearm just below the elbow before embracing like long-lost relatives.

As they stepped back from each other, Baker nodded toward the motorcycle.

"Nice ride."

Floyd crossed his tattooed arms over his chest, swelling a little with pride. "That's a 2008 Harley Davidson FXSTC Custom Softail. Rides like a smooth criminal straddling a bat out of hell."

Baker laughed. "Impressive."

"You ridin'?"

"No, regrettably. Not had a lot of time for it in recent years."

Floyd nodded politely. "The Army treating you well?"

Baker took a breath and turned to face his friend. "I'm not in the Army, Floyd. I haven't been for a long time."

They regarded each other for a moment before Floyd said, "Yeah... I figured. I'll be honest, I was surprised to hear from you. And a lot of the boys are skeptical about me meeting you. That's just me laying all my cards on the table here, okay?"

"That's all right. I understand. I expected as much, and I appreciate you coming here. It's a lot for me to ask, I know."

"The way I figure it, if Big D was back in town and asking for help, it must be something big. The Dogs owe it to you to at least hear you out."

Baker smiled. "You might regret saying that."

Floyd frowned. "So, it *is* big?"

"As big as it gets."

Floyd nodded and sat gently on the seat of his bike, facing Baker. "Break it down for me."

Baker took a moment, pacing back and forth, searching for the words that wouldn't make him sound crazy. He soon realized there weren't many to choose from.

"Okay," he began. "You need to understand that everything I'm about to tell you is classified."

Floyd shrugged. "Right... I ain't gonna call *The New York Times*, if that's what you're worried about."

Baker laughed. "Of course not. I only say that because by knowing what I'm about to tell you, you'll be subjecting yourself to an element of risk. All cards on the table."

His friend joined in with the laughter. "I'll take my chances."

"Fair enough. I work... well, *worked*... for the CIA. I was part of a unit that specialized in doing the kinds of things the American people are better off not knowing about. The kinds of things that allow everyday citizens to sleep at night, safe in the knowledge that truly awful things don't really happen."

"Such as?" asked Floyd, unfazed.

"Now *that* I can't tell you. But I've been to a lot of different places, done a lot of bad things justified as the greater good, and killed a lot of people."

Floyd shrugged and, with a wry smile, said, "What do you want? A medal?"

Baker chuckled. "I'm good, thanks. I have a bunch of them already, and right now they don't count for shit."

"Go on..."

"My unit worked exclusively for one man, who, in turn, reported directly to the president. My last mission was to take out a domestic terrorist we were told played a significant role in 4/17."

For the first time since Baker began speaking, Floyd looked genuinely shocked. "Shit. Really?"

Baker nodded. "Yeah. Problem was, I'm not altogether sure he was who we were told he was. But regardless, I had orders. My CO, however, ignored those orders and started asking questions. Then our second-in-command was ordered by Langley to kill him. So, he shot him in the head. No hesitation."

"Jesus. That's brutal."

"It's how we operate. Unfortunately, my former CO survived and is now working for GlobaTech Industries. He killed our second-in-command when we found ourselves on opposite sides of the same mission a couple of days ago in Prague."

"Prague? That shit was all over the news! That was you?"

Baker nodded. "Regrettably, yes. Hours after that went down, the CIA disavowed me and the remaining member of my unit, essentially marking us for death."

"I see. And you want help disappearing? Is that it?"

Baker shook his head. "No. I want help burning it all to the ground."

Floyd smiled, partly with disbelief. "What? The CIA?"

"GlobaTech. I want to kill my former CO, his new team, and then I want to destroy GlobaTech Industries. If I can do that, the CIA will have to take me back."

"So, you wanna do all this just to impress your old employer?"

"I'm not sure you comprehend how screwed I am, Floyd. The Central Intelligence Agency wants me dead. They're probably targeting me with a goddamn drone as we speak. If I don't get back on their good side, I'll be looking over my shoulder for the rest of my life. The only consolation to that being it's likely to be a very short life."

Floyd looked away for a moment. His expression hardened, and he hocked a glob of spit on the ground before looking back at his friend. "I hate those bastards."

Baker raised an eyebrow. "The CIA?"

"GlobaTech. Bunch of self-righteous pricks who think

they can police the entire planet. If I had my way, I'd drag each and every one of them behind my ride by the neck."

"Interesting..." said Baker, smiling. He turned toward the car and beckoned with a gesture of his hand. "I want you to meet some friends of mine, Floyd."

He got to his feet and took a step away. "Who are they?"

"Relax, brother. They're good people." He flicked his head toward the trio as they approached. "Guys, this is Floyd." They all murmured a greeting. He pointed to LaSharde. "Floyd, this is Charlie. Along with me, she's what's left of my old unit. That's Travis, an old Army buddy and an elite mercenary. The big guy is Devoe, who works for him."

Floyd nodded once. "Hey."

Baker moved to stand with them. "So, what do you think, brother? Are the Dogs of Lucifer up for causing a little chaos?"

Floyd looked at each of them in turn before glancing away to the Mexican sky in the distance, running a hand along his beard. When he looked back at them, he smiled. "Why not? Who's gonna notice more chaos nowadays, right? It'll be a tough sell, but I reckon the pack will ride with you."

They took each other's forearm again, and Baker put his other hand on Floyd's shoulder. "I appreciate this. Thank you."

"Well, don't get too ahead of yourself. The council haven't agreed yet."

"But you think you can convince them?"

He shrugged. "I reckon so. I take it you have a plan?"

Baker nodded. "I do."

"Okay, then. Give me an hour. I'll be in touch."

He mounted his Harley, revved the engine, and slowly

circled the lot before accelerating out and seamlessly disappearing in the increasing flow of morning traffic.

Baker watched him go, smiling fondly as he remembered what life in the gang used to be like.

"So, it went well?" asked Travis.

"It seemed to," replied Baker. "Now we wait, I guess."

LaSharde sighed heavily and walked away toward the car, shaking her head.

"What's her problem?" asked Devoe.

Baker turned to him. "The man Jericho killed, Chris Black... they were together. This is even more personal to her, but I think she's afraid because she always had Chris by her side. Just give her time and cut her some slack. She'll come around once things are in motion. She'll feel better when we're actually doing something."

"I hope you're right," said Travis. "We'll have enough of a fight in front of us. I don't wanna have to worry about who's watching my back."

Baker didn't reply. He had enough to think about without worrying himself to distraction over the fact his old friend had just raised a valid point.

26

Josh Winters sat leaning back in his chair, his feet resting on the corner of his desk. With his hands behind his head, he breathed slow and deep. His eyes were closed, relishing the feeling of the early sun shining through the windows of his office and hitting the side of his face. For just a moment, he was lying on a beach, sipping a cocktail, staring out at a clear blue ocean and not thinking about anything of consequence.

The intercom on his desk buzzed loudly in the quiet of his office, pulling him unceremoniously back to the real world. He twitched upright and pressed the flashing button.

"Yes?"

"Sorry, Mr. Winters," said the voice of his secretary, Kim, from outside. "Were you sleeping?"

"Me? Don't be silly, Ms. Mitchell. I don't sleep. I just power down and stand in the closet like a primary school teacher."

She giggled. "Your British humor is weird."

"Yeah, well, we like to stand out, I guess."

"I have an analyst here to see you. He looks worried."

Josh rolled his eyes and massaged the bridge of his nose. "Best send him in, then."

The intercom clicked off, and a moment later, the door to his office opened. Paul walked in, cradling a laptop under his arm and holding papers in his hand. He strode urgently toward the desk, setting everything down on the edge and staring impatiently at Josh.

"Well, you *do* look worried," he said. "What's up?"

Paul took a deep breath. "Sir, I think I've found them."

"Baker and LaSharde?"

"Yes." He opened his laptop and pressed a few buttons before spinning it around, so Josh could see the screen. He then spread the papers out across the desk.

"What am I looking at?" asked Josh.

Paul pointed to the screen. "My team and I have been monitoring the Cuyuta region of Guatemala for the last twenty-four hours, like you asked. We've seen no significant movement in or out of the village. Just the odd person coming and going, which you would expect."

"Okay..."

"I know you trust the intel you were given, so I wasn't doubting our targets are there, but I started thinking, if I were in their position, how would I move so that I wouldn't be seen? I mean, they probably know someone's watching them, right?"

"That would be my guess, yeah."

Josh was intrigued. He looked at his analyst patiently, wishing he would get to the point but allowing him the time. He began to realize this was probably how Adrian felt all those times he had asked him to do something and then had to endure his own long-winded explanations.

Paul continued. "I thought, what if we've been going about this all wrong? What if our assumptions that a heavily-armed force of mercenaries will lead a charge to try and kill Mr. Stone and his unit were inaccurate?"

Josh smiled. "It's actually Miss Fisher's unit, so I wouldn't let her hear you call it his... but go on."

"Oh, right. God, yes—she terrifies me." He paused as Josh laughed, realizing his admission was spoken out loud. "Please don't tell her I said that."

"Your secret's safe with me," Josh assured him. "On the condition that you arrive at your point sometime before the turn of the century."

"Right. Yes. Sorry." He composed himself. "I know it sounds crazy, but I thought, what if they're not there to recruit Travis Dean and his men to their cause? So, I began looking specifically at the smaller movement in the area that had previously been dismissed. That's when I found this."

He leaned forward and pressed a button on the laptop, to begin playing a video feed.

"And this is?" asked Josh.

"Satellite imagery from six hours ago. Two a.m. local time. Three men and a woman travel out of the camp to a makeshift landing strip nearby and board what looks like one of our choppers."

"One of ours? That's not possible."

"The images are unquestionably clear, sir."

Josh got to his feet and began pacing behind his desk. The cogs inside his mind turned, replaying the theory he and Jericho came up with to see if it held up in light of the new information.

He stopped and turned to Paul. "Tell me you tracked the chopper."

"We did." He gestured to the printouts. "These are stills of the last known location."

"El Paso?" asked Josh hopefully.

"A small town near the Mexican border called Anapra. They drove away in a car that was waiting for them, toward El Paso. We're waiting for more footage to pull through, so we can track it once it crossed into the States, but we ran an internal search of our own databases to see if anything was reported from our border patrols nearby and got nothing, so whatever they did, it worked."

"This is... this is good work, Paul. Thank you. I need to... yes... right... I need to... Thank you." He paced out of his office. "Kim, get Julie and her boys to meet me at helipad five, would you?" he asked as he walked past her desk without breaking stride.

If Baker and LaSharde were already in the United States, he knew he had little time to lose.

———

Thirty minutes later, Josh was standing with his back to a GlobaTech transport helicopter, enjoying the feeling of the sun on his face once more, accompanied by the light, warm breeze of a California spring. Dust danced lazily around his feet, and the sound of a perpetually active community that surrounded him carried on the wind.

Facing him, positioned in a loose semi-circle, stood Jericho, Julie, and Collins. They were kitted out in lightweight tactical armor, thigh holsters that contained their individual *Negotiator* handguns, and their Tech Sleeves strapped to their left forearms. Each of them had been sleeping when Josh's secretary called them in, but he would never have known to look at them now.

"I can't believe they're already here," said Jericho. "We shouldn't be reacting to this. We should be out in front of it. We *knew* what they were..."

Julie held a hand up to him. "Take it easy, big guy. Sir, what's our next move?"

"What this all boils down to is stopping another problem before it becomes a problem," he said. "Ryan is stuck in Washington, playing nice and pretending he doesn't know Cunningham is a piece of shit, even though they both know he knows he is. But our illustrious leader was explicit in his instructions to me. And I quote, 'Make sure those three reprobate sonsofbitches keep off the goddamn front page!'"

"Classic Schultz!" laughed Collins sarcastically.

"We will," Julie assured him. "But those two aren't going to worry about bad press, and if we're going to stop them, we can't be restricted by PR concerns either."

Josh held his hands up. "Hey, you don't have to tell me, all right? I spent years trying to stop Adrian from leaving a trail of destruction in his wake, but I finally realized that he wouldn't have been half as effective as he was if he did. He still made inhuman efforts to protect innocent life, but he did what he had to. Leave Ryan to me. You three need to focus on apprehending Baker and LaSharde and whoever else is with them. Key emphasis on the word *apprehend*. Is that clear? And Jericho, I'm looking at you when I say that."

Jericho took a long, deep breath, swelling his chest and shoulders to their full size and width. "If they shoot at me, I'll shoot back."

"I should bloody well hope so! Just don't shoot first. And if it gets physical, try to avoid forcing me to ask the question, 'Were they like that when you found them?', like last time."

"He will," said Julie, digging her elbow into Jericho's arm.

"Let me quickly paint the picture for you all. Officially, kinda, we're going after these two because the guy at the

CIA whose job it is to clean this shit up doesn't want to get his hands dirty. It benefits GlobaTech to not have them running around taking pot shots at us, so we took it off their hands. But make no mistake—the real reason the CIA, as a whole, wants nothing to do with this is because they're too busy running a covert, nationwide manhunt for Adrian. He's out there on his own, fighting for his life with each minute that passes, trying to figure out a way of stopping the president from taking over the world... as crazy as *that* sounds. He's not doing it because he's bored. He certainly isn't doing it because it's easy. He's doing it because it's right, and by God, we're going to help him.

"He's relying on me, and by association, the three of you to do what we can to make his life easier until such time as he can pull a trigger. Now we can't do that if we're facing a grand jury investigation on terrorism charges. Which means we get Baker and LaSharde off the streets quietly and then go back to focusing on what matters. Ryan doesn't need to know what's happening. He's too busy playing politics, which is exactly what we need him to be doing. Prague is behind us. El Paso is the legacy the three of you will leave behind when all this is over. Do it right."

Silence fell as the words hit home with each of them. After a few moments, Collins stepped forward. "Josh, I just wanna be the first one to say... that was a kick-ass speech. I mean it. Did someone write that for ya?"

Jericho moved to his side. "Yeah, seriously, that was moving stuff. I'm inspired. Truly."

"Now come on, you two. Knock it off," said Julie, joining them. "Josh was being serious, and he raised a good point. So, just be quiet while I find out if he'll repeat it for me as I record it... it would make a great self-help CD."

The three of them laughed among themselves as Josh

looked on, smiling with his arms folded across his chest. He knew every move they made right now was under intense scrutiny. And he knew the next few hours would be hard for Jericho. He had no issue with them lightening the mood.

"All right, you've had your fun," he said after a couple of minutes. "Get your asses on the chopper. You'll head to El Paso immediately. I'll brief you in the air once we get more intel."

"You got it," said Julie, climbing aboard.

As Collins stepped up behind her, a voice made them all look around.

"Got room for one more?"

They turned to see Rick Santiago standing before them, visibly struggling to stay upright but dressed and ready for a field mission nonetheless.

"What the hell are you doing out of bed?" asked Jericho, stepping toward him.

"You folks have found Damien and Charlie, right?" he said, more statement than question.

"Yes," answered Josh.

"Then I want in."

"No." Jericho moved in front of him and placed a large hand on his friend's shoulder. "You can barely move, Rick. You'd be nothing but a liability out there."

He shrugged the hand away. "Don't tell me what I would be, homie. You ain't in charge no more! Those bastards turned on me too. You got your eyepatch, I got this hole in my gut. If you're taking them down, I gotta be there. After everything you told me yesterday—about your boy, Adrian, and the prez, and the CIA—I gotta be there, Jericho. How can I sit this out? Would you?"

Jericho held his gaze. He felt like a hypocrite telling him to sit this out, but he was concerned for his well-being.

Seeing Santiago's set jaw and unblinking stare, he couldn't help but admire him. His fight. His determination.

He turned to look at Josh, who immediately read the look on his face and held his hands up. "Hey, don't look at me, Hercules. It's Julie's unit. She'd be responsible for him out there, so it's her call."

Jericho adjusted his gaze to Julie, who was sitting in the back of the chopper, leaning forward and resting her elbows on her knees, looking on.

She held his gaze for a long moment before turning to Santiago. "You're right. Jericho isn't in charge anymore. I am. As much as I don't want the extra responsibility... I guess you have as much right to be there as the rest of us. But you do what I say when I say it. Are we clear?"

"Yes, ma'am," he replied, struggling to suppress a smile.

"I don't need you running off on some maverick revenge kick and getting yourself even more messed up than you already are. You stay back, you let us do our job, and you'll get time to say your piece and get your closure, I promise you."

"Sounds fair, ma'am."

Julie sighed. "And honestly, if you ma'am me one more time, you'll have more to worry about than your guts falling out. Are we clear?"

He chuckled, which forced a slight grimace. "Yes, ma... Sorry. You got it."

She nodded. "All right, then. What are we waiting for?"

Collins took his seat, then turned and offered a hand to Santiago, who gladly took it. As Jericho went to step on, Josh moved to his side.

"Be careful out there," he said. "And remember what I said, okay?"

Jericho nodded. "Don't worry. I'm not Adrian."

"I know you're not. Arguably, you're worse. Look at you. You could pull their arms out of their sockets if you wanted to. I'm talking full-blown Wookie after losing at chess."

Jericho frowned. "Huh?"

"I'm just saying... I hope you got the closure you needed from your encounter with Black. These two are just pawns. You're the best out-and-out soldier I've ever seen, Jericho. This is a mission, not a crusade."

He placed a hand on Josh's shoulder. "You have my word."

"Thank you."

With that, he boarded the chopper, taking a seat next to Julie, opposite Santiago. They were airborne within two minutes, heading for El Paso.

27

The chopper cruised east, maintaining a steady seventy miles per hour. They had been in the air almost an hour, passing the time with idle chatter, staying sharp and motivated, although Collins had been unusually quiet, which hadn't gone unnoticed.

"You okay?" Julie asked him, shouting over the noise of the blades.

"Aye."

She exchanged a look with Jericho, who then nudged him with his elbow. "Ray, in the time that I've known you, I don't think you've ever given a one-word answer to anything."

Collins smiled. "Something just doesn't feel right, y'know?"

"About this mission?"

"Yeah. I know Josh explained how his analysts tracked these guys down, how they thought outside the box or whatever. But it just feels... I dunno... too easy."

Julie leaned forward. "Ray, when has *anything* we've done been easy?"

Before he could answer, static crackled over their comms, and Josh's voice sounded in their earpieces.

"Can you all hear me?" he asked.

They all confirmed they could, including Santiago, who had been given a spare comms unit.

"Good. We have some more intel for you. Satellite images have come through, and we've been able to track Baker and LaSharde's movements in El Paso."

"And?" asked Jericho.

"And it's not good."

"Ah, bollocks," said Collins, clapping his hands together in frustration. "I bloody knew it!"

"What have you found?" asked Julie, ignoring him.

"Well," Josh began, "they sat in a parking lot for about an hour. Baker spoke to a guy who showed up on a motorcycle. Then they drove around aimlessly for another hour before heading north on I-25."

"Who was the guy on the bike?" asked Santiago.

"We don't know," replied Josh. "He disappeared after the meeting, and we were unable to track him. There wasn't enough in the feed for facial recognition or enough to get even a partial shot of the license plate. My gut is saying he was a contact, perhaps of this Travis guy? Weapons or connections, maybe?"

"Sounds about right," said Collins. "Do we know where they're going?"

"We're not a hundred percent sure, but I have a hunch."

"Which is?" asked Jericho.

"They're heading to Santa Fe."

"Why there?"

Josh sighed, causing more static on the line. "There's a GlobaTech research facility there. It's where we're developing vaccines and medication to ship around the world to areas affected by 4/17. There are even some CDC employees on site."

"You think they're going to attack the facility?" asked Julie. "That's ballsy, given there's only four of them."

"No," replied Josh. "That's not ballsy. That's suicide. I don't think their target is the facility itself. I think the target is Jericho."

Silence fell inside the chopper as everyone exchanged glances filled with a mixture of worry and professional curiosity.

"We've said all along that we believe Baker and LaSharde want revenge on Jericho," he continued. "Well, probably on all of you, but he'll be their priority. Their endgame. My guess would be they're figuring on someone tracking them and telling us. Worst case scenario is they stand outside the Santa Fe compound, shoot the first security operative who goes to them, and that's your ballgame. The news will be all over it, which will mean more bad press for everyone. But they know they'll lure you lot out just by heading vaguely in that direction. Ultimately, they'll want to control the battlefield and kill you all as quickly as possible."

"So, this is definitely a trap?" stated Collins.

"I think that's a fairly safe bet, yes."

"So what?" said Jericho. "That doesn't change anything. There's four of them and four of us. And I can tell you that any one of *us* is worth ten of *them*. We head to intercept, do what we gotta do, and then get back to doing work that matters."

"You think it's that simple?" asked Julie.

Jericho shrugged. "Why wouldn't it be?"

More silence.

"Julie, what are you thinking?" asked Josh.

"I'm thinking we need to re-direct to Santa Fe immediately," she replied. "How far in front of us are they?"

"Don't worry. I've already spoken to the pilot," said Josh before going quiet a moment. "Based on when this footage was recorded and where you are now, they'll likely arrive at the facility maybe an hour, hour and a half before you."

Julie nodded. "Right. So, they will have time to establish themselves, which means we need to land prepared. We're on it, boss."

"Copy that," said Josh before the line fell silent.

Jericho turned to Santiago. "You sure you're up for this, Rick?"

"I wouldn't be here if I wasn't, homes," he replied casually.

"Okay." He turned to Julie. "Let's figure this out."

The three of them leaned forward and held their left forearms out in the center of their triangle. They activated their Tech Sleeves, quickly bringing up information about the facility—schematics, employee details, a map of the surrounding area. Each of them focused on one aspect, functioning with the instinctive, seamless precision of a unit far more experienced than theirs.

The ghosts of Prague were firmly in the past.

"Right," Julie began. "The facility stands alone near the intersection of Route 599. The area around it is mostly flat desert, so there's no way of approaching unseen. Being there first is a distinct advantage."

"The only other building around is a diner, maybe a half-mile down the road," added Collins. "It'll be a popular truck stop, given the close proximity to the freeway and the fact it's the only game in town, so chances are there will be civilians inside."

Jericho pinched the screen, zooming into the map

displayed on his Sleeve, then turned it to match the direction of their approach.

"The diner is the best option for them," he observed. "Think about it. We know they're unlikely to assault the facility with just the four of them. If their plan is to take us out—or me at the very least—they'll dig in at the diner, secure the perimeter, and wait for us to approach. But it's like you said, Jules. No way can we land without them knowing."

Julie nodded as she stared intently at her own Sleeve. "You're right. They'll see us coming no matter what. So, we should head straight for the facility."

"Why?" asked Collins, furrowing his brow. "We know they won't be there. We fast-drop out of the chopper behind the diner, storm the place, try to catch them off-guard. Easy."

"No, she's right," said Jericho. "If we land at the Globa-Tech site, we can warn the security team there of a potential skirmish, maybe arrange some back-up if we need it. Then we could try to lure them to us. It'll make taking them down much easier." He looked over at Julie. "Good call."

She nodded her gratitude, trying to suppress a smile.

Santiago shuffled forward in his seat and half-raised a hand. "So, I got a question, y'all."

"Shoot," said Julie.

He pointed at her arm. "Can I get one of those computer sleeve things y'all are wearing? That tech is tight, homie!"

They all laughed, but it was Jericho who replied. "If you decide to stick around when all this is over, you can have whatever you want, Rick."

He smiled. "We'll see. Will I be working with you?"

Jericho shook his head. "No. Once we're done here, we

all go back to helping Adrian Hell in his fight against the president. Then we leave GlobaTech quietly."

Santiago looked deflated. "Because of Prague, right?"

"Pretty much, yeah."

"Damn." He stared at the riveted metal floor of the chopper for a few seconds. "Well, if this is a one-and-done mission, so be it. I'm just glad to be along for the ride with you folks."

"Good to have you here, brother."

They bumped fists and relaxed back into their seats. Julie tapped away on her Sleeve, busying herself by looking over the intel once more. Collins gazed out of the window, watching the barren landscape slide away behind them as they sped toward Santa Fe. He had his elbow resting on the edge, stroking his chin as he focused on nothing in particular.

He still couldn't shake the feeling that something wasn't right.

The remaining flight time passed by quickly and mostly in silence. The voice of the pilot crackled into their headsets.

"We're approaching the Santa Fe facility," he announced. "Two minutes out."

No sooner had he spoken, Josh's voice followed.

"I have a clear visual of you," he said. "Looking good from here."

"Any sign of the targets?" asked Julie.

"As you suspected, their vehicle pulled in at the diner a little over an hour ago. All four passengers entered the building and haven't come out since."

"Okay." She looked at the three men in turn. "We stick to

our plan. Rick, would you liaise with the security team on site at the Santa Fe facility for me? Explain the situation and maybe patch them into our comms channel."

Santiago nodded. "No problem, boss lady. But... are you benching me with this? I can fight. I'm ready. I'm—"

"I'm not benching you. Jericho has vouched for your technical abilities, that's all. After Prague, I'll admit I'm anxious to make sure this mission goes off without a hitch. The best way I see of doing that is to play to everyone's strengths. Yours is tech, so I want you working alongside the security team to make sure our asses are covered."

He let out a taut sigh, resigning to the fact she made sense.

"Thanks," she said. "Ray, once we reach the diner, you and I will make the approach and head inside."

Jericho frowned. "Why does he—"

"Playing to our strengths, big guy. Don't get your panties in a bunch. As much as I hate to admit it, Ray does have a way with words..."

Collins smiled and tapped Jericho's arm. "Hey, ya hear that? Told ya she likes me!"

Julie turned to him with a look of disbelief. "How did you get *that* from what I just said?"

He waved her away casually. "It's okay. Ya don't need to admit it in front of everyone."

"Asshole," she muttered, rolling her eyes as he laughed before addressing Jericho again. "Anyway, my point is, if we want to diffuse this situation from the outset and take them down without any unnecessary violence, we need to talk them off the ledge. He can talk. And I'm more diplomatic than you, at least. Your presence will only antagonize them."

"So, what do you need from me?" asked Jericho, trying hard not to sound disappointed.

"You'll be outside by our vehicle. If it goes south and they run, they'll need to get past you. And if they make it past the two of us to get outside in the first place, chances are we'll be at the stage where we need you to do whatever the hell you gotta do to stop them."

He took a deep breath, swelling his chest and smiling a little, happy with his assignment.

Collins screwed his face up and frowned. "Hey! Why does he get the fun job?"

She raised her eyebrow. "Because you were an asshole a minute ago." She looked around the chopper. "Questions?"

The silence confirmed there weren't any forthcoming.

"Good," she said. "Now game faces on."

The helicopter began its descent, and within a few seconds they touched smoothly down onto the landing pad. Jericho reached over and slid the door open, stepping out first and moving to the side for the others to follow. Despite the draft from the blades, the heat hit him like an oven door opening.

Collins was last out. The four of them walked in a wide line across the empty section of the compound reserved for the chopper, heading for the main building. The entire facility was comprised of three low, separate buildings, linked together in a loose V-shape by corridors. The closest one to them had an enclosed entrance, with double doors under a walled canopy directly ahead. As they approached, the doors opened outward, and two men dressed in Globa-Tech uniforms appeared, holding submachine guns loosely in front of them.

"Miss Fisher?" asked one of them as the group neared the building.

"That's me," replied Julie.

He nodded a professional greeting. "I'm Carter, the head

of security here. Mr. Winters called ahead of your arrival and asked us to give you whatever you need."

She nodded back. "Appreciated, thank you. This is my team." She casually gestured to them but dispensed with any introductions, which she felt were unnecessary. "I'll need five minutes of your time right away for a de-brief. Can you also arrange transportation and weapons?"

"No problem, ma'am."

Collins and Jericho looked at each other and winced.

Julie smiled politely. "I appreciate your help, thank you. But please, don't call me ma'am."

The operative was visibly taken aback but recovered without missing a beat. "Of course. My apologies."

"No need. Let's just get this done."

The men turned on their heels and headed back inside. Julie followed with the rest of them right behind her.

"Ol' Carter dodged a bullet there, eh?" whispered Collins, leaning close to Jericho.

"Take notes," he replied. "If you ever wanna say something stupid or offensive to her, make sure she's distracted first."

The two of them chuckled together.

"I can hear you, y'know," Julie called over her shoulder.

The chuckling stopped.

"Sorry," they said in unison.

Santiago, who was walking behind, pushed in-between them both and muttered, "Pussies," as he hobbled ahead, eager to get to work.

Collins frowned. "Okay, you're new..."

Jericho patted him on the shoulder as they headed inside. "He's got a point."

"I know, but I don't need to hear it. She's a scary woman."

Inside the diner was quiet. The whirring of the coffee machine and the low mumblings of the radio were empha-sized in the tense silence. Baker and LaSharde sat opposite one another at a booth next to the window, sipping coffee. Travis stood next to the serving counter, his gun trained casually on the three staff and five patrons who had been bound and gagged and sat on the floor behind it. Devoe stood in the open doorway, leaning against the frame, looking out at the intersection and the freeway, enjoying the warmth of the sun on his face.

They had arrived almost an hour ago, quickly taking control of the diner and establishing themselves, ready for the next phase of their plan. They had seen the chopper in the distance just over ten minutes ago, accurately assuming it was Jericho and his team heading to the GlobaTech facility a half-mile along the road.

"Are you ready for this?" Baker asked LaSharde.

She shrugged. "Guess I'll have to be."

"It's not too late if you wanna back out."

"What? And risk letting Jericho get away with killing Chris? Kiss my ass, Damien."

He raised an eyebrow. "Fair enough. Then get your head in the goddamn game, will you? This is going to work, but I need you with me. I need you committed. When bullets start flying, I need to know you have my back."

She slammed her fist on the table, causing the salt shaker to topple over. Baker jumped in his seat. She leaned forward and pointed a finger close to his face.

"I'm gonna pretend you didn't question my loyalty just then. I've been with you since the beginning, goddammit. Since Colombia. Since Prague. Since Guatemala. I've not liked half the shit that's gone down, but I've been here regardless. So, don't ever insult me by doubting my loyalty again, you sonofabitch."

Baker sat back against the seat. He cast a glance across the diner toward Travis, who simply flicked his brow, silently confirming LaSharde's response was good enough for him. Finally, he nodded to her.

"Okay. I apologize. And I'm grateful to know you're with us on this."

She sighed. "I just want this to be over. Once we take out Jericho, we'll have GlobaTech on our asses. We need to be sure the CIA will take us back."

"I know that's a risk, but it's one we have to take. If we reach out to Jones now, he'll trace our location in a second—that's if they haven't already—and it could ruin this whole thing. We've come so far, and we're almost home. Jericho's head on a pike will keep the agency happy, which should open the door for us."

"And if it doesn't?"

Baker was quiet a beat. "If it doesn't? Well, GlobaTech are about to have a few job openings…"

He smiled, and after a moment, so did LaSharde. Before long, they were laughing.

Devoe looked across at Travis. Neither man spoke, but their hard expressions spoke for them. Both were beginning to wonder if taking the fight to GlobaTech was really the right move.

28

The white, GlobaTech-branded SUV cruised along the quiet road. Julie was behind the wheel, her visor down to shield her eyes from the glorious yet punishing midday sun. The ride was smooth, and thin clouds of dust danced alongside them as they sped toward the diner, where they knew they would find Baker and LaSharde and their new friends.

Each of them was armed with their *Negotiators*, strapped securely into thigh holsters, while Santiago prepared the Sig Sauer P226 he had insisted on being given to bring along.

Before leaving the Santa Fe facility a little under ten minutes ago, Julie had taken the time to brief the on-site security on the situation and potential threat, asking them to remain vigilant while she and her team handled things directly. Santiago had reconfigured their systems, granting them access to the same satellite feeds that Josh had back in Santa Clarita, as well as the comms channel they were currently using. That way, they could see what was going on in real time and communicate if necessary.

Jericho sat up front beside her, his arm resting casually out the window. He felt the warm breeze on his face, and for a moment, he closed his eye, embracing what he knew would be a short-lived reprieve. A brief calm before an unavoidable storm. His mind wandered, drifting through the multitude of memories from the last two weeks. From landing on the airstrip in Colombia to waking up in Santa Clarita with Josh staring at him... to Julie pretending to help him escape.

He glanced sideways at her, admiring the strength and determination she exuded with every breath. She was a natural leader, and he had no issue stepping aside, so she could take control of the team. His days of relishing the pressures of command were behind him.

"How ya feeling, big fella?"

Collins's question distracted him. He shifted in his seat and looked behind him.

"Just eager to put this all to bed. You?"

Collins shrugged. "I still don't like it, but it's our job, right? We'll be fine."

"We're here," said Julie, slowing as she approached the intersection.

The diner was up ahead on the right. A thin line of traffic queued in front of them, waiting to join the freeway. Once it cleared, she slowly neared the diner, pulling over opposite the small parking lot out front.

The four of them looked over. They could clearly see their four targets, who didn't appear to acknowledge their presence. There was no sign of anyone else.

"Ah, bollocks," said Collins. "I'm telling ya, this doesn't feel right."

"Yeah, homes," added Santiago. "Where is everybody? The customers. The staff."

"This doesn't change anything," said Julie. "They wouldn't kill anyone unnecessarily, so the worst case is they have hostages. We don't have eyes on anyone, so I reckon they're in the back, out of the way. This is a good thing. Less to worry about."

"Come on," said Jericho.

He stepped out of the SUV, took a couple of paces toward the diner and stopped in the middle of the road, stretching to his full height and width before resting a hand casually on the butt of his gun.

A moment later, the others joined him. They stood in a line, facing the large window, watching Baker, LaSharde, Travis and a fourth man stare back at them.

"Now what?" asked Collins.

"There are some collapsible barriers in the trunk," replied Julie. "You and Rick use them to form a perimeter around the diner. I'm not taking any chances."

They moved with efficiency and purpose as she had asked. She looked at Jericho.

"Last chance," she said to him. "If you're gonna start crushing people, I'd rather know beforehand."

His mouth curled into a discreet smile. "I'm the diplomatic last line of defense, as per my orders. *Ma'am*."

Her eyes narrowed. "Watch it, Gigantor."

"Just trying to psyche you up," he said with a shrug. "Go get 'em."

As Collins and Santiago returned to Jericho's side, Julie stepped forward, distancing herself from her team. She brushed her hand against the butt of her own gun for a final moment of reassurance.

"Damien Baker. Charlotte LaSharde. My name is Julie Fisher," she shouted. "I work for GlobaTech Industries. I'm here to detain you, pending a federal investigation into your actions in Prague. Put down any weapons and come out quietly."

She took a deep breath, holding it a moment, embracing the silence and the tension in the air, both palpable and consuming.

Despite being clearly visible inside, there was no obvious movement or attempt to respond from anyone. Julie stood her ground, patient and disciplined. Waiting. Thinking of all the ways this could unfold.

Then the door opened.

Damien Baker stepped out, followed a moment later by Charlotte LaSharde. He was wearing a leather waistcoat over a black T-shirt. She wore a knee-length poncho over her clothes, completely covering her arms.

"Jesus," whispered Collins, leaning over to Santiago. "We're the good... meet the bad and the ugly."

Santiago smiled but remained silent and focused.

Baker looked past Julie and locked eyes with Jericho. "You took your time."

Julie sighed. "Hey, asshole. Don't talk to him. Talk to me."

Baker shifted slightly and stared at her blankly. "Why?"

She planted her feet and squared herself toward him. "Because I'm in charge. He works for me."

He smirked. "Right. And who do you work for?"

"I already said—GlobaTech Industries. Are you deaf as well as stupid?"

His smirk faded. After a long pause, he looked past her once more to Jericho.

"So, how did you find us?"

Julie side-stepped slightly, moving into Baker's line of sight. "We found you because we're good at what we do. Now you tell me—why are you here? Why are you doing this?"

Baker shrugged. "If you're so good, you figure it out and tell me."

She rolled her eyes, hesitating for a split-second before replying, taking that extra beat to compose herself and not rise to his obvious goading.

"My guess, based on what we know about the two of you? You want revenge on Jericho for killing your old boss and probably on the rest of us for what went down in Prague. You think you lured us here to take us out, in the vain hope that doing so will get you back in the good graces of the Central Intelligence Agency." She shrugged. "But I'm just guessing..."

Baker regarded her for a moment before ignoring her completely. He looked past Jericho this time.

"Rick, good to see you, bro. How are you?"

Santiago acknowledged him with a casual flick of his head. "I'm all good, homes. How's the Nicaragua site looking these days?"

Baker remained impassive. Unfazed. "It's probably still in better shape than you are right now, you goddamn traitor. Black's knife didn't cut deep enough."

Santiago smiled. "Oh, it cut plenty deep, man. He's just a crappy aim. Ask Jericho."

LaSharde stepped forward. "You sonofabitch!" she yelled, though it was unclear whom she was directing the insult toward.

"Where are the hostages?" asked Julie, eager to change the subject and diffuse the situation.

"What hostages?" asked Baker innocently.

She raised her eyebrow. "You expect me to believe you walked into that diner, and there were no staff or other customers in there?"

Baker glanced over his shoulder. "Oh, *those* hostages.

They're fine. They're tied up in the kitchen, out of the way. I have no desire to piss the CIA off further by causing more collateral damage."

"How considerate."

Jericho looked on, his eyes shifting in all directions— watching Baker and LaSharde's movements and body language, watching Travis and the other man still inside, listening to the conversation.

Beside him, Collins muttered, "I'm telling ya, something isn't right..."

Jericho glanced at him. "What is it?"

"I don't know. But he's stalling."

"Why would he do that?"

"I don't know. But he is, Jerry. I'm telling ya."

"She can handle it. Just relax and watch her six."

Julie folded her arms across her chest. "I'm gonna need the both of you to surrender any weapons you might have. Same goes for your friends inside."

Baker screwed his face up, feigning regret and apology. "Yeah... that's not gonna happen, lady." He pointed at Jericho. "Hand him over to us, and we'll let the rest of you go."

LaSharde flashed a questioning glance at her comrade, her eyes narrow and her brow raised with surprise, which Julie noticed.

"Hand him over?" she asked, laughing and motioning over her shoulder with her thumb toward Jericho. "You're kidding me, right? I couldn't do that if I wanted to. And you couldn't take him if you tried, and we both know it."

"Think what you like," he replied. "One way or another, I'm taking that bastard's head back to Langley."

The mention of the CIA's headquarters made Julie think. She looked back at Jericho, who intuitively understood what she was thinking. He nodded once in agreement.

She turned to Baker again, smiling almost playfully. "You... you don't know, do you?"

For the first time since exiting the diner, Baker hesitated. He wavered slightly before responding despite maintaining his confident, stoic appearance.

"Know what?"

Julie laughed. "Oh, man, this is awkward. Ah... we've been tracking you from the moment you left your little hideout in Guatemala."

"So what?" shouted LaSharde. She moved closer to Baker, standing directly in front of Julie. "You think we didn't know you'd be tracking us? We expected it, you stupid bitch. And now you're all here, we're gonna—"

"No, you're not," said Julie, cutting her off. "See, we had no idea where either of you went after you pulled a vanishing act in Prague. We all got carried off to the U.S. Embassy, then shipped back to GlobaTech HQ. We've been tracking you for the last thirty-six hours, from the moment you snuck out of Cuyuta to the moment you walked into that diner. But *we* didn't find you."

Baker and LaSharde exchanged a look, which Julie interpreted as concern. Their brows furrowed. Their jaw muscles visibly clenched. It was Baker who spoke.

"Who told you where we were?" he asked.

Julie smiled and took a step to the side. Without looking around, she said, "Do you wanna tell them, big guy?"

Jericho moved to her side and took a long breath.

"Julius Jones called our boss," he announced. "The CIA handed you to us on a silver platter because they wanted nothing to do with either of you. See, regardless of what you might think, of how narrow-minded you are... I was right. Back in Colombia? I was right to question that order. See, Adrian Hell... oh, he's a stone-cold killer, all right—no doubt about that. But it turns out, he's not the enemy. Not this time. This time, he's trying to help. 4/17 wasn't what you think it was. Damien... Charlie... you're on the wrong side of this thing. Chris Black was his own worst enemy. I did what I had to do, and I wish it could've been different—honest to God, I do. But it wasn't. Now please, do the right thing here. If you come with us now, nice and easy, I promise Globa-Tech will do everything it can to help you."

Silence fell as his words landed, as if the world itself held its breath. The noise from the nearby freeway faded away. The roads in all directions were empty. Even the breeze had stopped. The dust settled around them.

Travis and Devoe emerged from the diner, each holding pistols by their side. They separated, slowly circling in opposite directions until they stood, at ten and two respectively, near the conversation.

Baker and LaSharde remained side by side, speechless, thoughts racing through their minds. Any hopes of rejoining the agency had been shattered in an instant. They knew Jericho wasn't bluffing. He had no reason to. The realization hit them both that it no longer mattered what happened next. Neither of them were ever going home.

Just a few feet in front of them, Jericho and Julie stood watching, their hands lingering near their holsters, ready to draw on a moment's notice. Behind them, standing beside the SUV, Collins and Santiago looked on with bated breath.

Collins had watched the two men from inside the diner move into position. He was ready. But still, something didn't feel right to him.

"Be ready," he hissed to Santiago. "This could get real interesting, real fast."

Santiago glanced sideways at him. "What d'you mean, *interesting*, homie?"

Collins thought for a moment before shrugging. "Ah... lots of screaming and shouting as people start shooting at us?"

Santiago looked back toward the diner. "Oh, man, I hate *interesting*."

Jericho allowed his hand to rest the butt of his gun. His good eye flicked between Baker and LaSharde, trying to get a read on their intentions.

"So, what's it going to be?" he asked.

Baker took a small step back. A second later, LaSharde followed him. They put a little distance between themselves. Each movement was subtle, casual but strategic. Julie noticed it first. The positioning meant that their four targets now formed a wide, loose semi-circle in front of them.

"I think they chose the hard way, Jericho," she said quietly.

He nodded. "I think you might be right."

They both backtracked to rejoin Collins and Santiago by the SUV.

"It doesn't have to be like this," Jericho called out.

"Yes, it does," replied Travis, speaking for the first time. "See, we were promised jobs at the CIA when all this is over. I aim to get what was promised to me. Baker's a good man, but his problems aren't mine." He snapped his gun up, taking aim at Jericho. His arm was steady, his finger inside the trigger guard. "If I hand you in alive, they might reward me more. What do you think?"

Jericho shook his head. "If you hand me over alive, they'll kill you before me. You're the mercenary, right?"

Travis nodded silently.

"Yeah, I've seen your file. Impressive. A little reckless for my taste, but there's no denying you're a hell of an asset. Trust me, you'll make ten times what Langley would pay you by staying as you are. You and your friend over there can still walk away from this. We're here for what's left of my old unit, not you."

"Well, I'm here for you."

Everybody held their breath. Eight pairs of eyes darted left and right, intently watching everyone else's movements, looking for the first sign of aggression. The silent stalemate felt like a lifetime for all involved.

It was LaSharde who finally broke the silence.

"Screw this," she muttered, just loud enough to be heard.

She brushed her poncho aside, revealing a double-barreled, sawn-off shotgun in her right hand.

Julie and Jericho reacted a fraction of a second before she pulled the trigger, diving out of the way as the first shot destroyed the front tire of the SUV.

"Shit!" yelled Collins, drawing his weapon and returning fire as he moved around the other side, desperate for cover.

Santiago did the same as Baker, Travis, and Devoe all began shooting.

Julie and Jericho regrouped behind the SUV, firing back every chance they got.

A cacophony of gunfire filled the air as the close-quarters shoot-out erupted on the deserted street. A repeated dull *thunk* sounded out like a drum beat as bullet after bullet tore into the SUV's bodywork, shredding it slowly. Another large, deafening blast from LaSharde's shotgun shook the entire vehicle.

Baker backtracked toward the diner entrance, searching for cover of his own as he unloaded at his former commanding officer. Travis and Devoe had already moved inside, seeking cover the moment the shooting started. Only LaSharde remained, stubbornly standing her ground as she quickly loaded fresh shells into her gun, eager to inflict as much damage as she could on her enemies.

"If you have a shot, take it," shouted Julie over the noise.

But no one did. They were pinned down, on the defensive from the start and forced to resort to blind fire.

Another two blasts from the shotgun, and LaSharde finally began to step away, pacing backward to rejoin her friends inside the diner.

Santiago peeked over the wing mirror, anxiously gripping his gun, desperate to prove his worth. LaSharde paused to reload. He saw his window. He quickly stood, ignoring the jolt of pain in his midsection, and took aim.

"Charlie!" he shouted. "It's over."

She looked up at him. Her face froze. She was in the middle of reloading, and the realization that he had her dead to rights hit her like a freight train. As she took a breath, sure it would be her last, one gunshot sounded out above all others, silencing the battlefield. LaSharde flinched and screwed her eyes shut, convinced she had been hit.

But the bullet that stopped the skirmish didn't hit her.

She opened her eyes slowly. In front of her, on the other side of the bullet-ridden SUV, she saw Jericho, Julie, and the third member of their team standing motionless, their mouths open, looking to her right. She followed their gaze and was just in time to see Santiago's lifeless body hit the ground, throwing dust up around him as he landed. His head rolled to the side, out of her line of sight, but the smoldering hole in the center of his forehead gazed blankly at Jericho and his friends, like a demonic eye, taunting them.

LaSharde looked back over her shoulder to see Travis standing in the doorway, his arm still extended and rigid, holding his gun. Whispers of smoke poured from the barrel.

"Get inside," he called to her.

She didn't hesitate, taking full advantage of the distraction.

Jericho was vaguely aware of the movement, but he couldn't tear his eyes away from Santiago's body. His brow furrowed against the flood of emotion. His jaw clenched.

Before he could react, Travis emptied the remaining rounds of his magazine into the SUV, forcing the three of them to duck down. Then he disappeared inside.

"Goddammit!" Julie snarled through gritted death. "Shit!"

Collins put a hand on her shoulder. "Hey, this ain't ya fault, Jules. This is on that piece of shit, Travis, and he's gonna get what's coming to him. Ya got my word on that."

Her breathing came fast and shallow, urging the rush of adrenaline around her body as quickly as possible. She wanted to fight. It was the only way she knew to deal with what had happened.

"Hey, do you hear that?" asked Jericho.

There was a distant rumble being carried on the breeze. It was impossible to tell from which direction. It sounded like it was everywhere.

"Yeah," replied Julie, suddenly aware of the noise. "What is that?"

"Oh, shit..." said Collins. "Guys, we got a big problem. Look."

He gestured to the road that led back to the GlobaTech facility. Heading toward them was a convoy of motorcycles. He counted twenty, but there could've been more.

The roar of the engines grew loud as they neared the diner, until it was all-encompassing.

Jericho tapped Julie's shoulder and pointed in the opposite direction. "Ah, this isn't good."

She turned to look. So did Collins.

From the opposite direction, another fleet of bikes appeared, close to the same size as the others.

"Who the hell are these guys?" asked Collins.

"I don't know," replied Julie. "But something tells me they're not on our side."

Jericho pressed a finger to his ear. "Josh, come in. Are you seeing this?"

There was a crackle of static before his voice sounded in their earpieces.

"I do," said Josh. "And there's more. Another group coming from the west, from behind the diner. I count thirty. Get your asses out of there, right now!"

"Negative," said Julie. "The SUV is totaled, and we lost Santiago. We're sitting ducks." She looked at Jericho and Collins in turn. "Guys, we've got nowhere to go."

29

The three of them stood and walked around the SUV, stopping in a line in the middle of the road. Baker and LaSharde re-emerged from the diner as the army of bikers formed a perimeter around them. With the freeway to their backs and all other sides blocked by enemies, Julie, Jericho, and Collins knew today could be their last.

So, they made a stand.

Baker paced slowly toward them, each step more arrogant than the last. The smile on his face said more than a thousand words. He had won, and he knew it.

"Oh, yeah... I forgot to mention my friends, didn't I?" said Baker. He turned his back momentarily to them to show off the Dogs of Lucifer logo on his leather waistcoat. "See, before I was military, I was part of a brotherhood. These bastards raised me. When I asked for their help, they didn't hesitate."

"I knew he was stalling!" yelled Collins.

"You're a coward, Damien," said Jericho, taking a step forward. "You're a disgrace to every man and woman who ever stepped up and served their country."

He scoffed. "You think that's what we did? Served our country? Jesus Christ, Jericho. We were mercenaries, just like Travis. Only difference was we knew where our next paycheck was coming from. So, spare me the self-righteous crap. This isn't about service. This is about loyalty. About respect. If you'd have just done your damn job, none of this would be happening. This is on *you*, Jericho. This is all on you!"

Jericho went to reply but stopped himself. He knew there was little point getting into a debate on ethics and who was right and wrong. The time for talking was over.

"You're going to die today, Jericho," Baker continued. "You and your new friends. You're gonna die right here in the street. I'm gonna lay you next to Rick for the world to see. Then I don't care what Jones said to you—he'll welcome us back with open arms for finally cleaning up the mess *you* caused."

LaSharde strode past Baker, toward the three of them, her shotgun leveled and ready to fire at a moment's notice. She looked at each of them in turn, then said, "All of you. Guns. Comms. On the ground. Now."

Julie hesitated, looking around slowly at the dozens of emotionless, bearded faces staring back at her. There could easily have been ninety of them. Maybe more. She didn't have the time, nor the inclination to count.

LaSharde stepped forward and slashed the base of the shotgun into the side of her head. The impact was dull and heavy. It sent Julie to one knee.

"I said now!" she yelled.

Julie's vision blurred for a second. The moment the fog began to clear, she stood straight and stared LaSharde right in the eye.

"That was your free shot," she said calmly. "The next one will cost you."

LaSharde held her gaze, smirking with the arrogance of someone who believed unconditionally that they had complete control.

"Now," she said.

Julie glanced at her teammates and nodded. Then she drew her *Negotiator* and placed it on the ground in front of her. Next, she took her comms unit from her ear and tossed it down beside her gun.

Reluctantly, Jericho and Collins followed her example.

LaSharde stamped on each earpiece, shattering it into the dust. Then she slid the guns away with a shove of her foot.

Baker moved to her side and placed the barrel of his gun firmly to Julie's forehead.

"Are you still happy to be in charge?" he asked her. "Do you want to go first? Set a good example for your boys?"

Every fiber of her being tensed until she thought she would burst. Her knuckles flooded white as she clenched her fists. She pressed against the gun, forcing him back a little.

"If it means I don't have to listen to any more of your bullshit, you bet your ass I wanna go first," she said.

He smiled as he slipped his finger inside the trigger guard.

"Wait!"

Jericho held up his hand. Baker turned to him, staring impassively.

"Yes?"

"This is between you and me, Damien. It always has been. I know the two of you would've followed Chris without question. Charlie, you especially. My argument doesn't matter to you. I get that. All you see is someone you once worked for that's now your enemy, and you're doing what you were trained to do. What I trained you to do. I get it."

Baker smiled humorlessly. "If you're trying to save her, it won't work."

Jericho shrugged. "Maybe. But let me give you a chance to get what you really want out of this. Then perhaps you'll see you don't need these two at all."

His arm wavered slightly, but the gun remained firmly pressed into the skin of Julie's forehead. "And tell me, Jericho. What do I really want?"

"Me. You wanna wrap your hands around my throat and beat me until I'm nothing. You wanna unleash all that anger you have toward me." He paused to turn to LaSharde. "And so do you, Charlie. You want to kick me to death for what I did to Chris. And I'm giving you that chance." He gestured to Julie. "Leave her out of this. Put down your gun. Call off your small army of Hell's Angels. Let's deal with this like soldiers. The two of you... and me. Hand to hand. To the death. Right here, right now."

Baker stepped back and lowered his gun, casting a questioning glance toward LaSharde. Silently asking her opinion. She stared back. Jericho could see they were considering it.

"Jerry, what are ya doin', buddy?" whispered Collins.

Jericho ignored him. "Come on, Damien. Charlie. Let's end this once and for all. Leave my team out of it. Let the hostages inside the diner leave here unharmed. Take me out yourselves and disappear. No one, including the CIA, need ever know where you went."

Julie turned to him. "Jericho, no. I am ordering you to—"

LaSharde stepped forward and swung the butt of her

shotgun once again. Julie saw it coming but wasn't fast enough to completely evade the blow. She tried to turn away and took the brunt of the impact on her shoulder. She staggered back but stayed on her feet. She quickly composed herself and stared at LaSharde, who was smiling at her.

"Bill me, bitch."

Julie smiled back. "Oh, I'm adding it to your tab. Don't you worry."

Baker stepped in front of LaSharde and ushered her back before turning to Jericho. "I'll tell you what. I'll think about it. God knows it's appealing, but I'm... just not sure it's smart. So, here's what I'll do. I'll think about it while you get yourself warmed up."

He looked over his left shoulder and nodded toward Devoe, who threw his gun to the ground and walked over, rotating his shoulders and flexing his considerable frame.

"Nice goin', Jerry," said Collins.

"Hey, you're alive, aren't you?" replied Jericho without looking around. He then looked at Julie. "If this doesn't work, grab your gun and start shooting until there's nothing left. You hear me?"

Before she could respond, he stepped forward to meet Devoe. The two behemoths stopped inches apart, standing to their full height and width. It had been a long time since Jericho had come across anyone remotely close to his size and dimensions, but Devoe matched him, muscle for muscle.

Travis and LaSharde circled to the sides, ensuring their weapons were trained firmly on Julie and Collins while maintaining enough distance to feel comfortable. Baker paced idly back and forth in front of what was left of the diner's large front window, looking on with intrigue and impatience.

Jericho's mouth twitched almost imperceptibly, a fleeting smile as he prepared to enter the only place he ever truly felt at home.

The battlefield.

Without warning, he dipped to his right and whipped a huge fist back across to his left, hooking a powerful punch into the side of Devoe's face. Almost no wind-up. Flawless technique. Inch-perfect execution.

He connected flush, just below the cheekbone. Devoe's head snapped to the side, and he subtly re-positioned his back leg to remain upright. He shook his head and stood back up, fixing Jericho with a hard stare.

Jericho's eye narrowed. He had literally broken men's faces with punches half as powerful as the one he just threw, and Devoe just stood and took it.

Devoe smiled, his ice-white teeth illuminated against his smooth, dark skin. "Not bad."

With a speed rarely seen in a man his size, he mirrored Jericho's movements and delivered a punch of his own. It was faster than Jericho anticipated, but he still saw it and immediately began to block. But at the last second, Devoe dropped his near shoulder and drove his fist down, into the side of Jericho's ribcage.

The blow winded him, forcing him to double over while he caught his breath. The moment he lowered his head, Jericho knew he had made a mistake. The follow-up blow to the back of his neck dropped him to his knees. A pulsating explosion of pain erupted behind his eyepatch.

He let out a grunt of discomfort as he felt massive hands grab the back of his clothing.

Devoe dragged him up and threw him across the road, sending him sprawling across the dusty blacktop. A ripple of laughter travelled around as the bikers looked on, enjoying the show.

Jericho knew he couldn't take much more punishment. The pain in his eye wasn't subsiding, which was limiting his movement and concentration. Devoe was strong, and if he allowed him to take advantage, he would end up dead.

He pushed himself up to one knee as he heard the thin crunch of Devoe's boots approaching. He took a painful breath and listened for the next shot. The disturbance in the air around him as a fist hammered down.

Then he spun around as he stood, launching his own attack. Getting his retaliation in first. The uppercut launched from his knees, all the way up into Devoe's chin. Jericho growled with the exertion, forcing every ounce of weight and muscle into the punch, determined to take his enemy's head clean off.

Devoe didn't expect it. He never saw it coming. It connected as sweetly as any punch ever had—just off-center on the mandible bone, on the edge of the chin. If any normal human being had eaten a shot like that, he would've been in a coma before he hit the ground. Devoe fell backward like a freshly-chopped tree, his eyes rolling up inside his head. But as he hit the ground, he allowed his own momentum to roll his body back and over, coming to a rest like a sprinter on the starting block.

Jericho didn't have time to react. As he straightened, Devoe charged and speared him back to the ground, almost cutting him in two with the impact. More wind was forced from his lungs, but Jericho scrambled to his feet, knowing that staying down would be the end of the fight.

As both men made it back to a vertical base, Devoe rained down blow after blow—an elbow to the temple, a stiff knee to the gut, another punch to the face. Jericho brought his arms up in a tight guard, doing his best to weather the storm. But the last punch made it through, and it rocked him to one knee yet again.

Devoe stood his ground, breathing deep and heavy.

Jericho coughed and wheezed and spat blood onto the ground.

"Shit," he muttered as he gasped for air.

The pain in his eye had faded, but he knew that was the adrenaline. He welcomed the flow of it like an old friend. He held a hand up to his face, his fingers pressing against the material of the patch, feeling across his forehead.

Jericho stared ahead, his jaw set, renewed purpose in his eyes.

He pushed himself upright once more and looked over at Devoe. The hatred etched on his opponent's face was a product of circumstance, not consequence. The venom in the man's dark eyes was instinctive. He was in a fight for his life, and he had just hit Jericho with everything he had left in his gas tank.

And Jericho got back up.

"Come on!" he yelled at Devoe. "Come on, you sonofabitch!"

Devoe lurched forward, swinging wildly from the hip. It was a desperate, Hail Mary attempt to end the fight with one blow.

Jericho had expected it.

He stepped forward and to the side, ducking beneath it and quickly spinning around to meet Devoe as he recovered. As he turned back, Jericho lowered his shoulders and relaxed his neck, then snapped his head forward. It was a perfect arc of dead weight, and his forehead connected firmly with the bridge of Devoe's nose.

More importantly, so did the metal plate that was keeping his skull in one piece.

Jericho felt bone and cartilage cave under the impact, shattering like glass. Once again, Devoe tumbled back like a felled tree. Except this time, he stayed down. He landed with a heavy thud, spread-eagled in the dirt.

As Jericho looked down, he saw the man was dead. Killed by the brutal and uncompromising connection. A significant portion of his face looked as if it were missing, but the truth was it had simply been crushed inward. The eyes bulged lifelessly, burst against their sockets as everything from the bridge of the nose down to the upper lip had been shoved inside.

Jericho leaned back and stretched, gritting his teeth against the constant agony circulating inside his own head. But he didn't have time for that now. The pain could wait. His fight was just beginning.

He turned a slow circle, getting his bearings and finding Baker. He ignored the squadron of bikers. He ignored Julie and Collins. He stopped when his gaze rested on his former subordinates.

Baker stood motionless, his eyes unblinking, his mouth a thin line of disappointment. LaSharde was beside him, her shotgun held low by her side, her eyes wider with shock. Behind them, Travis looked on, unable to form coherent thoughts or sentences. He had known Devoe a long time. They were like brothers, and he believed there was no one tougher.

He was wrong.

Jericho held his hands out to the sides, using more energy than he would've liked to stay standing. His breathing was quick and heavy.

"Who's next?"

Travis and LaSharde were frozen with uncertainty. Baker continued to pace outside the diner, his hands twitching, muttering to himself. His doubt was clear to see, and Jericho knew he had a small window of opportunity in which to take advantage.

Behind him, Julie and Collins looked at the wider scene, watching for movement, for any sign of imminent danger. It was Collins who saw it first. One of the bikers to his right dismounted his motorcycle. He crouched momentarily. When he stood tall again, he was armed. A handgun held low and tight to his leg.

"Ah, shite," he hissed. "We gotta go, boss."

Julie glanced around and saw more bikers doing the same to her left. They were preparing themselves. Waiting for a signal or a command.

She looked toward the diner and locked eyes with Baker. In that moment, she saw the conviction in his eyes. The exact second a decision was made.

It was now or never.

"Inside!" she yelled, setting off in a sprint, deviating slightly to scoop as many of their weapons up as she could on the way past. They were going to need them.

Almost immediately, Jericho and Collins followed, hoping Travis and LaSharde would remain disoriented just a few seconds more.

Baker saw them make their move and went to raise his gun, but Jericho didn't give him the chance. Despite his weakened condition and the agony he was suffering, he found the speed he needed. He knew that when you genuinely fear for your life, adrenaline can be almost endless. He ignored the pain he felt in every inch of his body and bore down on Baker like a locomotive, diving head-first into him and taking them both through the window frame and over a table inside the diner.

Bullets started flying a second later, just as Julie and Collins dove in after him, scrambling to their feet and seeking cover behind the counter. Jericho followed, dragging a reluctant Baker with him.

The cacophony of gunfire was relentless. The whipcrack as each round chipped away at the brick and plaster of the diner added to the claustrophobic symphony only found in a warzone.

The space behind the counter was short but wide. Julie and Collins huddled together, keeping as low as they could, riding out the initial onslaught. Behind them, Jericho had Baker pinned to the floor, crouching beside him with his hand around his throat.

"Call them off!" he screamed over the noise.

Baker stared up at him defiantly, spittle forming at his mouth as he tried to breathe through the pressure on his throat. He shook his head.

Jericho huffed with frustration and drove his elbow down into Baker's face, knocking him out. Then he joined the others.

"We're surrounded," he said.

"No shit!" replied Julie. She handed Collins his gun. "I could only pick up two. Sorry."

"Two... three... doesn't make much difference against a hundred."

"Well, let's not worry about that now. Find the hostages. Make sure they're safe."

"How are we gonna get them outta here?" asked Collins.

Julie took a long breath. "We're not."

"Okay, I respect the hell outta ya, Jules, but that's a Godawful plan. Just Godawful."

She rolled her eyes. "If you wanna try sneaking them past all those people out there shooting at us, be my guest. Personally, I'm kinda relying on the fact that both Josh and the security team at the Santa Fe facility can see what's happening. They will also know our comms are offline. So, I would like to think the cavalry is on its way, which means we just need to stay alive long enough for them to get here."

A scattering of bullets blistered the counter inches above their heads, forcing them to instinctively duck lower.

"Jesus!" yelled Collins. "Okay. But how long do ya honestly think we can survive this without getting hit? It's like Normandy Beach out there!"

She thought for a moment, then looked at her *Negotiator*. Then at his.

"You remember Prague, right?"

He shrugged. "Yeah…"

"Well, that gun you're holding is state-of-the-art. You saw what it could do to a hotel wall when you got curious… Wanna see what you can do to a fleet of motorcycles?"

She smiled at him mischievously. Collins exchanged a look with Jericho, who simply shrugged back. He then laughed.

"Oh, hell yeah! But if Josh or Mr. Schultz shout at me again, I'm blaming you."

"I'm more than happy to take responsibility if it means we're alive so that they *can* shout at us."

"Amen to that."

He adjusted the setting on his weapon, switching the ammunition type from standard rounds to explosive-tipped. He shuffled around Julie to the opposite end of the counter, to give himself the best angle. From his new vantage point, he could see their battered, bullet-ridden SUV. He could see LaSharde and Travis standing in open ground, roughly halfway between it and the diner. Just to the right of Travis, he could see the leg of Santiago's lifeless body. Away to the left, he saw the first row of bikes and maybe half of the second. Every rider was firing at them, as were LaSharde and Travis and the group of bikers away to the right that he couldn't see.

He assessed the world before him, searching for the best plan of attack. The best way forward. He knew he would only get one shot, as there was no reprieve from the hail of bullets pouring down on them. He had to make it count.

He made his decision and braced himself against the counter, remembering the kick he felt last time he fired one of these rounds.

He glanced over his shoulder. "Jerry, when I fire, it'll give ya a couple of seconds to head to the back and get those civvies, okay?"

"Got it," he called back.

"And make sure *Easy Rider* back there is properly out, would ya? I don't want him jumping on us when you're not there."

"He's fine," said Julie. "Just focus on your shot."

"I am. Now this should cause a distraction big enough for ya to get a few shots off yaself. I'm gonna aim left, so scooch to the far end and aim right, okay? And be careful— the recoil is a bitch."

Julie shrugged. "So am I."

She got in position and waited for Collins's signal.

He closed his eyes and took a deep breath.

"Come on, Ray," he muttered to himself. "Remember ya live for this shit."

Without a second more of hesitation, he popped up and fired once at their SUV. His bullet found its target, and the SUV exploded. The shell became instantly engulfed in flames as it was launched into the air. As Collins had hoped, the sudden eruption provided a rare pause in the otherwise ceaseless enemy fire. LaSharde and Travis dropped to the ground. Bikers dove for cover behind the motorcycles. Jericho dashed through the door behind the counter in search of the hostages.

"Now!" shouted Collins.

He and Julie popped up again, firing across each other, aiming another explosive bullet at the first bike they could see. A split-second later, two motorcycles were catapulted backward. The sound of metal bending and breaking rang out as they collided with other vehicles in their respective fleets like pins on a bowling alley.

They both ducked back behind cover, expecting a retaliatory onslaught any second.

"That was fun!" said Collins.

"Let's hope it buys us some time," replied Julie.

Once the door closed behind him, Jericho stood and looked around. He had entered the kitchen. It was deserted. Pans and plates of freshly-prepared or half-cooked food sat unattended on the sides. Grease stained the tiles underfoot. The area was rectangular, with two single doors on the opposite side of the room, either side of the corner. One led outside. The other, Jericho guessed, led to a storage room or refrigerator. He knew a third group of bikers were at the side of the diner, and therefore close by the exit.

He headed for the storage room.

A steel knife sharpener was jammed into the mechanism of the handle, preventing it from being opened from either side. Jericho quickly removed it and yanked the door open. A group of people were huddled together against the far wall, men in front of women. Three of the men were dressed in kitchen whites, so Jericho assumed they were the chefs. Another four were dressed either casually or in business dress. Customers. Behind them were three waitresses and three women dressed similar to the men. Thirteen people in total.

They looked terrified.

Jericho held out his hand, palm first as a sign of passiveness. "Relax, I'm here to help. Is anybody injured?"

They all shook their heads, but one of the chefs spoke to confirm. "No, we're all okay. W-who are you?"

"My name's Jericho Stone. I work for GlobaTech Industries."

"Oh, thank God!"

A ripple of relief filled the storage area as everyone slowly got to their feet.

"Okay, one step at a time," said Jericho. "We're not safe yet. My friends are out front fighting off a small army. We have limited ammunition, and we can't be sure help is on its way. Although we kinda hope it is."

The chef who spoke looked at the group before stepping forward, nominating himself as the spokesperson. "So, how do we get out of here?"

Jericho set his jaw. "For now, we don't. It's safer where we are."

Another ripple of murmuring sounded out but with a lower tone.

"Look, I know you're scared," he continued, sensing the concern and disappointment. "I know you want to get out of here and see your friends and family again—and I promise, I will do *everything* I can to make sure you do—but for now, I need you to trust me and let me do my job."

He noticed a couple of the men exchanging worried glances. He saw the doubt in their eyes. Their hands twitched. Weight shifted back and forth between each leg. He knew what it meant.

He stepped toward the nearest one and grabbed his collar, pulling him close.

"Hey! I mean it. You gotta trust me. I've trained most of my adult life to beat shitty odds like these. But a team is only as strong as its weakest member. I don't need you or anyone else thinking they're a hero or that they know better just because they watched *Die Hard*, all right? You might not like what I've said. You might not understand it. But I don't care. Right here, right now, in this room, I am the best at dealing with people who are trying to kill me."

He let go of the man, gently shoving him back into the group before turning to address everyone.

"You might think staying here is insane. But outside, there are over a hundred people, all armed with guns, all trying to kill us. They're bad people. Genuinely bad people. This is real. If you go outside, you will mostly likely be shot and killed because I can't save you all from a bullet. But the door to this room is made from steel almost a foot thick. That *can* stop a bullet. That will stop everything except a missile, okay? So, stay here and let me do my job."

The man nodded. "N-no problem, sir."

"Thank you."

One of the female customers half-raised her hand, as if asking permission to speak. When Jericho looked at her, she said, "Are you... are you okay? Forgive me, but you look like hell."

He smiled. "I'm fine. Don't worry about me. I just had a disagreement with somebody."

"Man..." said one of the chefs. "What does he look like?"

Jericho shrugged. "Like a corpse."

More murmuring rippled around the small group, and Jericho couldn't tell if they were impressed or scared.

The group re-huddled against the far wall, and Jericho turned to leave.

"What are you going to do?" asked one of the waitresses.

He looked back at her. "I'm gonna get myself a gun, then politely ask everyone to stop shooting at us."

She held his gaze for a moment and then he left, shutting the door behind him. He scanned the kitchen area until he found something he could use as a weapon. He settled on a nearby cooking knife. He picked it up, checking the blade was sharp before flipping it around in his hand, holding the handle so that the blade was pressed against his forearm, hidden from the enemy.

Then he headed through the other door and outside.

"I've got one fun bullet left," announced Collins. "You?"

"Two," replied Julie. "We get three apiece by default."

"I'm gonna blow up another motorcycle!"

"Hold on a second, *Commando*. They're not firing back yet. Let's just see how this—"

She was interrupted by the staccato roar of gunfire as the remaining bikers opened fire on the diner once again.

Collins looked at her. "*Now* can I blow something up?"

She shrugged. "Sure, why not?"

He chambered the last explosive round and prepared to fire, bracing himself for the inevitable recoil.

He peeked over the counter, glimpsing the landscape outside the diner and picking a target. The first motorcycle he hit took out three behind it, making a hole in the middle of the group he could see. Four or five more were parked close together on the right. He committed the position of the one in the middle of the group to memory, so he could quick-fire from cover.

He took a deep breath, steeling his nerves as he readied to expose his head to the ongoing barrage of gunfire. Two seconds was all he needed.

He nodded to Julie and pushed himself up enough to bring his gun level with this target. The exact moment his finger squeezed the trigger, a line of bullets splintered the counter inches from his face. Instinctively, he fell away from the counter, but the aim of his explosive round fell with him, and it blew a hole in the ceiling. The building shook under the impact as bricks and tiles rained down on them from above.

"Shite!" yelled Collins as he rolled out of the way, narrowly avoiding a large chunk of roof as it shattered on the floor beside him.

"Ray! Are you okay?" shouted Julie. "Are you hit?"

"No, I'm good. You?"

"I'm fine, but—uh!"

"Jules?"

Collins pushed himself up on all fours and looked over to see LaSharde kneeling beside Julie, raining vicious, unrelenting blows, one after another, to her face and body.

"Jules!"

As he scrambled to his feet, his legs were swept from under him, and he landed hard. His gun flew from his grip. He stared up to see Travis looming over him.

"Ah, crap..."

Travis reached down and hoisted Collins upright, jabbing him in the stomach and face before throwing him over the counter in the open diner. The shooting from the bikers had ceased, which Collins was thankful for. He figured they wouldn't risk hitting their own teammates.

He managed to get to one knee before feeling Travis's boot bury itself into his ribcage. He crumpled back to the floor, wheezing as he fought to breathe through the pain. As he turned his head, a fist connected with the side of his face, further hindering his struggle to find his feet again. White dots appeared before his eyes, and a dull pain erupted at the base of his skull. He scanned for his gun but couldn't see it.

He knew he had to do something to defend himself.

At the side of the counter, LaSharde had straddled Julie's waist and was continuing to hammer down fists and elbows. Julie did what she could, keeping her guard up and adjusting it to block either her face or body, depending where the shot was aimed. But she was struggling to read LaSharde as her visibility was limited from behind her arms.

"I'm gonna kill you!" screamed LaSharde. "You're gonna die for what you did to Chris—and to Damien!"

To Damien? What's she talking about? thought Julie. *We only...*

She glanced to her right, behind the counter, to see a pile of rubble stacked on Baker's head and torso. He had been crushed when part of the ceiling had collapsed.

Oh...

She wriggled her body and pushed with her hips, desperate to create a little space and leverage, to counter the attacks from LaSharde. But her opponent was tough and a knowledgeable fighter. Every attempt Julie made, LaSharde simply shifted her weight to counter the movement, keeping her pinned to the floor.

Blows were beginning to break through her guard. Her gun was out of reach. Julie knew that LaSharde would never stop until she was dead. Her mind raced for a solution. For a way out. But nothing was forthcoming.

She was getting beaten, and she didn't know how to stop it.

Jericho pressed his back to the wall as he shuffled toward the edge of the diner. Outside was bordered by a low wall that was more gesture than practical. The enclosed space it created housed large trash cans and discarded wooden crates. Beyond it was flat, dusty terrain. To the right was a long road that cut through from the west, forming part of the intersection currently flooded with the Dogs of Lucifer, which, in turn, led to the on-ramp of the freeway.

He reached the edge of the diner and peered around it cautiously. He estimated the back row of bikers was no more than ten feet from him. There were four of them standing in a line in front of their respective bikes, weapons aimed casually forward. They were fidgeting, as if they were trying to see something past their brethren in front of them. Whatever it was, it was stopping them from shooting, which Jericho was grateful for.

There was no easy move to make. Whatever he did needed to be swift and brutal. There was no room for error. He was the only thing separating the bikers from the civilians inside—whether the bikers knew that or not. He couldn't risk innocent lives on the chance that the Dogs of Lucifer weren't interested in an additional killing spree.

He had to neutralize as many as he could in one attack and hope it provided enough of a distraction for Julie and Collins to make a stand at the front.

The sun was high behind the diner, almost directly overhead. This played to Jericho's advantage. When they inevitably turned to look at him, the light would be in their eyes. It might not make much difference, but Jericho would take anything that could give him a slight edge over his enemy.

He took some deep breaths, testing himself against the pain still coursing through his body after his encounter with Devoe. The headache and the strain on his eye barely registered, and he willed his adrenaline to keep flowing, so that continued. He felt tweaks and stabs of discomfort in his chest and ribcage but nothing he couldn't ignore until later.

"Screw it," he muttered as he set off around the corner.

After three giant, stealthy paces, the closest biker to him was within reach. He couldn't afford any hesitation. Any mistakes. He had one chance at this. He rehearsed his intended movements in his head once, then twice... and then he moved with deadly purpose and unrivalled conviction.

He approached the biker's right side, knowing his footsteps would give him away. As the biker turned, Jericho whipped his right hand across, slashing with the concealed blade and slicing cleanly through the man's exposed throat. The cut wasn't immediately lethal, but it was precise and opened him up enough that it took him out of the fight before he realized he was in one.

In a fluid, continued movement, he brought the knife back across his body, left to right, sliding the blade effortlessly in the next man's side, between two of his ribs. The placement was executed perfectly, and the biker was dead before he hit the ground.

Jericho left the knife embedded in his victim and scooped up the handgun he had dropped. As the remaining two bikers turned, they each caught a bullet to the head.

He picked up another gun, and wielding both, he ran back toward the diner. He unloaded both clips into the swarm of leather-clad bikers chasing him down, who had now realized they were under attack and had begun to react.

Bullets chipped at the brick inches from his head as Jericho disappeared out of view behind the wall. But instead of sprinting into the assumed safety of the diner, he stopped and waited. Both guns were empty, and without a spare magazine, they were almost useless. So, he flipped them in his grip, grabbing both by the barrels. Ignoring the heat coming off them, he held them both, ready to swing.

He expected at least a few of them to follow him.

One appeared moments later. He had left himself enough space that he wouldn't be caught by surprise when someone rounded the corner. He struck efficiently and fast, landing five hard, unanswered blows with the butts of each gun. The biker dropped to the ground, unconscious. His gun flew from his hand. Jericho crouched to retrieve it, dropping one of his own in the process. He stood as the next two men stepped into view, their guns aimed low, as if unsure whether or not to fight back.

Pacing backward in the direction of the fire exit, Jericho aimed and fired, accurately snapping to each target and putting a round in each one, center mass in the chest. He threw the empty gun in his left hand, which caused the next man who appeared to flinch, momentarily distracting him. Jericho took out both his kneecaps with another well-placed couple of rounds before heading back inside the diner and locking the door shut behind him.

His breathing was rapid and shallow. His hand was shaking—a combination of nerves, excitement, and adrenaline.

He checked the magazine. There were seven rounds left.

He reloaded it and took a deep breath, trying to slow his heartrate.

"Well, that worked."

Julie caught LaSharde's arm as she tried to land another blow. Her nose was bleeding, and her upper lip was split near the corner of her mouth. She held on to the wrist with both hands and yanked LaSharde toward her as she thrust upward with her hips. The combined effort was enough to topple LaSharde and allow her to slide out from underneath.

She scrambled to her feet in time to block another clubbing swing from LaSharde, who grunted with the exertion.

"Why won't... you... die... bitch?" she screamed through heavy breaths.

Julie spat out some blood and smiled. "Because I'm having... way too much fun!"

She charged at her, dropping her shoulder at the last minute and tackling LaSharde, spearing her back to the floor—except this time, it was Julie on top. She took a different approach than her opponent had. She wrapped a hand around LaSharde's throat and squeezed, then placed her other hand over the nose and mouth.

LaSharde's eyes bulged almost instantly as panic set in. It was impossible for her to breathe. Her limbs kicked and flailed with desperation. Julie relaxed her body, dropping her weight onto LaSharde's hips, controlling her movements.

Julie stared down into the wide, dark eyes. Despite the panic, she could still see the anger and the venom looking back.

"You went to all this trouble to take down four people," said Julie. "And you still couldn't get it done. You risked innocent lives. You risked more bloodshed and conflict in a new world that's already seen enough of both for ten generations. And for what? Revenge? Redemption? You should be—"

LaSharde had reached a piece of rubble nearby and smashed it into the side of Julie's head. Her grip relaxed immediately, and she fell to the side, clutching her head, disoriented. Her hand was soaked with blood.

LaSharde rolled away, gasping and choking, taking every available second to recuperate.

"You okay?" shouted Travis, seeing her move away from the counter.

She nodded back but said nothing.

Travis refocused on Collins, who still couldn't get back to his feet.

"My friend is dead, you sonofabitch!" he screamed, thrusting another kick deep into Collins's gut. "He was my ticket outta this shithole. He was gonna get me in the door at Langley, and you ruined it!"

Collins coughed up blood, which immediately stained the dust and cracked tiling beneath him. He reached up and placed a hand on the booth near the broken window, trying to hoist himself upright.

"Heh... do ya honestly think the CIA would've taken you in?" asked Collins, smiling a crimson grin. "Look at the mess ya caused here. Believe it or not, the agency values discretion. Mostly because... because they're pieces of shit and don't want everyone to know, but..."

He got to his feet as Travis looked on, impassive and arrogant. He couldn't straighten his body, but he held his ribs and did the best he could, so he could look him in the eye.

"Ya failed, asshole," continued Collins. "Ya couldn't even get *this* job done, and ya got, like, a million people outside helping ya."

He chuckled as he cast a subtle glance over at the counter to check on Julie. He could see her legs. She was down, and LaSharde was crawling toward her like a shark smelling blood.

"Shite," he hissed under his breath.

He had to keep Travis distracted until he recovered enough to fight back. Then he had to neutralize him long enough to help Julie. But he couldn't see—

Collins took a deep, agonizing breath and relaxed. A huge grin crept across his face.

Travis scowled, gritting his teeth and clenching his fists. "What are you smiling at?"

"Heh! I was just thinking... how I'm not sure I can... beat ya. But then I realized I don't have to."

"What? What are you talking about?"

Collins finally stood straight, only to sit on the edge of the table and rock backward to immediately relieve some pressure on his ribs. Still chuckling, he nodded toward the door that led to the kitchen area.

Travis frowned and looked behind him at the exact moment Jericho launched a straight left. The thunderous blow caught him flush on the jaw, and Travis dropped to the floor as if he were made of lead.

"Ya took ya time..." said Collins.

Jericho winced as he took a deep breath. "Yeah, about that. I kinda—"

"Jules!" yelled Collins, pointing over to the counter.

Jericho looked around and, seeing LaSharde standing

over Julie, holding a large piece of rubble above her head, levelled his gun and fired three times. Each round punched its way through LaSharde's torso, the combined force of each impact sending her flying away, leaving thin trails of blood floating behind her. The rubble dropped onto the surface of the counter, smashing it.

Jericho dropped his gun and moved as quickly as he could over to Julie. He crouched beside her and rolled her onto her back. She was conscious but visibly dazed. Her pupils were dilated and unfocused. There was a deep gash on the side of her head. It wasn't life-threatening, but she had lost a lot of blood.

As he put a hand over her wound, she snapped back into the moment and began struggling against him.

"Hey, hey, it's okay," said Jericho. "It's me. Stand down, soldier. You're all right."

She looked in every direction before settling on him. She stared into his eyes, taking a moment to focus on his features.

"Jericho? Are you okay?" she said gingerly.

He smiled. "I'm fine, but we need to get you on your feet. We might have a problem."

She hooked her arm around his neck, and he lifted her upright.

"You say that like we've been on vacation until now," she said, dusting herself down and resting against the counter. She stared for a long moment at LaSharde's body, which lay twisted and blood-soaked at the end of the diner. Then she looked over at Collins. "Did you get your ass kicked again?"

He shrugged. "Apparently."

"So, what's the problem?" she asked Jericho.

"I found the hostages," he said with a heavy sigh. "They're safe and unharmed in the storage locker in the kitchen. I don't think they intended to hurt them. They just wanted them out of the way."

"That sounds like a good thing..."

"It is. But then I snuck out back and took out a few of these Dogs of Lucifer pricks. I think I pissed them off."

"Great."

"Jericho Stone!"

All three of them turned to look out front. Standing in front of the burning wreck of their SUV was the man who had met with Baker earlier that morning. He was holding a shotgun in his hand.

Jericho looked at Julie. "Told you."

"Damien Baker was a friend of mine," the man continued. "Me and him, we went way back. We started in the Dogs at the same time. We came up together. He asked for my help. He asked me to bring the Dogs of Lucifer with me. I didn't hesitate. This was nothing but a favor for an old friend. That was until you killed him. And his friends. And my brothers. So, now it's personal. Get your ass out here and face your reckoning."

The loud double-crunch of a shotgun being cocked echoed around the eerily still diner.

"Now what?" asked Collins, quietly. "There's still a shit-ton of bad guys looking to kill us. Our guns are somewhere under that debris back there. And I doubt you have enough bullets in that thing to get us all outta here alive, Jerry."

"We gotta try and talk him down," said Julie, struggling with each word. "It's the only way. We have to think about the civilians back there."

"Okay," said Jericho. "But when we get outside, spread out. That bastard has a Remington, which will fire a hell of a spread. If we're all standing together, one shot will split us all in half. If he starts shooting and we're separated, at least we stand a chance of getting to him before we all die."

Collins shook his head. "How depressingly logical of ya, Captain."

The three of them shuffled outside, casually forming a line and putting space between them. Jericho was front and center, standing a few feet away from the man with the shotgun. He looked him up and down.

"You're the guy who met with Baker, right?" he said. "We saw you via satellite."

The man nodded. "The name's Floyd. And these here are the Dogs of Lucifer."

Every biker still standing walked hurriedly toward them. Dozens of footsteps filled the air as close to sixty men, most bearded and all wearing the same leather waistcoat, formed a large circle around the trio.

Floyd gestured to the gun in Jericho's hand. "You're gonna want to put that on the ground."

Jericho looked around, his grip automatically tightening around the butt. "Oh, I beg to differ."

Floyd raised the shotgun and held it level, unwavering and calm. He paced forward until the barrel rested against Jericho's chest and smiled. "Put it on the ground, muscles. This ain't no place for a hero."

Jericho held his gaze but did as he was asked, seeing no other move he could make.

Floyd stepped back. "So, you all work for the mighty GlobaTech, huh? I'm not impressed. I don't recognize you or your company as having any authority over me."

"Well, that's not really up to you, is it?" said Julie. "Fact of the matter is, the world's in pieces, and we're the only ones in a position to fix it."

He swung the shotgun around in a slow arc, so his aim

rested on her. "D'you know what? Out here, even the police won't get involved in our business. So, what makes you so special, huh? What gives you the right to waltz your asses along my road, in my city, and start laying down the law to me?"

"Hey, buddy," said Collins, doing his best not to react to the pain he was feeling. "Ya got this all wrong, pal. We ain't here for you or any of ya YMCA friends. We came for Baker and LaSharde, to detain them, so they can face justice for all the bad shit they've done. You ask me, I never expected them to come quietly. Turns out I was right. We did what we had to, and now they're dead. Job done. We just wanna go home. We ain't got any beef with any of ya."

"That's right," added Jericho. "We can make sure the authorities don't come looking for you when all this is over. We can keep your names out of the news. The world has enough to worry about without a bloodbath in New Mexico. Let's just call this one a tie and all walk away, yeah?"

Floyd kept the shotgun trained on Julie but looked at each of them in turn.

"Yeah... that isn't gonna work for me. You see, we don't have anything to fear from your so-called authorities. You said it yourself—after 4/17, the world has bigger things to worry about than a group of bikers who are simply helping maintain order in their own neighborhood. This is our civic duty."

"Threatening GlobaTech operatives?" asked Julie sardonically. "You know we've been appointed by the United Nations to keep the peace on a global scale, right? Whatever the hell else is going on in Washington right now, if you attack us or kill us, there won't be anywhere you can hide from the whirlwind of shit that will come looking for you. Do you understand that?"

Floyd smirked. "You think very highly of yourself, bitch. I'm gonna kill you first."

She rolled her eyes. "Do you know what? I am sick and tired of being called a bitch today. I'm actually very nice!"

He laughed. "I ain't ever gonna find out... *bitch*."

He took a breath and moved his finger over the trigger.

Julie closed her eyes.

A single gunshot rang out, followed a moment later by a muted squelch and a heavy thud.

...

...

...

Julie opened her eyes. Floyd lay in a heap on the ground, a thin trail of blood pouring from a large exit wound on the side of his face.

"Huh?"

She looked at Jericho and Collins, who were as confused as she was. All around them, the bikers shuffled nervously, exchanging looks and aiming their gun in every direction.

Then they heard the chopper.

And the trucks.

From both directions, large, white personnel carriers with GlobaTech markings skidded to a halt. Four in total. Armed operatives poured out of the backs of them, swarming into the circle of bikers and asserting violent and unquestionable authority without hesitation. The ones who didn't get knocked down surrendered their weapons and offered no resistance.

Within minutes, the remaining members of the Dogs of Lucifer were outnumbered almost two-to-one.

Julie sank to her knees, mostly because she was too dizzy but in part because she was so thankful to be alive, she didn't know what else do to.

"Sonofabitch..." said Collins, smiling.

Jericho looked up and saw the chopper land behind the diner. Then his focus rested on the diner itself. Now it was all over, he could see past the instinctive fight for survival and see the world for what it was. The diner was a mess. Half the roof was missing, all the windows had been blown out, and the brickwork looked like a sponge.

"Christ..." he muttered.

A small group of operatives appeared from the side of the diner. Jericho recognized two of them as the men who greeted them when they landed at the Santa Fe facility—which felt like a lifetime ago.

He nodded to them.

"Carter, am I glad to see you."

"Are you all okay?" he asked, dispensing with any small talk.

"We'll live," confirmed Jericho. "There are thirteen civilians in the back, shut inside the storage room in the kitchen. They're fine too."

"Thank you," said Carter. "The medical team should be here any moment. We'll get you all checked out."

Collins shuffled to Jericho's side. "Talk about playing for the crowd... what kept ya?"

Carter smiled apologetically. "Mr. Winters made contact the moment your comms went offline. We were monitoring the situation, but we weren't allowed to intervene without approval from Washington."

Collins raised an eyebrow. "Seriously?"

Carter nodded. "As much autonomy as GlobaTech has, certain decisions need higher approval now we're linked to the U.N. Mr. Schultz eventually gave the order for us to move in, but it took some convincing, from what I understand."

"Bastards..."

Carter and his unit moved inside the diner. Jericho and Collins lowered themselves to the ground and sat in a circle with Julie.

"Can you believe that?" said Collins. "They weren't even sure they could come and rescue us! Jesus!"

Julie had her hand to her head. She removed it and stared at her bloody palm. Then she looked up at Collins and Jericho in turn. "Honestly? I can't say I blame them. This is ten times worse than Prague. If not in innocent casualties, then from a PR standpoint. Now this is over, news crews are gonna be all over this place within the hour. I'm surprised Schultz agreed to send in the cavalry at all."

Jericho nodded. "Yeah, especially since we're getting fired the moment Adrian Hell's finished doing whatever it is he's meant to be doing. But I'd bet my last dollar it was Josh who fought for us."

Julie looked at him and smiled. "You finally put your trust in us, then?"

He shrugged. "I don't know about all that, but I trust the two of you, and... yeah, I trust Josh. He's a good man."

Collins laughed. "Well, ain't this touching. For what it's worth, if I were stuck in the trenches, ain't nobody I'd rather have beside me than the pair of you." He lay himself down gently in the middle of the road. "Now, if ya don't mind, I'm gonna lie here for a minute, enjoy the fact no one's kicking the crap out of me, and try not to cough up any more blood until the ambulance arrives."

Jericho and Julie looked at each other and smiled, holding each other's gaze for a long moment.

Collins sighed, loud and exaggerated. "Oh, for the love of all things holy... I can hear the tension between the two of ya from over here. Just make out already, will ya?"

Julie leaned over and punched his leg. He grunted and then started laughing. A moment later, both she and Jericho joined in.

As the sun beat down on the chaos that consumed the intersection in the middle of the Santa Fe desert, the three of them laughed together, grateful they had each other and happy to be alive.

THE END

DEDICATION

When I was much younger than I am now, I was a casual reader. I'd go through phases where I could either devour two books in a week or not pick one up for a month. But I would always read what my father recommended. He was an avid reader and a big fan of the classic thrillers by such legends as Alistair McLean, Wilbur Smith, and Len Deighton.

My dad passed away in 2010 after a lengthy battle with cancer. Not a day goes by that I don't miss him, and one of my biggest regrets is that he never got to read one of my books. Whether they are good or bad is ultimately a matter of opinion, but I know he would have loved them regardless.

With my ambitious literary project, the *Thrillerverse*, beginning in September 2018, I'm revisiting my old works and giving them a polish. This book has the potential to play a more pivotal role in my bibliography than it ever has before. Given how big of a role my dad played in helping me discover my love for books, it's only fitting this novel pay tribute to him.

For Jim.

20/10/46 – 23/01/10

A MESSAGE

Dear Reader,

Thank you for purchasing my book. If you enjoyed reading it, it would mean a lot to me if you could spare thirty seconds to leave an honest review. For independent authors like me, one review makes a world of difference!

If you want to get in touch, please visit my website, where you can contact me directly, either via e-mail or social media.

Until next time...

James P. Sumner

JOIN THE MAILING LIST

Why not sign up for James P. Sumner's spam-free news-letter, and stay up-to-date with the latest news, promotions, and new releases?

In exchange for your support, you will receive a **FREE** copy of the prequel novella, *A Hero of War*, which tells the story of a young Adrian, newly recruited to the U.S. Army at the beginning of the Gulf War.

Previously available on Amazon, this title is now exclusive to the author's website. But you have the opportunity to read it for free!

Interested? Simply visit the below link to sign up and claim your free gift!

smarturl.it/jpssignup

Lightning Source UK Ltd.
Milton Keynes UK
UKHW041059191222
414155UK00004B/165